Side-Lined
Sacking the Quarterback
Off Season
Forbidden Freshman
Broken Pottery
In Bear's Bed
Office Advances
A Biker's Vow
Hershie's Kiss
Theron's Return
Incoming Freshman
A Lesson Learned
Live for Today
Locky in Love
The Injustice of Being
Watch Me
Coming Clean
Professor Sandwich
Big Man on Campus

Good-Time Boys
Sonny's Salvation
Garron's Gift
Rawley's Redemption
Twin Temptations
It's a Good Life

Cattle Valley
All Play & No Work
Cattle Valley Mistletoe
Sweet Topping
Rough Ride
Physical Therapy
Out of the Shadow
Bad Boy Cowboy
The Sound of White

To Bed a King

By Amber Kell

Hellbourne
Back to Hell
Matchmaker, Matchmaker
Switching Payne

Supernatural Mates
From Pack to Pride
A Prideful Mate
A Prideless Man
Nothing To Do With Pride
Talan's Treasure
More Than Pride
Protecting His Pride
Overcoming His Pride

Cowboy Lovin'
Tyler's Cowboy
Robert's Rancher

Yearning Love
Taking Care of Charlie
Protecting Francis
In Broussard's Care

Dangerous Lovers
Catching Mr Right
Accounting for Luke

Planetary Submissives
Chalice
Orlin's Fall
Zall's Captain

The Under Wolves
A Gamma's Choice

Magical Men
Keeping Dallas

By T.A. Chase

Out of Light into Darkness
From Slavery to Freedom
The Vanguard
Two for One
Where the Devil Dances
Stealing Life

The Four Horsemen
Pestilence
War
Famine
Death

The Beasor Chronicles
Gypsies
Tramps

Home
No Going Home
Home of His Own
Wishing for a Home
Leaving Home
Home Sweet Home

Every Shattered Dream
Part One
Part Two
Part Three
Part Four
Part Five

Rags to Riches
Remove the Empty Spaces
Close the Distance
Following His Footsteps
Anywhere Tequila Flows
Walking in the Rain
Barefoot Dancing

By Jambrea Jo Jones

By Devon Rhodes

Vampires & Mages & Werewolves Oh My!
A Pint Light
Through the Red Door
Locke, Stock and Barrel

Wet Your Whistle
Christmas of White

Anthologies
Gaymes: Rough Riders
His Hero: A Ring and a Promise
Unconventional at Best: Rough Awakening
Unconventional in Atalanta: Out of Service
Unconventional in San Diego: A Sliver of Sunset

Collections
Homecoming: A Detour Home
Feral: Pride and Joey

Unconventional in San Diego anthology

FATE'S BRIDGE
CAROL LYNNE

COMING IN THIRD
AMBER KELL

THE UNICORN SAID YES
T.A. CHASE

BLOOD ON THE MOON
JAMBREA JO JONES

A SLIVER OF SUNSET
DEVON RHODES

Unconventional in San Diego
ISBN # 978-1-78430-711-0
Fate's Bridge ©Copyright Carol Lynne 2015
Coming in Third ©Copyright Amber Kell 2015
The Unicorn Said Yes ©Copyright T.A. Chase 2015
Blood on the Moon ©Copyright Jambrea Jo Jones 2015
A Sliver of Sunset ©Copyright Devon Rhodes 2015
Cover Art by Posh Gosh ©Copyright August 2015
Interior text design by Claire Siemaszkiewicz
Pride Publishing

Published in 2015 by Pride Publishing, Newland House, The Point, Weaver Road, Lincoln, LN6 3QN, United Kingdom.

Pride Publishing is a subsidiary of Totally Entwined Group Limited.

FATE'S BRIDGE

Carol Lynne

Dedication

For Jambrea, Amber, TA, Devon and Stephani. Love you all!

Chapter One

Roman Gschwind lifted the glass of merlot to his lips as he watched the patrons of the seaside bar revel in their full-moon madness. He'd decided a week earlier that Unconventional was not only aptly named, but the strangest club he'd ever visited.

"Another?"

Roman glanced at his youngest brother, Alexi. Why a vampire with Alexi's lineage would tend bar for a living was beyond reasoning. Their maker, Aldric Gschwind, was one of the oldest and most powerful vampires in existence. Alexi, like Roman, had amassed a great fortune over the centuries, but unlike Roman, Alexi had turned his back on the money and position that came with being one of only five sons of Aldric. They weren't a biological family, but Aldric had forever tied them together by gifting them with renewed life as vampires. So, even though Alexi wasn't technically his brother, in the eyes of other vampires they were both sons of Aldric.

"Roman! Do you want another?" Alexi asked again.

Before Roman could answer, someone slammed against his shoulder. He slowly rose off the stool and turned to face the rude wolf shifter who'd dared touch him.

Alexi jumped over the bar and pushed himself between Roman and the shifter. "He didn't mean it," he said in an attempt to soothe Roman's outrage. "He's drunk." He squeezed Roman's shoulders. "There's no challenge in taking him on."

"Get rid of him before I drain him," Roman growled. He brushed Alexi's hands off him before taking his seat.

For two weeks he'd bided his time, sipping wine and watching humans and paranormals come and go from the bar, all in an effort to see the surfer that Alexi claimed was Julian reincarnate. It had been nearly one hundred and sixty-three years since he'd last held the only man he'd ever loved, and the mere thought of Julian roaming the beaches of California had prompted Roman to drop everything and fly from his home in New York City to San Diego.

Roman was thrumming his fingers on the bar when Alexi returned. "Tell me again."

Alexi sighed. "Like I've said a hundred times before, I was working the bar when a group of surfers wandered in. The smallest of the group came up and ordered two pitchers of beer and five glasses." He leaned his forearms on the bar, putting himself closer to Roman. "It was him. His hair was blonder and his skin darker from the sun, but I'm telling you, I'd recognize those amber eyes anywhere, and when he smiled, he had the same dimples as Julian."

Roman swept his hand in the air behind him. "So, why hasn't he returned?"

Alexi shook his head. "I don't know. I did notice someone bothering him last time he was in. Maybe that's the reason he's staying away."

"Who?" Roman stared into the bar's mirror at the people crowded together behind him.

"I don't know his name. He was a vamp, but not a regular customer." Alexi tapped Roman's empty glass. "Another?"

Roman pursed his lips. "No." The wine at Unconventional was suitable for their patrons, but Roman was accustomed to much better. "Tell me if you see the vamp again, and get his name." Whether or not the young surfer was a reincarnation of Julian, it was against their laws to harass humans.

"Of course." Alexi dipped his chin in a sign of respect to his elder brother before moving to fill an order.

Where are you? Roman turned to face the door as he had so many nights. After several minutes, his last memory of Julian invaded his thoughts.

Roman wiped Julian's forehead with the cold rag. The smell of Julian's decaying flesh filled the bedroom, but Roman couldn't leave his love to die. "Let me change you. Please? I beg you."

Julian barely had the strength to shake his head. "I don't want to live forever as damaged as I am," he croaked.

"But you'll be with me," Roman reasoned. "I can't watch you die, knowing I have the power to save you."

"You promised you wouldn't turn me," Julian whispered.

"That was years ago, before I realized I couldn't live without you." Roman removed the cloth from Julian's forehead and dunked it in the cool water before replacing it.

"If you love me enough...I will return," Julian gasped before closing his eyes forever.

Roman felt the customary pain seize his chest at the memory. The gangrene that had killed his human lover had been so unnecessary. If only Julian had allowed the surgeon to remove his entire leg after the accident that had cost him his foot.

"Vamp attack!" someone yelled from the doorway. "Two men down," he continued, beckoning for help with a wave of his arm.

The hairs on the back of Roman's neck began to prickle as he slid off his stool.

"I'll go," Alexi shouted over the chaos.

"No." Roman stormed toward the door, pushing people out of his way as he strode toward the smell of fresh blood.

"Over there," the stranger directed.

Roman froze the man in place with one glance. "Do not follow." He knew it could be a trap, but his instincts had protected him for over eight hundred years. Besides, there were few vampires alive who could overpower him.

By the time he reached the bodies, the sweet aroma filling the air had his cock hard and throbbing. "Julian," he whispered into the steady ocean breeze. He didn't need visual confirmation to know his love had finally returned to him.

When the sight of the bloodied men came into view, Roman only had eyes for the smaller of the two. The right side of Julian's throat had been torn as if a rabid animal had attacked him. "No!" He'd waited too long to lose Julian again.

Roman sank to his knees before scooping Julian into his arms. It was obvious from the amount of blood pooling around Julian that his attacker hadn't been after a midnight snack. Roman pressed his lips to Julian's wound, hoping he'd be able to sense a heartbeat.

Faint. So very faint.

Roman stared up at the stars and let out a warrior's cry at the injustice. The only way he could save Julian was to turn him, yet he'd promised he'd never do that.

"Fuck," Alexi cursed as he stopped beside Roman. "You have to turn him."

"I can't." Roman buried his face against Julian's blond hair. "I promised I wouldn't."

Grumbling, Alexi dropped next to Roman. "Give him to me. You may have given your word, but I didn't, and I'm not about to put up with another century of your bad mood."

Roman handed Julian to Alexi with only a moment's hesitation. He was certain Julian would be angry with him, but he vowed to let Julian yell at him daily for the next five hundred years if only the two of them could be together.

Roman watched as Alexi lapped at the broken skin on Julian's neck to seal it shut. Within seconds, the wound began to knit together. Alexi bit into his own wrist before holding it against Julian's parted lips. Because of their bloodline, it only took a few crimson drops of Alexi's essence to start the process.

"Drink," Roman encouraged Julian when Alexi held his wrist to Julian's mouth.

Julian took several long pulls before sinking back into unconsciousness. "Now you must bind him," Alexi said, passing Julian back to Roman.

Roman nodded. It wouldn't be easy to chain the man he loved, but the transition could be violent if Julian's body didn't accept the change. He stood with Julian cradled in his arms. "You might try to help the other one," he suggested.

Alexi glanced at the fallen man to the left. "He's already dead." He brushed his fingers down Julian's cheek. "I wasn't wrong about him."

"No, you weren't, and I will be forever grateful for what you've done." Roman wasn't used to expressing his emotions, so the declaration seemed to take Alexi by surprise.

"I would have done it no matter what." Alexi continued to stroke Julian's face. "He is quite beautiful."

Roman took a step back, pulling Julian out of Alexi's grasp. It was natural for a vampire to feel a paternal bond toward those he had sired, but it was rare for a sexual bond to form. Yet the expression on Alexi's handsome face was anything but paternal.

"He's mine," Roman growled.

Alexi met Roman's narrow-eyed gaze with one of his own. "I think you may not have a choice in that, *brother.*"

Roman stiffened. "Are you challenging me?" Alexi was four hundred years younger than Roman. Despite the fact that the same sire had turned them, Alexi had to know Roman was more powerful. For the first time since his sire had informed him of his new brother, Roman felt real fear when he stared at Alexi.

Alexi broke eye contact. "No." He turned toward the other victim. "I'll deal with him. Get Julian home before he wakes."

Roman heard the regret in Alexi's voice and wondered if the sexual bond Alexi had already formed with Julian could be broken out of sheer will. "Thank you."

* * * *

Bodi Rain opened his eyes and immediately squinted at the bright light that filled the room. A room he didn't recognize. *Shit.* He lifted his hand to scrub at his face, only to feel a tug on his arm. "What the fuck?" He stared at the chain attached to his manacled wrist.

"It's okay," a deep voice said from the shadowed corner. "You've handled the first part of the transition better than expected, so I'll be able to release you soon."

Transition? "Who the hell are you?" Bodi asked while struggling to free himself.

A man stepped into the light. "Do you recognize me?"

"No." Bodi would definitely have remembered meeting a guy as hot as the one standing beside the bed. A sharp pain shot through his temple as the memory of his attack came back to him. "Are you with him?" He looked around the room. "Is he here?"

"The man who bit you? No. He left you to die outside Unconventional. My brother and I saved you."

Bodi stared up at the mystery man. "Who are you?"

"Roman Gschwind." He wrapped his hands around the scrollwork of the metal footboard. "Does that name sound familiar?"

"No," Bodi admitted. He scanned his body, searching for injuries, but saw none. "If you saved me, why aren't I in a hospital?"

"Because you would have died before we could get you to one." Roman cleared his throat. "I'm sorry, but we had no other choice but to turn you into one of us."

"One of us?" Bodi couldn't believe what he was hearing. He knew all about the creatures that prowled the streets of San Diego, but he never thought he'd become one of them. "What am I?"

"Do you know the name of the vampire who attacked you and your friend?" Roman asked, changing the subject.

"Yaz, or something like that. Dude was nuts. He's tried to talk to me a couple times, but I'm not into vamps." Bodi licked his lips and frowned at the coppery taste. His stomach sank when he realized what he'd just tasted. "Am I vampire now?"

Roman nodded. "It was the only way."

Something in Bodi snapped at the confirmation. He began to pull at the chains with all his strength, watching as the metal cuffs bit into his skin.

"Julian!" Roman yelled, moving to restrain Bodi.

"Who's Julian?" Bodi asked.

Roman sank to sit on the edge of the mattress before lowering his head.

"Roman?" Bodi prompted when Roman didn't answer. Roman lifted his head and Bodi sucked in a breath at the blank expression on Roman's handsome face.

"What is your name?" Roman eventually asked.

"Bodi. Bodi Rain." He grinned at Roman's confused expression. "Yeah, I'm *that* Bodi Rain."

Roman's black eyebrows drew down in a scowl. "I don't know what you mean."

"The *surfer*. Winner of damn near every tournament I enter. Cover of every surfing magazine that matters. Any of that ring a bell?"

"But you're so small." Roman ran his palm across Bodi's stomach. "So delicate."

Bodi watched as his muscles rippled under Roman's touch. "Maybe compared to you, but I can assure you, I'm average."

"You're wrong. You're unlike any man I've ever known," Roman whispered.

Despite the fact that he'd just been informed he'd been turned into a fucking vampire, Bodi's body responded to Roman's touch. *Really?* When the hell was his brain going to catch up to the situation? A vampire?

"Wait!" he yelled as the biggest issue finally hit him. "Vamps can't go out in the sun, right?"

"Not for the first three hundred years or so." Roman removed his hand from Bodi's stomach, but didn't stop staring at him as if he was a midnight snack. "After the first two hundred, give or take, you'll be able to handle dawn and twilight. I understand where you're going with the question. Unfortunately, unless competitions are held at night, your career is at an end. Better that than your life, I believe."

Bodi closed his eyes. He had a good chunk of money in the bank, so that wasn't the real issue. Truth was, he loved the attention he'd gained from surfing professionally. He craved the admiration. Thankfully, he'd never taken his gift on the board for granted so he'd invested his money wisely. "I can catch waves at night though, right?"

"Yes. You'll have to feed first, of course, but as long as you're inside before dawn, you can enjoy everything the world has to offer."

Holy fuck. Bodi hadn't considered the bloodsucking side of his new life. "You mean I have to find some unsuspecting human and have them for dinner every single night?"

One corner of Roman's sexy as sin mouth tipped up in a bemused grin. "It's against the law for us to harm humans. Besides, we need supernatural blood to survive." He pressed his palm to his chest. "Because of my age, if you choose to feed from me, you will only need blood every three days in the beginning. As time goes on, you will require less and less."

Bodi's gaze zeroed in on the bronzed skin of Roman's neck. He wasn't sure if the warm coloring of Roman's complexion was due to age or ethnicity, but the thought of putting his mouth to Roman's neck got his body's attention. "How often do you feed?"

"I feed only from those turned by my sire, so I meet with a brother once a year to take care of that necessity."

"So, you're my sire?" Bodi asked. He'd need to get the book *Vampirism for Dummies* or he'd end up bugging the hell out of Roman with questions.

Roman sat quietly for a long time before retrieving a wallet from his back pocket. "There's something I need to share with you." He removed a small sepia photograph and held it in front of Bodi's face. "This is Julian. He was the love of my life."

It didn't take an idiot to see the startling resemblance between himself and the dude in the picture. "That's why you called me Julian."

"Yes." Roman withdrew the picture and gazed at it for a moment before putting it back into his wallet. "Julian died of gangrene over one hundred and sixty years ago. I begged him to let me change him, but he made me promise I would never do that to him."

"He'd rather die than become a vamp?" Although Bodi didn't like what had happened, it was sure a lot better than dying. What a fucking idiot Julian had been. He'd had Roman in his bed and still chose to rot away? *Fool.*

"Julian lost his foot in a buggy accident a month before he passed away. Before that, we'd talked about me turning him, and he'd agreed, but wanted to be a few years older first. After the accident, he refused to undergo the transition because even vampire blood cannot regrow what has already been taken."

Despite the explanation, Bodi still thought Julian was an idiot. "So what does he have to do with me?"

After an uncomfortable silence, Roman licked his lips. "Because he was reborn in you. I know most humans don't believe in reincarnation, but most supernaturals have the ability to identify souls as they pass from body to body throughout time."

Bodi started to rub his face at the uncomfortable announcement, but the chains stopped him. "Release me."

Roman shook his head. "I can't until after you've had your next feeding. Once the transition is complete, you'll be freed."

Bodi didn't like it, but again, he knew absolutely nothing about his new vamp gig. "So, I've got this dude's soul, and I obviously look like him. What's that mean?"

"Julian promised to return to me," Roman replied. "When I saw you in the parking lot, I knew he'd told me the truth, but you were dying, and I'd promised not to turn you. One of my brothers, Alexi, was with me. He took the necessary steps to keep you alive." He started to say something more but closed his mouth.

"But I'm Bodi. Even if I have someone else's soul, I don't remember you." Bodi winced at the pained expression on Roman's face.

Roman nodded once. "Will you give me a chance to get to know you?"

"Sure, we can hang out or whatever." Bodi was used to sleeping around, so fucking wouldn't be a problem either. "More if you want," he added.

A loud knock at the closed bedroom door drew their attention.

"Come in," Roman ordered in a gruff tone.

Bodi recognized the tall, muscular man from Unconventional step into the room. At well over six-foot-four, the bartender looked as good as he had the first time Bodi had set eyes on him. He glanced between Roman and the newcomer, trying to decide which man was hotter. Roman's black hair rode just past his shoulders while the bartender's brown hair was cut extremely short. Both men had droolworthy bodies, but Bodi felt an unmistakable sexual pull toward the bartender. His cock hardened almost immediately, and there was nothing he could do about it.

"How're you feeling?" the bartender asked.

"He's fine," Roman answered. "Bodi, this is Alexi Gschwind. Your sire," he ground out between clenched teeth.

Chapter Two

Roman's heart broke as he witnessed the instant attraction between Alexi and Bodi. He knew he should excuse himself. He needed more information about a sexual bond, because the way he understood it, the connection was more powerful than the traditional link between a sire and transitioned *child*.

"Have you been fed?" Alexi asked.

Bodi shook his head but didn't speak.

Roman fisted his hands when he noticed the erection pressing against the zipper of Alexi's jeans. "I planned to feed Bodi after I explained the situation."

"I'll do it," Alexi announced, moving closer to the bed.

Roman knew he had no right to ask, but he couldn't give up without a fight. "Please, Alexi. I know you want him, but please let me do this."

Alexi scrubbed his hands over his short brown hair. It was obvious that if any other man had asked the favor, Alexi would have turned them down, but Roman wasn't any other man. "We need to talk."

"Yes." Roman stood. "We'll be right back," he told Bodi, who was openly staring at Alexi's cock. He followed Alexi out of the room and down the hall to the kitchen. By the relaxed set of Alexi's shoulders, Roman didn't think he'd have to fight for the right to feed Bodi, but he was sure Alexi had something to say about it.

"We have a problem," Alexi said while he crossed his arms over his muscular chest.

Roman remembered the tented blanket at Bodi's groin before glancing at the front of Alexi's jeans. "Yes, that much is obvious."

"I need to fuck him like I need to breathe," Alexi proclaimed. "That said, I know what his soul means to you, so we're going to have to work something out."

Roman had no doubt Bodi would welcome Alexi into his bed. The hard part would be to convince Bodi to let Roman into his heart. "He doesn't remember me."

Alexi chuckled. "Drop your walls and let him see the man you were before Julian died. I know you've built them up to protect yourself, but you have to give Bodi a reason to knock them down."

"What do you suggest?" Roman asked his brother.

Alexi started toward the spare bedroom. "Feed him. Date him. Talk to him. Fuck him. That's more than you did for Julian, and he fell in love with you."

"I didn't have to share Julian either," Roman pointed out. He'd lived a long life and had taken part in epic scenes of debauchery, but everything had changed for him when he'd fallen in love. Back then, the thought of someone else touching Julian in a sexual way would have driven him to murder.

Alexi opened the bedroom door with Roman on his heels. "Roman's going to feed you, but it'll be the three of us in bed together."

Roman swung his gaze to his brother. That scenario wasn't one they'd discussed, and one he wasn't at all comfortable with. How could he hope to form a bond with Bodi if Alexi was in the room?

Bodi was writhing on the bed, obviously delirious with lust. Roman stepped forward and grabbed the rag he'd used earlier to wipe Bodi's sweating forehead and face. He glanced back at Alexi, who seemed to be in a frenzy to rid himself of his clothes. "Have you ever heard of anything like this?"

Alexi tossed his boots to the side of the room. "No, but I'm sure Father could give you answers if they're so important to you." He used his incredible strength to tear the jeans from his powerful body before climbing onto the bed. "All I care about right now is fucking."

"Please unchain me," Bodi begged Alexi. "Need to touch you."

Roman had assumed Bodi's transition had been easy, but the tortured expression on the man's face led him to believe the change hadn't started until Alexi had first walked into the room. Was it possible? He reached into his pocket. Calling his father without prior warning was a breach of protocol, but perhaps one of his other brothers would know what to do.

When Alexi reached for the manacle securing Bodi's left wrist to the chain, Roman charged forward. "Stop! Let me make some calls before you release him," Roman warned. Because he was the elder and stronger brother, Alexi paused.

"I need him," Alexi growled.

Roman pushed his own needs aside. He couldn't stand to see Bodi and Alexi in their current condition because it wasn't pleasure that drove them—it was pain. "Take him if you need to, but leave him bound until I find out what the hell's going on."

Alexi insinuated himself between Bodi's spread thighs before Roman could turn his back on the pair. He stared at his phone and tried to concentrate on the number pad as he dialed Mao. He could have easily transported to Mao's home, but he refused to leave Alexi and Bodi alone.

Mao grunted into the phone, a clear sign his brother was in the middle of fucking.

Instead of pleasantries, Roman got right down to business. "Have you ever experienced a sexual bond with someone you've turned?"

Mao grunted once more before rattling off a command in Chinese.

Roman wasn't sure if a man or woman was on the other end of the order, but whoever it was must have obeyed quickly because Mao answered Roman within seconds. "You turned someone?" Mao asked in the smooth, confident voice he was known for.

Bodi's cries of passion were so loud in the room that Roman was forced to plug his left ear to hear Mao. "Alexi turned someone who would have died otherwise."

Mao chuckled. "A man, from the sounds of it."

Roman gripped the phone tighter. "Just answer the question. I need to know if you've ever experienced what seems to be happening between the two of them, because I've never seen anything like it."

"Fuck!" Alexi howled as the sounds of skin slapping against skin grew even louder.

"Once. Many years ago," Mao finally replied. "It's not something to interfere with if that's what you're thinking."

Unease hit Roman at the sound of Mao's voice. Mao was the eldest of their father's *children* but rarely had anything to do with the vampire who'd sired him. "I need to know if it's safe to unchain Bodi. Other than Alexi's initial gift of blood, Bodi's not been fed," Roman relayed. He glance at the bed and winced. "They're like wild animals right now."

"It's the transition. From what I hear in the background, they're both going through a change. I take it Alexi also tasted Bodi's blood?" Mao asked.

"Yes. He had to seal the wound on Bodi's neck to stop the bleeding." Once he'd looked at Bodi and Alexi, Roman couldn't take his eyes off the pair. Their fucking was so incredibly raw and violent, but neither of them seemed to care.

"The phenomenon only occurs under rare circumstances. The human's unique genetic makeup prompts a mutation in both human and vampire. Who is this man?"

"His name's Bodi." Roman bit his bottom lip as he watched Alexi's cock plunge again and again inside Bodi's sweet hole. It was obvious Alexi had already come a number of times fromthe milky white fluid escaping around Alexi's solid erection as it continued to fuck Bodi. "He has Julian's soul," Roman finally admitted to his brother.

Mao swore in his native tongue. "I think he has more than Julian's soul inside him. You should have been the one to turn him."

"I know, but I'd promised Julian that I wouldn't. Alexi was there when we found Bodi, so he did it to save him," Roman tried to explain.

"Well, congratulations, brother, I think you've just tied the three of you together."

Roman shook his head. "Bodi doesn't remember me."

"He will. After the transition, Julian's soul will most likely reach out to you, but Bodi won't understand it. Unfortunately, it'll go one of two ways. Either he'll accept what his heart is telling him to feel, or he'll rebel and put all three of you in danger."

"So I should keep him chained?" Roman's gaze went to the cuffs biting into Bodi's tanned skin as his body continued to thrash under Alexi.

"No." Mao sighed heavily into the phone. "This particular kind of transition is as much mental as it is physical. Keeping him chained may prevent him from attacking you, but mentally it'll do greater harm. You need him to accept both of you, otherwise, he's likely to tear himself apart from the inside out."

Roman would know if Mao was tied to someone, so whatever had happened had occurred before Roman had been turned. "What happened to your sexual bond mate?"

It was several seconds before Mao answered. "He walked out into the sun."

Roman sucked in a breath. Suicide was extremely rare among vampires, and the thought of Bodi doing the same went a long way in making his mind up for him. "What do I need to do?"

"Spend as much time with him as you're able. Let him know there's nothing wrong with fucking one man while loving another." Mao made a noise deep in his throat that sounded to Roman suspiciously like emotion. "Do everything you can to convince him his feelings will be reciprocated no matter what his body urges him to do, and I warn you, Bodi's body will need Alexi's body as much as his soul needs your heart. It's not an easy balance to maintain, but it's the only way the three of you will survive intact."

"Please," Bodi begged as red tears began to slide down the side of his face.

"I need to go. Thank you for being honest with me." Roman moved to the side of the bed.

"Just do a better job handling this than I did," Mao returned before ending the call.

Roman dropped the phone into his suit jacket pocket before removing his clothing. Naked, he took the key from the chain around his neck and unlocked the manacles imprisoning Bodi's wrists. The way Alexi and Bodi were going at each other, Roman wasn't sure where he fit, but he needed to follow Mao's advice.

Roman pressed his lips against Bodi's temple. "Shhh," he soothed as he used the sheet to wipe at the bloody tears. "This is all part of your transition." He met Alexi's gaze. "He needs to feed."

Alexi nodded and slowed his thrusts. "I can't pull out yet."

"Have your fangs dropped yet?" Roman whispered in Bodi's ear.

Brow furrowed, Bodi just stared at Roman in reply.

Roman took Bodi's non-answer as a no, so while he would have loved the feel of Bodi's lips on his neck, he tried to remember what was most important. He pressed the soft flesh of his left wrist to his mouth and bit through the skin. The moment he sank his teeth into the vein, his cock went steel hard, which was a normal reaction when a vampire tasted blood, even if it was his own.

"Here." Roman held his wrist against Bodi's mouth. "Drink."

At first, Bodi refused to open his mouth, but within moments, he latched on and began to suck.

Roman knew he needed to watch Bodi closely. The initial feeding after a vampire's transition was dangerous because gluttony often overruled need.

"That's enough," Alexi commanded after about twenty seconds had passed.

When Roman tried to pull away, Bodi wrapped his hand around Roman's forearm. The struggle didn't last long, however, because Roman would always be the stronger of the two.

Alexi growled when Bodi's entire body went limp. "You gave him too much."

Roman licked his wound, cutting off the supply of blood, before staring down at Bodi. "Do you feel better?"

With his eyelids drooping, Bodi grinned up at Roman. "Better," he slurred.

"He needs to sleep," Roman told Alexi.

Alexi gestured to his erection after pulling out of Bodi. "And what am I supposed to do with this? No matter how many times I come, it won't go down."

Roman's initial reaction was to turn away from Alexi's glistening cock, but the phone call with Mao stopped him. He glanced back to Bodi, and once he was sure Bodi was resting peacefully, he swung his legs over the side of the bed.

"Come with me," Roman instructed as he left the bedroom. He walked straight to Alexi's liquor cabinet and pulled out a bottle of red wine. "We need to talk."

"I can't help my body's reaction to him," Alexi said from the doorway to the living room.

"I know." Roman poured them each a generous glass. He'd witnessed many things in his years on earth, but never had he seen the kind of frenzied fucking that had just taken place, and he needed to wrap his mind around the situation before he said or did something that would spell disaster for all three of them.

"I spoke to Mao." Roman held Alexi's wine out and waited for the naked vampire to cross the room.

"Do I want to hear what he had to say?" Alexi took the glass from Roman before sitting on the couch.

"Probably not." Roman chose to sit in a chair across from Alexi as he reiterated his conversation with the eldest of their sire's *sons*. By the time he finished, his glass was empty and Alexi was staring at him as if he had two heads.

"So you'll be forced to keep me around." Alexi seemed unhappy but resigned.

Roman refilled his glass before passing the bottle to Alexi. "Yes. If you leave, you'll be putting yourself and Bodi at risk."

"And you? I saw your face when I was fucking him. Are you going to be able to handle it? Julian was yours alone, but from the sound of it, Bodi can't be." Alexi ignored his glass and tipped the bottle to his lips.

Roman sat back in his chair and stared at the dark red liquid as he lifted it to his mouth. The thought of sharing Julian sent outrage coursing through his body, but he hadn't felt that way with Bodi. Sure, it bothered him to see Bodi and Alexi having sex, but he hadn't felt like ripping the skin from Alexi's body at the sight.

"I don't know," Roman finally said, trying to keep his gaze off Alexi's erection. "I think the big question is, how are you and I going to make this work for Bodi?"

Alexi chuckled. "It's not like we've never fucked."

True. Roman had often gone to Alexi for their yearly feeding, and sex had always played a role, but jacking each other off or the occasional fuck wasn't nearly the same as sleeping in the same bed every night. Sadly, he wasn't sure if he even liked Alexi enough to spend that much time with him, but he did know Alexi had always been there for him. Unfortunately, Roman liked structure in his life, and he doubted Alexi knew the word.

"My home is in New York," Roman reminded Alexi. "Are you willing to relocate?"

One moment Alexi was across the room and the next he was on his knees, insinuating himself between Roman's legs. "Doesn't really matter if I am or not, because I doubt you'll be able to convince our surfer boy to leave the waves."

Roman ran his palm over Alexi's short hair. He hated California, but Alexi was right. The next several decades would be hard enough on Bodi without taking him away from his home. "Can we at least move to a different house? I think Bodi would prefer something closer to the beach, and I'd much rather have a house that feels like a home."

Alexi wrapped his hand around Roman's flaccid dick. "I thought you liked my place?" He licked the head while maintaining eye contact.

Without the desire that came with feeding, it took a few moments for Roman's cock to respond to Alexi's attention. Roman watched Alexi circle his pink tongue around the crown of his hardening shaft. "Unlike you, I'm not ashamed to spend my money on things that'll make us more comfortable."

Alexi scraped one of his fangs against the tender skin, drawing blood. "If you'll agree to stay in San Diego, I suppose I'll let you spend your money on a new house," he said before latching on to the bulbous head of Roman's erection.

Roman couldn't keep a groan from escaping as Alexi gave him the best blow job he'd had in years. With each suck from Alexi, Roman felt his resistance to the idea of a threesome melt away. There was only one obstacle that remained.

"What if Bodi's soul never recognizes me?" Roman whispered, afraid that if he said it any louder he would jinx himself.

Alexi pulled back enough to answer. "Just be yourself, and either way, Bodi will fall in love with you."

Roman wasn't so sure. Despite the similarities in their appearances, Bodi was so different from Julian. Bodi, with his shoulder-length blond hair and choice of career, seemed a better fit for Alexi's lifestyle. *Damn.* Roman wondered if he had the ability to change after so many years of self-discipline. He glanced down at his naked body. With his legs sprawled and Alexi between them, devouring his cock, Roman realized there were definite advantages to a more relaxed way of life. It was on the tip of his tongue to ask Alexi if he wanted his ass, but Alexi beat him to it.

"Let's go back to the bedroom." Alexi stood before holding out his hand. "It's been years since you let me fuck you, and I want to be with Bodi in case he wakes up."

With his cock at full attention, Roman followed Alexi back to Bodi.

Chapter Three

Alexi sat back on his heels and watched while Roman moved a still-sleeping Bodi to the right side of the bed. He knew Roman had misgivings about the situation with the three of them, but Alexi couldn't have asked for a better scenario. For centuries, he'd lusted after Roman, but before Julian had captured Roman's attention, Roman hadn't been the kind of vampire to give anyone more than a day or two of his time.

After Julian's unfortunate death, Alexi had hoped he could help Roman heal but, once again, his brother had built up the walls that surrounded his heart and refused to let anyone else in.

Alexi liked to believe it was fate, disguised in a five-foot-eight-inch package, who had finally brought them together. Of course, Roman had no idea Alexi had always loved him from afar, and Alexi wasn't about to tell on himself. He ran his gaze up Roman's lean, sculpted body and groaned. "Pass me the lube."

Roman handed Alexi the small bottle. "I can't believe Bodi's still affecting your body." He drew his finger down the length of Alexi's erection.

Alexi grinned. The sexual bond he'd formed with Bodi had nothing to do with his current condition. Nope, his desire was aimed at Roman. "Do you need help?"

Roman reached down and circled his hole. "I can handle it."

After popping the top on the bottle, Alexi coated his cock. "How long's it been since you've trusted someone enough to bottom?"

"When was our last feeding?" Roman's face flushed. "Trust isn't something I'm good at."

It was the nicest thing anyone had ever said to him, and Alexi acknowledged the compliment with a subtle nod as he stretched out over Roman's perfect body. He fit the crown of his shaft against Roman's hole before pausing to take a deep breath. In the past, their coupling had always been a direct result of the feeding frenzy that occurred when vampires were strong enough to go months without taking blood.

The moment Alexi pushed inside Roman, he knew what he felt had nothing to do with the frenzy and everything to do with the vampire under him. He lowered himself to lie fully on top of Roman. The feel of Roman's soft breath against his lips almost had the words he'd longed to say slipping from his mouth, but he knew better. Roman's heart belonged to Julian's soul and always would. He closed his eyes as he sank his cock fully into Roman's warmth.

Roman's body stiffened for several heartbeats before he wrapped his arms and legs around Alexi. "You feel different," Roman whispered.

"*We* feel different," Alexi wanted to say. He slowly withdrew before thrusting his hips—sinking his length as deep as it would go. "Just thought I'd slow things down for a change."

Roman stared up at Alexi. "I think I like slow."

Alexi rested his forehead against Roman's as he continued to slide in and out. The squeeze of Roman's body around his girth was like nothing he'd ever felt before, and he knew he would do anything to build the kind of life with Roman and Bodi that he'd always dreamed of living. Excluding the occasional get-together, vampires were solitary creatures by nature, but Alexi had never enjoyed spending time alone. Roman might have enjoyed centuries of living apart from humans and vampires, but Alexi had always preferred to be surrounded by them. Working at Unconventional had been the perfect fit, but he wasn't sure if Roman could handle being around the noise and chaos each night, and he had no doubt Roman would want to be at Bodi's side regardless of the situation. If Bodi needed Alexi's sexual attention like he had earlier, the hot little surfer would need to stick close to Alexi.

Roman broke eye contact as he moved his legs higher around Alexi's torso. "I need you to fuck me hard," he murmured against Alexi's lips.

With a groan, Alexi withdrew his cock before repositioning Roman to lie on his side with his left leg draped over Bodi's groin. Alexi spooned Roman's back. Although Roman didn't say it, Alexi had a feeling the emotions sparking between them had been too much for Roman to handle, but that was Roman. Other than for Julian, Roman's emotions were buried so damn deep, Alexi knew it would take years to uncover them.

"Okay?" Alexi asked as he pushed back inside.

Roman ran his palm up Bodi's bare chest and rested his head on Bodi's shoulder. "Perfect."

A spike of jealousy hit Alexi when he realized Roman's words were meant more for Bodi than himself. *Someday.* For the moment, he would silently love Roman in his own way.

Alexi closed his eyes and hammered in and out of Roman as he had Bodi earlier. The only difference was the need driving him to climax, because it wasn't emotional with Bodi, not yet anyway. His connection with Bodi was purely sexual, although he hoped a much deeper bond would soon form between them.

"I'm close," Roman panted. He reached back and gripped Alexi's hip with the same hand he'd used to pet Bodi's chest only moments earlier.

Alexi continued to plunder Roman's ass despite the warning, but his overwhelming need ratcheted up a notch seconds later. He didn't understand what had happened until he heard Bodi's soft voice.

"It wasn't a dream," Bodi said, loud enough to be heard over the sound of Alexi and Roman's moans.

Fuck. Alexi felt as though his body was being torn in two as the need to have Bodi once again clawed at him. He buried his face against Roman's neck. Despite his physical response to Bodi, Alexi refused to withdraw until he was certain Roman had been satisfied. "Come," he demanded.

Bodi sat up and reached between Roman's and Alexi's bodies to explore the connection between the two. "You're screwing your brother?"

Alexi shook his head. "Not my brother in the human sense of the word." He barely remembered his biological brothers.

"So in your world, it's okay to do what you're doing?" Bodi asked as he pressed a finger against the length of Alexi's cock and let it slide in and out of Roman's ass on each thrust.

When Roman cried out his climax at Bodi's invasion, Alexi felt cheated. He slowed his hips and waited for

Roman to wring out his orgasm before withdrawing completely. Despite the fact that he hadn't come, Alexi rolled off the bed and stalked to the hallway bathroom. After wetting a washcloth, he began to clean himself as he condemned his own foolish pride. It wasn't Bodi's fault, or Roman's for that matter, and if they were going to make a relationship between all three of them work, Alexi had to get over his jealousy.

Alexi rinsed the washcloth under hot water before carrying it back to the bedroom. "We should talk before morning," he said after noticing the time.

"Talk later, I need you," Bodi whined as he rolled to his stomach.

It took all Alexi's self-control not to climb on the bed behind that fantastic ass and bury himself deep, but he had to stay strong. "Roman and I need to talk to you first."

In an effort to keep his hands to himself, he tossed Roman the washcloth before moving to lean against the wall. He regarded Roman first. "You want to start? I think Bodi deserves to know what Mao told you."

Roman narrowed his gaze at Alexi. "We still don't know if Bodi's soul will ever recognize me."

"Right, but he deserves the truth regardless," Alexi shot back. He secretly hoped Roman would get angry, because he'd much rather deal with a pissed off vampire than an indifferent one.

Roman did a quick clean-up before tossing the wet rag to the floor. "Fine," he ground out.

While Alexi listened to Roman tell Bodi the truth about their situation, he watched both men closely. Bodi appeared to take everything in with a surprising amount of calm while Roman appeared to get more anxious the longer he talked.

"What about my parents?" Bodi asked, interrupting Roman.

"I never knew my parents, but maybe Alexi can answer that." Roman glanced at Alexi.

"They're still your parents," Alexi said. "Unfortunately, unlike you, they'll continue to age." He still remembered his parents' deaths like they happened yesterday instead of centuries earlier. "It won't be easy when they pass, but it never is, no matter who you are."

"But I can still see them?" Bodi hugged his legs closer to his chest.

"Sure, if they'll accept you, but you need to prepare yourself for rejection. It's not an easy thing for most humans to come to terms with." Alexi uncrossed his arms and took a step toward the bed. They weren't finished talking yet, but the hard part appeared to be over with and only the details were left to discuss.

"I'm not worried about that," Bodi replied. "They accept everyone. It's just who they are."

"Good." Roman brushed Bodi's hair away from his face. "Do they live close?"

Bodi shrugged. "Cabo, but I try to get down once a month to see them." He sighed. "I bought 'em a place on the beach so I could take advantage of the waves. The sunshine feels different down there for some reason. Maybe it's because there're fewer people on my parents' slice of paradise, but there's absolutely nothing better in the world than catching a few waves before stretching out on the warm beach to bake."

Alexi frowned at the sympathy he felt for Bodi's plight. His connection with Bodi was supposed to be purely sexual, so the fact that he felt like wrapping his arms around the young surfer, to ease his obvious distress, bothered him. For centuries, Roman had been the only man who'd garnered that kind of response from him. He tilted his head to the side and studied the way Roman soothed Bodi with his touch.

"You'll get used to surfing at night," Roman told Bodi.

"Yeah? And will I get used to being so damn cold all the time?" Bodi bit his bottom lip as he snuggled against Roman.

Alexi moved to press against Bodi's back. "As you age, your body will start to warm." He pressed his palm against the center of Bodi's chest. "Do I feel cold?"

Bodi shook his head. "Sorry. I guess I'm still having a hard time accepting that I'm not the same man I was when I woke up this morning."

Alexi nuzzled Bodi's neck before placing a soft kiss on the sun-bronzed skin. "Don't apologize. You're adapting at an alarming rate."

"If you say so." Bodi yawned.

"Sleep," Roman urged. "Dawn is upon us."

Alexi met Roman's gaze. He didn't want to go back to his own room, and silently tried to convey the fact without words.

Blindly, Roman reached down and grabbed the blanket before covering all three of them. "We'll talk more this evening."

Alexi rested his hand on Roman's hip, caging Bodi between them. He closed his eyes and brushed his thumb back and forth, feeling lighter that Roman allowed such a touch. He still wasn't sure how things between the three of them would work, but he was determined to do whatever it took to keep both men in his life until he turned to ash.

Chapter Four

Alexi walked out of their new ten-million dollar La Jolla home to the impressive deck that faced the Pacific Ocean. It was just after three in the morning, and he'd known exactly where to find Bodi and Roman, although he hadn't expected to find the group of twenty or so surfers that had gathered to watch Bodi do his thing.

"He's magnificent," Roman said from his position at the wrought-iron rail.

Alexi pressed the full length of his body against Roman's back before moving Roman's long black hair to the side, exposing the column of Roman's neck. "He has quite a crowd gathered," Alexi murmured as he pressed a kiss to Roman's cool skin.

"More each night." Roman tore his gaze away from Bodi and glanced over his shoulder. "He's adapted nicely to surfing in the dark."

Alexi looked at the full moon. "It's not dark tonight."

Roman shrugged. "It's not the sunshine he's used to, either."

Alexi knew Roman still felt guilty about eliminating the warmth of the sun from Bodi, but Bodi seemed to take the changes in stride. Never in all Alexi's years had he known someone to adapt to vampirism so quickly.

"He's happy," Alexi pointed out as he slid his arms around Roman. "And he makes us happy."

Roman answered with a noncommittal grunt.

Alexi grinned because he knew he'd made his point. "Bodi's always lived for the adrenaline rush. What could be more exhilarating than the life he's now living? He gets fucked more times a day than a porn star, he'll be around to enjoy the ocean for centuries and he's in love for the first time in his life."

"How do you know he's in love?" Roman asked.

"How do you not? It's in his eyes every time he looks at one of us." Alexi turned Roman to face him. "You're so consumed with Julian and whether or not he's in there somewhere that you haven't accepted the gift Bodi, so obviously, has given you."

"Julian told me he'd return if we were meant to be together," Roman said.

"If it weren't for Julian, you wouldn't have been at Unconventional the night Bodi was attacked. Maybe we've been looking at this whole thing all wrong. What if Julian's only job was to bring you someone you *could* spend the rest of your life with?" Alexi wanted to bring his own love for Roman into the discussion, but he wasn't sure Roman was ready to hear the L-word, so instead, he improvised. "I'm living the life I've always wanted and that's because you and Bodi are in it."

The corner of Roman's mouth quirked up. "When did you get so sappy?"

"The first night I woke up with you and Bodi at my side and realized I could feel the sun on my skin without leaving my bed."

Roman cupped the back of Alexi's neck and leaned in for a deep kiss before breaking away again. "It's time Bodi came inside," he growled against Alexi's mouth.

* * * *

Bodi stared at the glass of red wine in front of him. Before his transition, he'd preferred beer, but he could no longer handle the bitter taste. Like everything in the last few months, he'd just shrugged at the unexpected development and moved on. He knew Roman and Alexi were confused by his ability to adapt to the new lifestyle so quickly, but the fact was, he was a vampire now. He'd never been the kind of person who held grudges or expected others to cater to him. Although he loved his parents with all his heart, they had always drawn attention, and, unfortunately, as a kid, he'd borne the brunt of people's ridicule because he'd been the easy target. Instead of letting it break him, he'd embraced the beauty of being different. So, while he could have spent years being bitter that his former life had been taken from him, he'd decided to welcome his new existence with open arms.

"More wine?" Alexi asked.

Bodi shook his head. "Where's Roman?"

Alexi leaned his forearms on the bar in front of Bodi. "Roman received permission to take Boris Yazinski off the street."

"Who?" Bodi ran his hand up Alexi's forearm. It was hard to be around Alexi and not want to fuck.

"The man who attacked you. It's taken a while for the elders to decide what should be done, but their decision was handed down, giving Roman permission to seek retribution," Alexi explained.

"What does that mean? Why's Roman seeking retribution? Shouldn't I be the one to do that?" As odd as it sounded, Bodi hadn't given much thought to the man who'd tried to rip out his throat. He'd been so busy adjusting to the changes in his life that he hadn't had time to dwell on the past.

Alexi reached out and cupped Bodi's cheek. "Sweetheart, you're not strong enough to handle Yaz."

Bodi turned his head and pressed a kiss to Alexi's palm. "I don't like the thought of Roman getting hurt because I'm too weak to fight my own battles. I understand that something needs to be done with Yaz, but it was my friend he killed. I should have a say in what happens to him."

"I'm sorry, but it doesn't work that way. Our laws were put in place centuries ago for a reason. The council looked into the situation and determined that, although Yaz is a relatively new vampire compared to some of us, he *does* know the penalty for killing a human."

Bodi glanced at the front door, willing Roman to walk through it.

"Roman knows what he's doing. He may be gentle with you, but he's a powerful badass when he needs to be."

It was hard to think of Roman as anything but kind, but Bodi trusted Alexi. "I just want him here with us."

"Are you starting to remember him?" Alexi asked as he served a fresh drink to the mage on Bodi's left.

Bodi shook his head. Roman asked the same question nearly every evening when they woke, and enough time had passed that he felt like a failure on each occasion that he was forced to say no. "What if I never do? Will he leave me?"

Alexi paused in the process of mixing a margarita. "You're in love with him," he stated.

Bodi wasn't sure how Alexi knew what was in his heart, but he couldn't keep his feelings to himself any longer. "Well, yeah. I think I started falling for him that first night when he showed me the photograph of Julian that he carries around. I remember thinking at the time that I'd give anything to have someone look at me like that."

"Have you told Roman that you're in love with him?"

"No, but I haven't told you either." Bodi realized what he'd confessed and waited for Alexi's reaction.

Alexi reached out and grabbed Bodi under the arms before lifting him across the bar. "You didn't have to. I see the way you feel each time you look at us."

Bodi heard several customers whistling and urging Alexi on. It wasn't the first time the two of them had given the crowd a show. In the first few weeks following his transition, Bodi hadn't been able to go more than two hours without some form of sexual contact from Alexi, but it was starting to get better. At least Bodi could wait until Alexi went on break now.

"Why haven't you said anything?" Alexi asked as he ground his erection against Bodi.

Before Bodi could answer, two things drew his attention away from Alexi. The hush from the crowd, and the overwhelming smell of blood. Looking over his shoulder, he saw Roman standing in the doorway. Splattered with blood, Roman looked like the badass vampire Alexi said he was.

"Home," Roman growled.

* * * *

Roman entered their newly purchased beach house first and strode straight through to the master bedroom. The adrenaline coursing through his body from the evening's hunt made it impossible to think of anything but claiming what was his. He stripped out of his drenched clothes before lying in the center of the mattress. Yaz's blood had soaked through the thin material of Roman's pants and shirt, leaving him covered in his enemy's life force.

Alexi stalked into the room. "You need to fuck?"

Instead of answering, Roman wrapped his hand around his cock and began to stroke its hard length.

Alexi ripped his shirt off. "Get undressed," he told Bodi.

"What's wrong with him?" Bodi asked, pulling off his sneakers.

"He's still in the throes of bloodlust. Follow my lead," Alexi explained as he finished with his clothes. He knelt on the foot of the bed and met Roman's gaze as he waited for Bodi to join them.

"It's done." Roman wanted to pull Alexi down on his cock, but he knew he'd only end up hurting Alexi if he tried to fuck while still in the grips of bloodlust. It wasn't a common condition for vampires to be in, but it was to be expected after killing one of their own species.

Once Bodi was at his side, Alexi leaned over and began to lick Yaz's blood from Roman's thighs. The cleansing of a loved one after battle went back to the beginning of their existence, but Roman had never been gifted with the intimate act because the only man he'd ever loved wouldn't have understood the barbaric ritual. The fact that Alexi and Bodi were cleaning their enemy's blood from his body touched Roman more than anything he'd ever experienced. It was in that moment that he realized Bodi and Julian were two entirely different people. He had no doubt they shared the same soul, but Julian's desire to return to Roman wasn't strong enough to take over Bodi's own desire to be in control.

Roman watched as his two men slowly cleaned the blood from his body. As he did, he saw Bodi for the man he *was* not for the man Roman had thought he wanted. He tried to imagine Julian adapting to life as a vampire but couldn't, because in his heart he knew that Julian would never have welcomed the transition, no matter what they'd initially agreed to. Perhaps fate had used Julian's soul to bring Bodi into his life. What if Alexi had been right and Bodi was the one he'd been meant to have all along, and Julian had merely been the bridge that had brought the two of them together?

Roman groaned when Alexi looked up at him. He realized what he would have missed if he'd turned Julian instead of waiting for Bodi. *Alexi.* Julian hadn't like to be around other vampires, so Roman would have had to adapt to life without Alexi in it. Maybe he wouldn't have realized the sacrifice he'd made, but he knew now, and he couldn't imagine a better life than one with both Alexi and Bodi in it.

"I'm at peace," Roman whispered.

Alexi reached for the bottle of lube. "Yeah, it's comforting to know Yaz isn't lurking around anymore."

Roman smiled. Alexi believed he felt peace because he'd ripped Yaz's limbs from his body, but his state of mind had absolutely nothing to do with the retribution he'd wrought on the rogue vampire.

Alexi tapped Bodi on the arm. "Turn around."

Bodi grinned and moved until Roman had the perfect view of his ass.

"How do you want to do this?" Alexi asked as he began to lube Bodi's pucker.

"I'll make love to Bodi while you fuck me," Roman answered.

"You mean, while I make love to you," Alexi corrected.

"Yes. I'd like that." Roman rolled to the center of the bed and waited for Bodi and Alexi to claim their spots on either side of him.

"Are you okay?" Bodi asked. "You seem different. Is it the bloodlust?"

"No." Roman gathered Bodi in his arms. He needed to tell Bodi the truth. "I understand now that I was always meant to be with you and Alexi. Julian's gone, and although I loved him, he wasn't what I needed."

Bodi twisted to look over his shoulder. "You mean that?"

"I do." Roman pressed his palm against Bodi's chest. "I think Julian loved me enough to bring the three of us together. Since his death, I've been blind to everyone because I thought only he could make me feel whole again. It was because I sensed his soul in you that I opened my heart enough to love again, and now I realize Julian's job was done the moment I held you in my arms the first time."

"I love you, too," Bodi replied. He reached behind him and directed Roman's cock to his hole. "I was so afraid of disappointing you."

"Never." Roman pushed the head of his shaft through the ring of muscles until he was buried to the root inside Bodi. He moaned in pleasure when Alexi impaled him in one smooth thrust.

Roman scraped Bodi's neck with his fangs as he began to drive in and out of him. The wounds weren't deep enough to feed, but they did bead up with enough blood to heighten Roman's pleasure. He latched on to Bodi's neck and sucked as he made love to his surfer. It still amazed him that after months of living life in the dark of night, Bodi still smelled like sunshine.

After several minutes, Bodi pushed back against Roman's groin. "Harder."

Roman released Bodi's neck and grinned at the hickey before it magically disappeared. "I thought we were making love," he reminded Bodi of Alexi's earlier proclamation.

"In my eyes, every time you touch me you're making love to me, so why can't we make love harder, deeper and much faster?"

Chuckling, Alexi pulled out of Roman before rolling to his back. "Should we double his pleasure?"

Roman thought about it. Although they'd tried many positions since getting together, they'd yet to both penetrate Bodi at the same time. "You think he can handle it?"

"Only one way to find out," Bodi chimed in.

Roman withdrew before easily lifting Bodi to sit astride Alexi's lap. "Have you ever taken two cocks at the same time before?"

Bodi shook his head as Roman poured more lube down the crack of his ass.

"Tell us if it's too much." Roman directed Alexi's erection to Bodi's stretched hole. He watched as Bodi's body seemed to swallow Alexi's heavily veined shaft in one gulp. Damn that was sexy. Grabbing his own erection just under the head, he got to his knees behind Bodi and slowly pushed his bulbous crown into Bodi's body.

"I'll heal if you two split me wide open, right?" Bodi asked between groans.

"Yeah, but there's no sense in being in pain, so if it's too much, just tell us." Roman fought the desire to drive in to the hilt.

"I'm fine." Bodi began to rock back, taking more of Roman's length.

Roman grunted with each inch of progress. By the time Bodi was fully seated, Roman was so close to orgasm he couldn't speak. A sense of nirvana overtook him, as he became one with his two men. Evidently, he wasn't the only one who felt the moment envelop them, because Alexi and Bodi went completely still.

"Meant to be," Alexi finally whispered.

"Yes," Roman agreed. He pressed his forehead against Bodi's spine. "Please tell me I can move now?"

"Yeah," Bodi panted.

Roman slid out two or three inches before pushing back inside. He repeated the motion several times before he felt Bodi's body clench around him.

"Can't. Hold. It," Bodi cried out as he came.

"Fuck," Alexi growled.

The warmth of Alexi's cum against his cock pushed Roman over the edge. His hips bucked as he shot his load into Bodi. The scent of perspiration and their combined climaxes threatened to overwhelm him as his body continued to quake with the force of his orgasm.

When Bodi sank onto Alexi's chest, Roman gave in to his exhaustion and collapsed against Bodi's back. The three of them had enjoyed sex for hours at a time, but he'd never felt as drained as he did at that moment.

Roman struggled but eventually calmed his breathing enough to slide off Bodi onto the mattress beside Alexi. He rested his cheek against Alexi's shoulder and watched Bodi sleep. "He truly is the best thing that could have happened to us," he told Alexi.

"I agree." Alexi kissed the top of Roman's head. "You're really not disappointed that he can't remember Julian?"

Roman brushed Bodi's hair away from his face. "According to Mao, we could have lost him if he'd remembered and couldn't handle it. I take peace in knowing I love Bodi for who he is. Julian will always have a spot in my heart, but he's gone, and I accept that now."

"That's good." Alexi drew Roman even closer. "We'd better rest before Bodi wakes and wants to go again."

Roman had no doubt Alexi was telling the truth, but there was one more thing the two of them needed to discuss. "I'm sorry I spent so many years pushing you away."

"Don't be. Like you said, it wasn't our time."

"This is our time," Roman proclaimed as his eyes drifted shut.

Julian waited until he heard steady breathing coming from Alexi and Roman before he opened his eyes. It hadn't been easy to hide his existence from the three men, but he'd known Roman would never fully give himself to Alexi or Bodi if he continued to carry a false sense of responsibility for Julian.

"I'll always love you," Julian whispered to Roman, "but it's time for me to go."

A slight glow lit Bodi's sleeping body as Julian bid farewell to his life on earth.

COMING IN THIRD

Amber Kell

Dedication

For my ménage loving fans!

Chapter One

"Do you think he'll cooperate?"

Niall stopped. He pressed his body flat against the wall at the sound of his uncle's voice. He'd planned to go clubbing, confident everyone had already left for the night. Normally by this time they were all off at social events or, as Niall privately called them, 'sucking up to the queen parties'.

Crap.

"He'll do what I want. It's time for him to marry. I've even made a list for him to choose from." His mother's tone pierced icy shards of disdain through his skin.

"What if he doesn't like your choices?" his uncle persisted, ever the sly voice of innuendo and scandal. There were weasel shifters less sneaky than Niall's Uncle Virnen, and none as mean.

"Then I'll persuade him." They laughed together, two partners pleased to crush others in their pursuit of common goals.

Niall's stomach gurgled and swirled in protest as he pulled his magic around him. The hair on his arms and neck rose, reacting to both the dangerous situation and his escapist magic. He raced past the doorway, breath held and nerves clenched to the edge of pain. A single drop of sweat slid down his hairline and worked a straight path down his nose. He twitched.

Fuck.

The rumble of voices concocting evil plans followed him down the hall. He didn't need to hear any more. He'd known his days were numbered. Mother had planned Niall's life since she'd first strategized how he should learn to walk. She also choreographed his whippings when she thought he'd twitched a pinky out of line.

Now they'd come up with a way to hold him in the painful, steel bear trap of marriage. Before he could say no, they'd have him shackled and bound. He had no futile belief they'd truly give him any say about anything. They might present him with the illusion of a choice, but reality wouldn't match the pretty fiction they created to get him to go along.

Tonight he would take control. For once he'd stop letting others run his life and do something for himself. Tomorrow they'd drag him back to his broken life but tonight was his. He'd be caught and punished, but they'd whip him even if he did nothing. His mother's guards relished the taste of his pain and the marks on his body. More than one had licked at him while he dangled from magic draining manacles, dripping out his life force.

His own guards had broken him out of his last captivity and more than a few of his mother's guards had met with an unhappy accident.

Burying his past horrors deep, Niall swiped a set of keys from the rack in the garage. The red convertible suited his mood tonight.

Although the queen's guards saw him leave the estate, no one moved to intervene. His mother must not have sent out word to keep him confined. For once, his luck ran true.

Niall lowered the convertible's hood. The breeze whipped around him, ruffling his hair and granting him an unprecedented wave of freedom.

What if I just keep driving?

They'd hunt him. His mother's trackers would find him, capture him and teach him a lesson about never wandering away again. He had no self-delusional belief he'd ever escape the guards permanently, unless through death.

The magical tracking devices on him alone could trigger a hunt if he didn't return first thing tomorrow. He might have slipped the leash for the moment but he could still be yanked back like a dog on a magical spiked choke chain.

It took several turns down narrow alleys before he found the building he'd heard about. The unremarkable outside didn't hint at the secrets inside. Niall had eavesdropped on some of the other fae talking about the bar and the hot hook-ups they found there. Tonight he'd be the one on the prowl.

A spot of street parking opened up and Niall slipped the car neatly inside. Hopefully it was a harbinger of good luck. He put the top back up before sliding out of the car and slammed the door behind him. If his hand shook a bit when he locked the door, he ignored it.

The bouncer at the door stopped him. "Identification?"

Niall pulled out his driver's license and handed it over.

The bouncer took out a little flashlight and flickered it over Niall's identification picture. A special coating reflected Niall's fae stamp with a swipe of the light.

Each paranormal received a special symbol to represent 'other than human'. Nothing would've shown if Niall wasn't paranormal.

"We don't get a lot of fae here." The bouncer's hungry graze slid up and down Niall's body. "If you're still here when I get off, I'll look you up."

"Thank you." It would be dangerous to tell him trolls weren't really Niall's type. Trolls tended to react with violence when rejected. He accepted his license back then scooted inside. Hopefully he'd have found a new companion before he had to figure out a reasonable excuse for brushing off the troll.

Music greeted him as he entered. Not a loud pounding rhythm but a quiet accompaniment to the people speaking inside. An enthusiastic group of dancers was displaying their best sexy moves on a small dance floor, but they hadn't reached the stripping-off-their-clothes stage yet.

He was only going to do this once. Get it out of his system then never revisit this desire again. Even if he found the perfect couple, his mother would see to it he didn't return.

Niall glanced over the crowd and decided to start with alcohol. He needed liquid courage before he tried to find a pair of men for the night. Going into a situation would take some reconnaissance and booze before he could determine who to approach.

Fantasies crowded his brain. If he really planned to experience a ménage, he had to do it now, before his mother married him off to a rich asshole to build up the family coffers. His only joy then would be to pull out this amazing memory to relive on those rough nights with his new husband.

Niall should've known better than to think they'd give him a choice of partners. Fifth in line for the throne—and gay—Niall had thought he'd be free of his mother's mating manipulations. He should've known better. Pure, blind optimism had never worked for him before.

"Are you old enough to be here?" the bartender asked. She flashed Niall a friendly smile even as her assessing gaze swept over him.

"Yes." He pulled out his driver's license to show it to her before she had to ask. It never paid to argue about his age. It would take another hundred years or so before he appeared older than twenty. Bartenders and liquor store clerks always gave him the stinkeye.

"Fae?"

"Yes." He didn't elaborate dark or light fae. It was rude enough of her to ask about his kind.

She gave him a narrow-eyed stare. He returned it with one of his own. After a minute, she smiled then handed back his card. "Here you go."

"Thank you." He shoved it back into his pocket. "Could I get a beer? Whatever you have on tap is fine." He didn't care what he drank. He needed something for his hands to fiddle with while he looked around for companionship.

She slid a frosty mug filled with a frothy medium gold brew over to him. He accepted the drink with a nod before turning to lean against the bar. He had a good vantage point where he stood. Couples were dancing while others stood around talking. He sipped his beer while he figured out who to approach. Paranormals were more open to ménage than humans so he didn't worry anyone would be offended by his request, but he didn't want to be rejected either.

A pair of men sitting at a booth in the corner caught his eye, but when they looked at him, he glanced away. They were big, buff and oozed dominance. He could tell they'd be too much for him. Niall got hard as he imagined the two larger men wrestling it out in bed over who would top him first. Shaking his head, he tried to clear the tempting image from his mind.

He needed something different. A couple he could brush away the next morning and wouldn't leave him longing for them later.

Taking another drink of his beer, he froze when a slim-fingered hand slid down his back before settling around his waist. "Looking for some companionship, honey? I'm Angelo. My friends call me Angel."

Angel had kind blue eyes, a sweet smile and smelled of the sea. Too bad Niall needed something different tonight.

"No thank you."

Angel frowned. "Are you here with someone?"

Niall offered him an apologetic smile. "No, but I'm looking to hook up with a couple tonight. If I wasn't, I'd take you up on your offer."

Did people still use the term 'hook up'? He'd read that in a book once.

"Really? You'd be interested in me?" The surprise in the Angel's eyes twisted Niall inside out. The handsome man shouldn't have any doubt of his appeal.

Standing on his tiptoes, Niall gave the kind man a soft kiss on his lips. "Yes."

A smile of surprisingly white teeth was his reward before a serious expression crossed Angel's face. "You need to be careful. A lot of men would take advantage of a sweet thing like you."

Niall didn't bother with his usual spiel. The guy didn't need to know Niall had enough magic to bring anyone to his knees, except his mother. Even two strong alphas couldn't crush him if he didn't let them.

"Do you know any couples here who might welcome a third?"

Angel gave him a sideways hug. "Let's take a look at who's here tonight, shall we? I just got here a few minutes ago. How about those two?" He pointed a finger at the two big men Niall had spied earlier.

Niall shook his head. "They look like they could chew me up and spit me out."

Angel laughed. "Nah, they're pussycats. Come on, sweetheart. Let's get you your ménage then maybe you can owe me a date later."

Niall nodded even though he'd never be able to carry through with his promise. This was it before his mother dragged him to the altar, either the wedding or the sacrificial kind. "Fair enough."

He let Angelo pull him over to the couple. They were talking to each other in low tones with expressive hands and appeared to be in the middle of an argument.

Up close, Niall could see the man on the left had dark red hair and brilliant green eyes. He was larger than Niall had thought from across the bar. His companion was just as big as the redhead but with midnight black hair and dark eyes. They ended their argument when Angel and Niall approached.

The redhead raked Niall from head to foot with a heated glance. "Hey, Angel, who's your friend?"

Niall became the intense focus of two pairs of eyes. He resisted the instinct to hide behind his new friend. If he wished for a fling, he had to be made of sterner stuff.

Angel didn't hesitate to approach them. "Hello, you two—this is Niall. Niall, the dark-haired man is Luka and the redhead is Jovan. Are you guys done arguing now? Because if you're not, I'll take Niall home with me. He was kind of looking for a couple but..."

"Go away, Angel." Jovan stared at Niall, his words slicing deep despite his intent stare.

Niall's heart sank to his stomach. He'd thought the attraction mutual. It was demoralizing not to be desired. Maybe he'd misinterpreted their attention.

Before he could speak, maybe apologize for bothering them, Luka grabbed his arm and pulled him away from Angel. "And leave your present here."

Angel reached over and squeezed Niall's shoulder. "If you decide not to go with these guys, come get me. I'll be watching the game for the next hour."

"Thanks, Angel." Niall kissed him on the cheek. Angel blushed, making the two men at the table laugh.

"You're trouble, little man." Angel patted him on the back then wandered toward the group by the television.

Determined, Niall turned back to the two men. He could've sworn their eyes glowed in the dim lighting of the club.

Shifters?

This could be very interesting. He'd heard good things about a shifter's sex drive. Jovan stood and stepped away from the table. He tugged on Niall's arm and motioned for him to join them in the booth. Niall scooted in, his heart hammering against his chest. He could do this. He left a good two feet between him and the redhead before he stopped scooting along the bench.

"Don't sit so far away, baby." Luka wrapped an arm around Niall's waist and pulled him over until they touched hip to hip. "How are we going to know if we're compatible or not?"

"Sorry." Niall twisted his fingers together. "I'm new at this. I've never had a ménage before."

Or anything else, but he refused to admit that much. A low vibration tickled along his arm.

"Did you just purr?" Jovan asked his partner.

"Of course not," Luka denied. He slid his nose along Niall's neck. "You smell amazing."

"Hey, share." Jovan scooted over until he pressed against Niall's other side. Heat from both sides took away the chill of the air conditioner. Shifters ran hot, and not just in the looks department.

Niall took a deep breath, his heart pattering an uneven beat. The combined scent of two gorgeous, needy men made his head spin and his cock harden. He pushed back down the magical surge flaring up at the idea of the three of them tumbling in the sheets together. He had to keep control. His magic could fly out of hand if he didn't watch it.

"May I kiss you?" Luka touched Niall's cheek with his fingertips and tilted Niall's face toward him.

"Yes." His voice came out a little higher than usual. Great—he sounded like an idiot, but he'd never been the object of such intense focus before.

Luka grinned. "You're fucking adorable."

Niall opened his mouth to argue only to have Luka kiss him. The bar noises faded as his entire world narrowed to the brush of Luka's warm lips and the minty flavor of his tongue sweeping across Niall's. Luka must've eaten a breath mint before they kissed.

"Don't hog him to yourself." Jovan kissed the back of Niall's neck. Shivers shot down Niall's spine. He pressed closer to Luka, trying to capture more of his taste and scooting away from his intense response to Jovan. Luka slid his tongue across Niall's lips, distracting him again.

He melted into Luka's touch.

"My turn." Jovan plunged his fingers into Niall's hair then pulled him back. Niall only had the chance for a short noise of disappointment before Jovan spun him around.

Where Luka's kisses seduced, Jovan's conquered. Every thought evaporated from Niall's head. His lips vibrated from the purring noise rolling between them.

"I guess I'm not the only one who purrs," Luka commented.

Unbidden power poured through Niall's body and crackled across his skin.

Jovan jerked back. "What are you?"

"I'm fae."

Jovan touched his lips. "You have a lot of magic inside you for such a little guy."

Niall scowled. No matter the amount of magic, he still couldn't overpower his mother. "I'm not that little."

"Mmm, you taste delicious." Jovan stroked Niall's head, petting him gently. "What do you think about coming home with us?"

Niall bit his lip. Here was his chance. He could run out of the bar and back to the safety of the castle or take a chance for the first time in his life. Could he throw away caution and go home with this pair?

"Shh, you don't have to make up your mind right now. Let's eat something and get to know one another first." Luka rubbed Niall's back almost as if he could sense Niall's sudden bout of nerves. Maybe they could smell it on him.

"If you let him, Luka will mother you to death," Jovan whispered in his ear. His hot breath bathed Niall's left lobe in a sensual fog.

Luka growled. "Hush! Just because you don't like my fussing doesn't mean Niall won't." Luka laced his left hand with Niall's right and gave his fingers a gentle squeeze.

Niall caught a trace of pain in Luka's eyes. "I like it. I'm just not used to people wanting to take care of me unless they need something from me." *Or to help me recover from a brutal beating.* His guards had pieced him back together more than once.

Luka kissed Niall's forehead. "Jovan, order us something to eat. We want our new friend to have enough energy to keep up with us. Do you have any dietary restrictions, Niall?"

This was where things could get tricky. "I'm a vegetarian." He winced.

"No meat at all?" Jovan's appalled expression had Niall laughing.

"No meat. I don't mind if you eat it. I just can't." The one time he'd tried had ended in a horrible stomach purging he'd pretty much do anything to prevent again.

Jovan's exaggerated sigh of relief had him chuckling again. "At least it isn't some ethical bullshit that will make me have to give up my leather pants."

Niall choked on the beer he had just swallowed. Luka helpfully patted him on the back, a gesture that would've been more helpful if he hadn't finished the motion by dipping his fingers into the top of Niall's pants and fondling his ass.

"Trust me, I wouldn't make you give up your leather pants. That would be a crime." He let his imagination take over. A spontaneous daydream of Jovan strutting around in tight leather pants had Niall wriggling in his seat.

Jovan's hard mouth curled into a wicked smile. Damn, maybe he *could* read Niall's mind. Jovan waved the waitress over when she passed.

"Hey guys, nice to see you two again. What can I get for you tonight?" The waitress pulled a pad of paper out of one pocket and a pen from behind her ear.

Jovan spoke up. "Good evening, Samantha. We'd like a triple order of spicy chicken wings, a veggie wrap and a double order of fries. I think our friend here needs a second beer, and please bring us a bottle of your best Scotch and a pair of shot glasses."

"Anything else?" she asked after she finished jotting down their order.

"Nope. Just keep the beer flowing." As Jovan slid his hand up Niall's thigh, his pinky finger wandered a bit on its own.

"Two will be more than enough." Niall needed courage, not amnesia. If he took a chance on these two, he didn't want to forget their encounter in a sea of alcohol.

"Be right back." She flashed them a bright smile before rushing off. More people had entered the bar, increasing the noise and heat levels.

Jovan eyed the newcomers milling around and seemed to come to the same conclusion as Niall. "It might be a while before we see her again. The bar is getting crowded."

"That's all right. We're not in a hurry." Luka kissed Niall's cheek again.

Niall could bask in the shifter's attention forever.

"We're a package deal, you know." Jovan's gaze slid back and forth between Luka and Niall.

"I know. I wouldn't dream of getting between you." *Unless they were both naked.*

Heat rushed to Niall's cheeks. He pulled his hand out of Luka's and folded them together onto his lap. "I just thought I should mention this has to be a one-time thing. I'm certain my mom will have my husband picked out soon."

He might not want a marriage, but once bonded he wouldn't stray. Unless he could find a loophole—or maybe death—he'd be wedded soon.

"Husband?" Jovan asked, his tone hard. "We won't play with a cheater."

"No! Damn, I'm telling this badly. My family has a tradition of arranged marriages." Not happy marriages, but arranged ones. The fae didn't worry about things like compatibility and romance. If the marriage didn't work, Niall could dissolve it after fifty years. When a species lived for centuries, a forever mate rarely meant forever.

Niall's father had run off with his boyfriend after only twenty-five years with Niall's mother, a year after Niall's birth. He hadn't seen his father since. His mother still considered his father's desertion the ultimate betrayal because it had harmed her image at court. Mutual divorces were fine. Being so evil your mate runs away was not.

"And you're okay with an arranged marriage?" Luka asked.

"I don't want to die." *Crap!* Niall froze. Maybe the club had drowned out his response?

"Die?" Jovan turned Niall's face toward him. "Tell me."

He should have a stronger backbone after dealing with his mother for years but he couldn't deny Jovan's request. His entire life spilled out like a giant confessional.

"Poor thing." Luka wrapped Niall in his arms and cuddled him close.

"And you're just going to let your mother run the rest of your life?" Jovan asked. His disapproving tone had Niall tensing.

"Can we not discuss my future? I'm more interested in the present." He dared to press a kiss to Luka's throat. Distraction worked better than answers.

Jovan stroked a hand down Niall's hair. Niall turned and kissed Jovan again. Jovan had a surprisingly sweet flavor, while gentle Luka tasted spicy.

As they waited for their drinks, Niall went from one pair of lips to the other. He lapped at Luka's mouth, then Jovan's, absorbing their differences and putting them in his memory banks to retrieve on a rainy day. He anticipated a lot of storm clouds in his future.

The waitress' cheery voice broke into the sexual haze taking over his mind. "Here you go, boys. Now keep it clean over here. I don't want to have to get out the hose."

Jovan bit Niall's bottom lip before sliding away. "Let's feed you, pretty one. You're going to need your strength." His wicked smile did little to settle the excited energy rushing through Niall's body.

She set three glasses on the table, the click of glass against glass almost silent in the noisy club. "You okay, cutie? I don't need to rescue you, do I?"

Luka's froze beside him and Jovan slid a possessive hand across Niall's thigh. Neither spoke. Did they think he'd object and cry foul?

"I'm fine. Thank you for asking."

Samantha's concerned look didn't fade but she nodded. "I'll be back in a bit with your food. Try not to strip down before I return."

"I make no promises." Jovan kissed Niall before he could pick up his beer.

The waitress' snort barely registered as Niall gave up his will to Jovan's embrace. Luka's softer touch slid down his back. Niall arched into Luka's fingers, offering himself up.

"You are beautifully responsive," Luka purred into Niall's ear.

He shivered, lust shooting through him. How long could he take this sensual assault and not come in his pants?

"Ease off, Jovan. We don't want our sweet boy uncomfortable while we eat." Luka's sharp tone broke through Niall's needy haze. How could Luka sound so determined when Niall had to work hard not to slide beneath the table and suck them off, one after the other? He didn't share that information. Jovan might take him up on the idea.

Jovan feathered two more kisses across Niall's lips before leaning back. Niall followed, wanting more.

"No, sweet, Luka is right. I don't want you coming quite yet."

"I recover fast." He might come quickly the first time but he could go again many times. His mother's people were known for their virility.

Luka kissed Niall's cheek. "I'm sure you can, sweetness, but the smell of your spunk while we eat would make it difficult to concentrate."

Right—shifters. "Sorry, I didn't think of that."

Luka rubbed a reassuring hand up and down Niall's arm. "Which is why we told you. Have you ever been with shifters before?"

Jovan growled.

"Shh, it's not like we expected him to be a virgin."

Chapter Two

Jovan scooted away from touching Niall. He couldn't risk any contact while the sweet fae shared his past experiences. Anyone who had touched the pretty man should be eviscerated. Jovan's inner cat purred at the idea. It was a great plan—both halves of him approved. They were both already prepared to kill Niall's mother with great delight.

"I-I've never had sex before." Niall's soft confession struck Jovan harder than a jolt of lightning.

Jovan and Luka scooted closer to Niall. "Never?" Jovan smiled at the excitement in Luka's voice. They were both obviously of the same mind over how they viewed anyone else touching Niall.

"Never." Niall blushed.

Jovan's inner cat wanted to lick Niall from head to toe. His fingertips tingled as his claws threatened to burst from the tips. How easily they could scratch off Niall's clothing and claim him in front of the entire bar. He envisioned the crowd watching them with envy.

"Jovan!" Luka's stern tone snapped him out of his contemplation of Niall's neck and the idea of setting his teeth against the fae's pale skin and leaving his mark, something deep and scarring. A keep out sign to let others know they weren't welcome. Maybe Luka could mark the other side and give Niall an almost complete marking collar.

A smack against the back of his head jerked his gaze away from Niall. He glared at Luka instead.

"What?" He rubbed at the sore spot.

"You were about to shift in the middle of the bar. Stop growling before Niall decides you're too freaky and runs away."

He snapped his attention to Niall's apprehensive gaze. "Sorry, sweet." He cupped Niall's left cheek. "I didn't mean to frighten you."

"I'm not frightened, but I didn't know what to do. Are you upset I'm a virgin? You can fix that soon enough."

"No. I'm far from upset. I want to mark you." No point hiding his urges—Niall would learn about more of them soon enough.

"Y-you can't. I'm going to be mated. My mother..." Jovan stilled at the fear in Niall's tone. What had Niall's mother done to him to create such terror? He'd suspected when Niall had said his mother was putting pressure on him that he'd glossed over parts.

"We won't do anything you don't want. Will we, Jovan?" Luka's tone indicated Jovan had better agree.

"No we won't." If they did end up mated, Jovan would take great joy in making sure Niall's mother never went near him again.

"Okay." Niall leaned companionably against Luka.

"Here you go." The waitress set her large tray on the corner of the table then transferred plates of food to the spaces before them.

Niall's eyes lit up over his veggie wrap. "That looks good." A pile of French fries sat beside the wrap. He grabbed a spare plate and dumped a good portion of fries on it before handing it over to Luka. "I don't need all these."

Luka grinned. "Thanks."

Niall nodded then gave Luka a sweet kiss. Jovan would've used more force but Luka's glassy-eyed smile and oozing pheromones told Jovan Luka hadn't felt any lack.

Luka licked his lips.

Only a few words were spoken amongst them while they ate, mostly "pass the ketchup" or asking for more wings.

"What do you think, sweetness?" Jovan asked after sucking the remainder of sauce off his lips.

"About what?" Niall had devoured his food, whether because of hunger or nerves Luka didn't know.

Luka stroked a hand down Niall's back, a gentling technique he'd used on Jovan more than once.

"About going home with us." He kept the growl out of his tone and tried to appear nonthreatening. Not an easy task when his inner beast urged him to throw Niall onto the closest flat surface and fuck him hard.

Niall nodded, a short, abrupt motion. "Yes, please."

"Check!" Jovan shouted, waving his hand at Samantha as she passed carrying a feast of food on her tray.

She tilted an eyebrow at him. "Let me drop this food off then I'll bring your bill over."

"Fuck that." He didn't have time to waste. He had two hot men to please. Jovan tossed a handful of money on the table, probably more than twice what they owed.

Niall gave a sweet squeaking noise when Jovan grabbed his wrist and pulled him along the booth and to his feet.

"Don't scare him," Luka muttered as he slid out of the other side. Bracketing Niall, they headed out of the bar. When it became too crowded, Jovan followed Luka, his guiding light. He adored his kind alpha mate. Others underestimated Luka because of his gentle ways but Niall had seen Luka's harder edges. Luka only smoothed them around Jovan. Their love allowed Luka to show his softer side.

The cool night air soon had Niall shivering. Luka pulled him from Jovan's grasp to settle Luka's jacket around his shoulders. "Here, you look cold."

Niall smiled at Luka. Jovan shouldn't be jealous — he knew Luka loved him above all others — but Niall's easy affection for Luka pulled a little envy from him. He suspected Niall could be the third they'd been seeking for the past twenty years. Sweet, magical Niall, who thought they'd ever allow someone else to touch him or let him leave them.

Foolish fae.

Luka settled Niall in the back seat of his Mercedes then tossed Jovan the keys.

"You're letting me drive?" Luka might love Jovan but he had an unhealthy obsession with his car.

"Yeah." Luka's eyes slid to Niall then back and Jovan understood.

Luka didn't have the concentration to drive. He trusted Jovan to get them home.

Jovan gripped the keys, the metal biting into his hand. No one before Niall had ever thrown Luka enough to have him relinquish his keys. Maybe he *should* be jealous.

He slid behind the wheel and started up the car. The engine purred, a deep, satisfying sound not unlike a cat. Jovan smiled.

"Don't forget we have Niall with us," Luka reminded him.

"I won't forget." His inner feline growled a warning of its own. They had to watch over their fae. They couldn't mate properly with shattered bits.

Niall had told him he couldn't be their forever third. He wouldn't stay past tonight and once he married he wouldn't be back to see them again. Jovan's heart ached as he put the car into gear and drove away. Already he could see heartache in the distance.

Jovan tilted his rear view mirror until he could see Niall's reflection. "Unzip your pants."

Niall whimpered. "We're in public."

"Tinted windows. No one will see you." Luka twisted in his seat to watch the show.

"You offered yourself to us for the night. Did you change your mind?" Jovan wouldn't tolerate disobedience.

"Sorry." Niall rushed to unfasten his pants.

"You're not helping his nerves," Luka scolded.

"I like him nervous." The thrill of the unknown added a kick to Niall's first time. Luka could offer all the reassurance he wished, but Jovan planned to play with their entertainment for the night. When Niall went to lie with his hand-picked husband, he'd be dreaming of them.

Jovan's cat screamed. Neither of them liked the image of Niall with someone else.

"Do you need me to drive?" Luka kept his voice low.

"No. I've got it." No way would he admit he couldn't stand the idea of Niall leaving them to marry some idiot fae. They would have to do something to change his mind.

"Ohh, you are beautiful everywhere, aren't you." Luka's soft cooing voice ramped up Luka's desire.

Jovan tilted his mirror down but the seats blocked his view.

"Touch yourself but don't come. Luka's picky about his leather seats," Jovan ordered.

"I might make an exception for you, sweet boy." Luka's voice dipped into a raspy purr. Jovan hadn't known his lover could make that sound.

Niall's soft moan had Jovan adjusting himself with one hand while he steered with the other. He took a sharp right onto their street, unconcerned about the squeal of tires.

Luka patted Jovan's arm. "Easy, we don't want him injured."

"Just trying to get home." He abandoned trying to watch Niall. If he spotted the fae's bare cock, he'd crash into a tree.

"Let's get there in one piece. Niall isn't going anywhere tonight."

Niall's loud pants had Jovan's cat growling. Having Niall where he couldn't touch or taste had his inner beast scrambling to get out. His cat didn't care if he needed long legs to drive—it wanted to pounce.

Tires screeched as he pulled into their driveway. He tossed Luka the keys. "Get the house open. I've got Niall."

Not giving Luka a chance to object or speak or anything else, Jovan got out of the car then opened the back door. He scooped Niall up in his arms. The fae squeaked and flailed to get his balance.

"Hold on to me." Jovan cuddled Niall closer.

Niall grabbed Jovan's shirt, leaving his erection exposed through the opening of his jeans. His cock dribbled pre-cum from its wide tip.

Jovan's ass clenched at the sight. "Wow."

"I know—it's ridiculous." Niall sighed.

"You're gorgeous," Luka disagreed. "Good things come in large packages."

Niall's startled laugh warmed Jovan.

Luka's voice broke through Jovan's fixation on Niall. "Bring him inside. We don't want the neighbors to call the cops for public nudity."

Since their closest neighbor was three miles away, Jovan doubted they'd have neighbor issues, but when Niall shivered in the cold night air, he rushed through the door Luka had left open for them.

Speeding through the house, he reached their bedroom within seconds. He set Niall on the bed then tore at his clothes, unconcerned over fabric integrity or future use.

"Hey, I need those later!"

"I'll give you new ones. Covering up your body should be a crime." Jovan kneeled at the bottom of the mattress to admire Niall's physique. The fae lacked the bulky build of Jovan and Luka but had a nice set of muscles of his own. He needed there to be a difference between Luka and Niall. Although he loved Luka, sometimes he craved something different.

"I like to work out. It's one of the few activities I'm allowed to do." Niall blushed. The color chased across his skin. Jovan lapped at the reddish tone, trying to taste the difference with his tongue.

Niall giggled.

"I think he likes that." Luka came up behind Jovan and started undressing him.

Jovan stood to allow better access. Once Luka had stripped Jovan down, he removed his own clothing. Jovan's cat's possessiveness rose to the surface. It snarled its readiness to claim the gorgeous creature on their bed. He crawled up the right side of the mattress beside Niall before glancing back at Luka. "Heads or tails?"

Luka's eyes glowed in the dim light. "Mmm. Tails."

"Don't I get a vote?" Niall's hesitant tone had them returning their attention to their nervous new love interest.

"You get to say if we're doing anything that hurts, but other than that, no. You came with us knowing we would take charge, didn't you?" Jovan couldn't completely stop his need to dominate but he would curb it a bit if Niall became too overwhelmed.

"Yessss," Niall hissed.

Jovan glanced down in time to see Luka swallow Niall's cock, a time-honored way to end arguments. Smiling, he kissed Niall's right cheek. "Let me know if anything gets to be too much for you."

They wouldn't stop. Nothing except Niall truly not enjoying himself would make them change their ways. Until then they would taste, tease and sexually torture the pretty man on their bed. Jovan couldn't wait.

He normally would've climbed on top of Niall and trapped Niall with his body but that position would block the lovely sight of Luka sucking Niall down, and he refused to ignore such beauty.

"Oh fuck, I'm going to come." Niall arched his back and tilted his neck, exposing a long column of pale skin. Jovan's gums ached, and his canines threatened to emerge, to bite down and claim this sweet boy as his own.

"*Resist.*"

Luka's voice punched through Jovan's needy haze. Yes, his mate was right. He couldn't bite Niall or leave any permanent scars. Fuck. His inner cat lashed its tail. Jovan hadn't felt this out of control since he'd claimed Luka twenty years ago.

Brushing off the odd compulsion, he turned his attention to Niall's lips. Soft and inviting, he slid his own across the alluring landscape. A groan vibrated between them—whether from Jovan's kiss or Luka's sucking Jovan didn't know, but he swallowed it down as if it were his own.

One kiss led to another, tongues dueled and their teeth clacked together from the pressure of wanting to get closer. Niall grunted against Jovan's lips, his body convulsing through his orgasm.

When they broke apart to suck in air, Niall smiled down at Luka. "Fuck, you're gorgeous."

Luka crawled up Niall's body, licking his lips. "And you're delicious. I'd be happy to suck you anytime."

"Next time I get a taste." Envy speared through Jovan.

"How about now?" Luka plastered his mouth against Jovan's, sharing the taste of the fae's cum. Sweet with a trace of bitter and mixed with Luka's natural spice, Niall's essence tasted better than catnip.

Jovan hummed his approval.

"Ours."

Luka's declaration confirmed Jovan's fear. Niall was their missing third. In Jovan's family, mates always came in threes. Even the elders didn't completely understand why, but there had never been a duo in his family's mating tree. Luka and Jovan had been searching decades for their third. Now, they'd found him in a gentle-natured fae...who planned to leave them to wed a hand-picked groom not even Niall could muster any enthusiasm over.

Fuck that.

No way would he allow Niall to get married to some fae asshole who would never understand what a treasure he had. They'd have to do something to protect their mate.

They broke apart and slid onto either side of Niall in a synchronized motion. Jovan had lost count of the number of men he'd shared with Luka over the years. Lions weren't supposed to be able to identify their mate until they were intimate. Except this time, Jovan's lion was taking over and the beast insisted Jovan remain theirs.

"I'm certain he's our third," Luka whispered into Jovan's mind.

"Me too." This added an entirely new level of issues. How could they keep a fae lover determined to do his duty to his family? Or afraid not to? They couldn't fight against the entire fae kingdom.

"Did you change your mind about fucking me?" Niall's soft voice broke into Jovan's thoughts.

"No." He flashed what he hoped was a reassuring smile. "Just trying to decide who gets to top you first."

Luka flipped over and spread his legs. Their wide bed allowed him to move around for their often-acrobatic lovemaking. "How about Niall fucks me while you take him?"

"Luka, you always have the best ideas." Jovan smiled at his mate. "Grab the lube."

Reaching into the bedside table, Luka pulled out a large bottle.

Niall's eyes widened. "Wow, you guys must have a lot of sex."

"I'm sure you've heard of our high sex drive. Shifters enjoy pleasuring their mates." Jovan stroked a hand down Niall's leg before wrapping his fingers around Niall's impressive erection. "You have an excellent libido as well, I see."

Niall's embarrassed laugh charmed Jovan. "I have a lot to be excited about. You two are any gay man's wet dream."

Luka lapped at Niall's neck. Obediently, Niall tilted his head back to allow him even more access. Jovan took a deep breath, fighting back his beast. This casual hook-up had turned into a deep craving.

Luka met his gaze. *"Control yourself!"*

Jovan nodded. He couldn't scare Niall with the force of his need. It would kill him if he frightened their new lover.

"Are you okay?" Niall reached out a hand toward Jovan.

The simple act soothed Jovan's beast more than all the demands in the world. Niall trusted Jovan not to hurt him.

"Fine." His voice had the rough texture of his beast's roar but there was little he could do about that. "Are you ready for me to prepare you?"

Niall nodded. "Yes."

"Watch me." They both turned their attention to Luka, and Jovan growled. Luka had taken their momentary distraction to climb on his hands and knees. He reached one hand behind him and was pressing his slicked up fingers into his hole.

"Oh damn, that's something," Niall whispered.

Jovan nodded his agreement.

Luka flashed them a brilliant smile over his shoulder. Jovan rarely told his mate how much he appreciated him, always thinking the words were unnecessary between mates. From Luka's expression, maybe he should offer them more often.

"Luka, you're beautiful in your need."

"You are," Niall agreed, bobbing his head up and down.

"Then fuck me, Niall." Luka spread his legs and tilted his ass up higher.

Niall moaned. "Oh hell. Keep that up and I'll spill before I get inside you."

Jovan laughed. He'd lost count of how many times Luka's beauty had almost ended things before they began. "You can do it, Niall. Slide into Luka and I'll prep you."

"I can't believe this is really happening." Only because of his enhanced hearing did Jovan pick up Niall's soft whisper.

"It's definitely happening, sweetheart, but if at any time you feel uncomfortable you can call it off and Luka and I will understand." He didn't want Niall to feel as if he had to go through with anything he wasn't ready for.

Luka nodded his agreement. They had no wish to make Niall feel like he had to have sex with them.

"Oh, I want this. I'm just hoping it won't turn out to be some sort of dream."

Jovan pinched Niall's thigh.

Niall yelped. "Ouch."

"See, it's real."

Luka laughed. "Now fuck me."

"Yes, sir." Niall accepted the bottle of lube Luka handed over. With shaking fingers, he applied a thick coating across his erection.

"I'm a shifter, babe, it's hard to hurt me," Luka said.

"Shush, I'll take care of you if I want." Niall moved over until he kneeled behind Luka.

Jovan crawled over to watch Niall's entry, ready to pull him back if he rushed from inexperience. Luka might claim to be tough but Jovan could tell Niall wouldn't forgive himself if he injured Luka. Niall pressed into Luka in a slow, measured motion. Pausing halfway in, he rubbed soothing hands down Luka's back. "Almost there."

"More, damn it. Niall, fuck me!" Luka's voice reached an outraged pitch at Niall's slow motion.

Jovan held back his laughter. He didn't wish to distract them. Instead, he turned his attention to his own task. Rescuing the abandoned bottle, he dripped lube on his fingers then circled Niall's hole before dipping lightly inside. "That's it, lovely—relax. I'm going to loosen you up a bit. Go ahead and give Luka what he wants."

"You're a bit distracting." Niall moaned and pushed deeper inside Luka.

"Oh, fuck the fates, you're divine." The bed rocked as Luka met Niall's invasion with rapid motions of his own.

"Let me know if I'm too rough." Niall slid out of Luka and into Jovan's touch.

He pushed his fingers deeper inside Niall's hole. "Now that you're in, you can't be too rough with Luka—he likes it that way."

Niall pressed a kiss between Luka's shoulder blades. "You can have rough sex another night. Tonight I want to worship you."

Jovan swallowed back the ridiculous lump forming in his throat. What the fuck was wrong with him? Niall's gentle regard for the tough lion shifter beneath him twisted Jovan's heart. No one besides Jovan had ever cared about Luka. None of their previous hook-ups had worried about anything other than shoving their cock inside Luka and getting off.

Luka's soft expression when he turned to regard Niall over his shoulder had Jovan catching his breath. "Thank you."

Luka and Niall kissed and once again Jovan couldn't stop staring at the sight. When Niall lifted his lips he cast a glance over at Jovan. "You're slacking on the job."

Jovan grinned. "Sorry, I'll get right back to work."

Coating his index finger with a bit more lube, he pushed it in, unerringly pressing against the spongy bit inside.

"Oh, yes." Niall jerked inside Luka's body.

Luka whimpered. "Stop messing around, Jo! Let's get this going right."

"He's a virgin—he'll take a bit more prep." Jovan slid in a second finger. Once Niall moved easily, he added a third.

"Please. I need more. If you don't fuck me soon it will be too late," Niall pleaded.

"Easy, babe. I've got you. Hang on." Finally certain he'd loosened Niall enough, Jovan pushed his cock inside. "Relax."

Niall took a long slow breath. "I'm fine."

"Let me know if you aren't." He used more gentleness than he'd bothered with anyone else before. Their occasional hook-ups hadn't received any more care than they'd dished out.

"I'm ready. Move," Niall demanded.

"Bossy bottom." Jovan kissed Niall's shoulder.

"I'm a bossy top, too." Niall pushed inside Luka. The lion shifter grunted.

"Do that again," Luka ordered.

"You can't be bossy, I'm in charge now." Jovan growled. He slid into Niall, pushing him deeper into Luka.

It took them a little time to find their rhythm. Jovan fully opened his mating bond with Luka and almost came from the emotions pouring out of him.

"I'm going to come," Luka warned.

"Do it." Niall squeezed around Jovan.

Jovan tightened his grip on Niall as he pounded out his desire. "Come, my beauty."

Niall grunted and his smooth motions became jerky and uneven. He gave a long groan and yanked Jovan's orgasm from him. Drained, Jovan pulled out, mindful of his mate's ex-virgin status.

He collapsed on the bed, careful to avoid crushing Niall.

Luka moved them around until they all cuddled together, away from the sticky spot on the sheet. No one spoke for several minutes. Jovan stroked his hands up and down Niall's body, skating his fingers across the fae's luminous skin.

Luminous? "Are you glowing?"

Niall sighed. "Yeah, sorry. It's a fae thing."

"How beautiful." Luka's voice dripped with wonder.

Niall couldn't argue.

Chapter Three

Niall blinked. Daylight speared between the curtains and into his eyes. His entire body ached. Not a single muscle had gone unused. Damn, that had been fun. Now in the cool reality of the morning, he had to sneak out.

Crap, he didn't have any clothes. Maybe Jovan wouldn't mind if he borrowed something to wear—he could have one of the servants return them later.

They'd fulfilled his fantasy—now he needed to go back to his real world. He didn't have to glance at his phone to know his mother had probably called him all night. He'd turned it off on the way to their house, knowing that even silent, the vibration would've driven him insane.

Niall slid to the bottom of the bed, trying to wiggle out without waking his bedmates. Halfway down his wrists were grabbed from both sides.

"Where are you going, sweetness?" Jovan's husky voice had him hard all over again.

Damn. He needed to leave.

"Home. It's time to go home." The words made his chest ache like an open wound but delaying the inevitable would only bring torture and cold cement rooms.

He couldn't ignore their tugging since they had iron grips on his wrists. The lion shifters pulled him back up and pinned Niall between them.

"Leaving without a goodbye?" Luka's hurt expression melted his resistance.

"Look, it's not that I didn't want to say goodbye properly, but I hadn't even planned on spending the night." He tried for honesty. The two sexy shifters had claimed to be all right with being a one-night stand, but this morning they were a bit clingy. Niall would've loved to wallow about in their bed for weeks but the cost would be too high.

Luka kissed him. Distracted by the shifter's hot mouth and Jovan's seductive touch, he almost gave in again. A loud pounding on the front door jerked him out of the passionate haze.

"Who the fuck is that?" Jovan growled.

Niall sent out tendrils of magic. "My guards have found me. Time for me to go." He tried to keep the despair out of his voice but from Luka's sympathetic expression he hadn't succeeded well at all. At least his mother hadn't sent *her* guards—they would've beaten Niall on the way back home.

"Want us to kill them?" Luka asked—a surprising offer from the half of the pair Niall had considered the gentler shifter.

"Um, no. Thank you." Killing the guards would trigger a fae/shifter war. Niall refused to be responsible for the guards' deaths. They might not be able to stop his mother's abuse but they did pick up the pieces and block punishments when they could.

More banging had Jovan jumping into action. "I'll get the door." Jovan snatched his pants off the floor and put them on before leaving the room.

"I'll get you something to wear."

Niall turned in time to see Luka slide out of bed and head to the large dresser in the corner. He opened a drawer and pulled out a pair of sweats and a T-shirt. He held them out to Niall. "Here."

"Thank you." Approaching his guards completely nude wouldn't have been a new experience. They'd seen him in far worse shape, but he preferred to keep his humiliation level as low as possible.

The shirt fell to Niall's hips and he had to roll the sweats to his ankles in order to walk, but at least most of him was covered.

Luka's wistful expression speared Niall's heart. "I was hoping to make you breakfast before seeing you off."

"Sorry—" He broke off his apology when Luka kissed him. Every thought dissolved from his mind and his focus narrowed to Luka. Luka's lips, his touch, the breath sliding across Niall's cheek had him hard and needy.

"Niall!" Jovan's shout jerked them apart.

"Sorry." Pulling up his magic, he flashed it over his body in a waterless bath. He refused to greet the guards smelling of cum.

Luka dressed silently beside him. "Neat trick. Do me."

"I thought I already did."

Luka's laughter relaxed him. Niall hadn't realized how stressed he was over leaving the shifters. Every instinct screamed he was making the wrong move. His fingers trembled as he tightened the waistband drawstring.

"You still smell of me." Luka's satisfied tone made Niall smile.

"I'm glad." At least he could take one memento out of this situation.

Once he had his shoes and socks on and had straightened himself as much as possible, Niall smiled at Luka then headed down the hall. Time to go back to reality. With each forward motion, the mantle of his life weighed heavier until his steps took on a slow reluctant rhythm.

He entered the living room to find Jovan blocking anyone from entering.

"Don't try to stall. Bring him out now!" Niall recognized the voice of his head guard, Tesner.

"Don't fuss, I'm coming." No sense trying to run out the back—they'd follow and the punishment would be greater.

"No!" Jovan snarled. He spun away from the door to walk over and wrap his arms around Niall. "They can't have you. You belong with us."

"I wish I could, but I need to go back home." His eyes burned with tears. If only he could stay there, but he didn't even dare imagine such a perfect scenario. His mother would have no problem hunting down the two lion shifters in order to bend Niall to her will.

"Do you want to?" Jovan's golden eyes dared him to lie.

"No, but I have to." He placed a hand on Jovan's neck. "I won't forget you, either of you."

Luka crowded Niall's other side until they were both wrapped around him. Niall pulled the lion shifters in closer for a three-way kiss. Heat burned his palms where he rested them on his lover's necks but the discomfort vanished before he could worry about injuring the pair.

"Take care of each other." He stepped away and this time they let him go. Niall nodded to the guards, his head held high. "I'm ready to go."

"A ménage, my lord?" Tesner asked.

Niall raised an eyebrow at the guard. "And?"

"Nice." A round of approval swept the group of four guards.

Niall shook his head at their antics. A quick sweep revealed the guards his mother had planted as spies were missing. "Where are the others?" Not that he wanted to see them but better to know their location than have them get the jump on him later.

Tesner smiled. "We thought we'd leave them behind. It doesn't take an entire garrison to retrieve one wayward prince."

"Thank you." He doubted his mother would've used the same reasoning. She'd have no problem dragging him out in shackles with as many witnesses as possible.

"No problem. Now, tell us about the shifters." Tesner's suggestive leer had the rest of the men laughing.

"It was nice."

"What kind of shifters were they?" Tesner frowned.

"Lion shifters."

"You took two lion shifters to bed?" Anvin, Tesner's second in command, asked.

"Yes." He said nothing else.

Anvin continued to chatter. "Impressive. They're known to be rough in the sack." Silence descended among the group, as if they were waiting for him to give details of his exploits.

"Well, you'll have to find your own and see." Niall kept his voice neutral.

"Or I could try that couple out myself. You're done with them, aren't you, my prince?"

Niall didn't feel his body move but somehow he ended up with his hand wrapped around Anvin's throat. He lifted the soldier with one hand despite Anvin outweighing him by fifty pounds. Magical energy surged through him.

I could crush him.

The thought sung through him like a tantalizing promise. Yes. If he destroyed Anvin then the guard couldn't touch Niall's lions. He liked that plan.

"Let him go, my prince." Tesner tugged at his wrist.

Niall flicked his hand and flung Tesner with his magic. The captain flew across the front yard.

"I swear I won't touch them." Anvin gasped through Niall's grip.

Satisfaction surged through him. Niall dropped the guard. "Good."

He smoothed his shirt then headed for the limo. Never before had magic poured through him like a heady tide of energy. For a minute, he knew he could live on that power alone.

"Fuck, he's power drunk." He heard someone whisper.

One of the guards raced to open the door for him. He slid into the back seat without another word. He had nothing to say to the guards as they joined him in the vehicle. Niall closed his eyes and watched the colors swirl beneath his eyelids.

"You've come into your magic, my lord," Tesner whispered beside him. "Now you need to pull it back."

Niall sighed. Opening his eyes, he saw the captain watching him with a worried expression. "What's wrong?"

Tesner audibly swallowed. "I-I've never felt this much power before. If you don't pull it back, it will start to eat away at us."

The strained faces of the other guards in the limo shocked him out of his inner fascination with the colors. "Sorry."

Niall focused on the waves of energy swimming in the air around him. Holding his hands palms out, he pulled the magic back into him. A loud pop echoed in his ears as magic vacated the area around them and sank into Niall.

"Wow."

Niall didn't know which guard had spoken. He shrugged and leaned against the headrest. He rubbed the spot over his heart as they drove away. A steady ache squeezed his chest the farther they traveled.

"Do you want to know how we found you?" Tesner asked.

"It doesn't matter." No one could hide from her. Niall hadn't even tried. "I wasn't hiding. I just wanted one night."

One magical moment he'd never get again.

"Your mother put a locator spell on you," Tesner continued.

"Figures." She wouldn't want him to get too far out of her control. "Thanks for waiting until this morning to come."

"You're welcome. I hope you enjoyed your time away." Tesner patted Niall's shoulder.

"It was great." Now he had to face the consequences of his actions.

The drive back to the castle only took half an hour but it might as well have been years. Niall's heart weighed heavier with each mile traveled. If he'd been driving he would've turned around and gone back to the shifters. Good thing he didn't have hold of the wheel.

The driver pulled into the long drive and stopped with an unnecessary screech of tires.

"Sorry. Fevran is a new driver," Tesner apologized.

Niall nodded but still didn't speak. The driver could've been one of his mother's spies and it still wouldn't make a difference. He could almost feel the cell doors closing behind him in his posh prison.

Fevran opened the door and everyone piled out. Niall allowed the escort, noting Anvin's careful distance from him as they walked. The fae guard wouldn't be putting himself within Niall's hold again any time soon. Tesner had no such scruples. He patted Niall on the shoulder. "Clarabelle is waiting for you in your suite."

"Thank you." He appreciated the warning. His mother was hard to deal with on a good day, and after being rousted from the lion shifters' bed, this was no longer a good day.

He opened the door to his suite and braced himself.

"There you are!" His mother's cold tone chilled him to the bone. Memories of childhood punishments flashed through him—icy, empty rooms, bare walls and little food until he broke down and gave her what she wanted or apologized for an imagined slight.

His magic flared out. He quickly pulled it back in before Clarabelle could comment on his sudden surge of power. He sometimes wondered if the other fae in court knew of his mother's torture of him. Did they condone her abuse or was it just easier to look away?

"What are you doing here, Mother?" He made his tone as unwelcoming as possible. She had broken protocol entering his suite without his permission.

"Where were you last night?"

"Out." Niall dropped down in the chair opposite his mother. At this moment he didn't care what she did to him. Nothing could feel worse than leaving his lovers.

She looked smaller somehow. Maybe spending the night sandwiched between two huge shifters had changed his world view.

A high flush crossed Clarabelle's face, more likely anger rather than embarrassment. "I expect a better explanation, and I don't need permission to come in here. I can do whatever I want to you."

He stiffened his spine. Showing signs of weakness would end in a whipping. Best give the illusion of strength and let her think he'd do something about her behavior.

"I am of legal age. I have no problem informing the queen's guards of your transgression if I find you here again." He clasped his hands to hide the shaking. Shifters might be able to smell nerves but his mother had no such skill.

"I bet you were tramping about." She ignored his statement. No doubt she would devise a hellish punishment for him later.

The words should've hurt like most of the ones that had come out of his mother's mouth in the past, but Niall had bigger problems now—like the hole in his heart. "Is there a point to your visit, Mother, or did you just come by to insult me?"

He let the power build in his eyes. He was done taking crap from anyone today. It must've shown in his face because she cleared her throat. "I've brought you a list of suitable marriage candidates."

She pointed to the table.

Shock that she had given him a choice, even a limited one, had Niall picking up the paper without comment.

"I underlined the ones who would give you the most political advantage. Shame you're gay—Varia is looking for a mate."

"Varia might be second in line for the throne but she's seeking a female mate." Niall scanned the list. "Crenshi is two hundred years my senior."

"He can give you a guiding hand."

"Selando smells of garlic."

"His family controls most of the food in the palace."

Niall resisted the urge to crumple the paper and toss it in the trash. Memories of the lion shifters twisted Niall up, bittersweet strands of longing entangling him like a spiderweb. He brushed the clinging bits of melancholy away. He didn't have time for sentiment while sparring with his mother. "How about you throw a party, Mother? That way I can see all your candidates at once."

He kept his breathing shallow, hoping to avoid throwing up. His stomach gurgled unpleasantly. The mere thought of mating with one of the men on his mother's list made him ill. Best to pretend to go along with her plotting while planning his escape. Fae didn't do well living on their own but if Niall didn't take the chance, he might as well slit his own throat and be done with it.

"Really?" Clarabelle smiled, an expression almost more frightening than her scowls. How did she deserve any happiness when she'd tortured him for years?

"Yes, that's the only way I can compare them to each other." He'd pick the least objectionable man to marry. At this point, he didn't care which one. They were all pompous asses who would live beneath Clarabelle's thumb. She'd let her guard down once he'd wed. After the wedding, he'd make a run for it. He didn't like the plan but defying her now would only lead to his death.

"That's smart thinking. I didn't expect you to be so willing." Her narrow-eyed gaze warned him to keep his enthusiasm low. He bowed his head as if under a great strain instead of feverishly plotting.

"I want a mate, Mother. I just might not want the same one you do." His perfect mates were living in a small house a few miles away. But they didn't need him—they had each other.

"I'll have my secretary draw up the invitations. We'll have it during the next full moon, in two weeks. I'm proud you're finally willing to be useful for once."

Blood filled his mouth where he bit his tongue. He nodded to her when she stood but didn't dare speak again. The moon charged fae powers and Niall would be able to properly judge his future mate by their matching energy. All mating dances were held during the full moon for just that reason. Niall doubted any of the men his mother chose would do anything for him. He'd grown up knowing them all, if not well, but maybe his adult perspective would be better than his childish one.

"Well good, then. I'll go now. Get some rest. We want you looking your best."

"Yes, Mother."

She kissed his cheek. Niall thought he hid his revulsion well. He didn't relax until the door shut behind her.

It opened again a short while later. "I can't believe you agreed to a mating party." Tesner plopped down in the chair beside him.

Niall shrugged. "It's not like she's going to give up and say never mind. She wants me mated. I want me mated. It's probably the last time we'll agree on anything."

Their choices of mates were miles apart but that didn't change the facts.

"What if your mate turns out to be like your mother?"

"I'll run. I'm not putting up with that bullshit any more. I'm not a small child to be bullied. I have my own skills." If only he could use them against his mother.

"I'm sorry I couldn't do anything when you were younger. She threatened to kill my sister if I interceded. I tried to tell the queen once but your mother intercepted me and had the rest of the guards beaten as an example." Sorrow wound through Tesner's voice, a dark ribbon of pain that never healed.

"I never knew." Over the years he'd just assumed the guards had looked the other way. What kind of monsters didn't care if a little kid was banished to what was basically solitary confinement? He'd seen pictures of human prisons that were nicer than his timeout chamber.

"You had enough to worry about. But now you can escape. Leave here and strike out on your own. If you stay, you'll be under your mother's compulsion your entire life. It could be twice as bad if you take a husband she's pre-approved."

"You know what will happen if I try to escape before the wedding. I'm going to go along with her plans for a while." Niall pointed to the piece of paper. "The list is on the table, check it out for yourself. I'm not sure what you think is going to happen."

Tesner snatched it up and scanned the sheet. "Oh damn, these aren't good. It looks like your mother is hoping for someone to help her take over the throne by putting you up as a figurehead."

"You sound surprised." Niall couldn't stop a bitter laugh from escaping. His mother had never done one positive thing for Niall in his life. Why would his marriage be anything but another power grab?

"Your mother is a dangerous woman. If she suspects you aren't going to pick someone, she'll make your life worse than before. Better to run now."

"I told you I'll go through with the wedding. It's after that I'll make my move." Niall leaned over and took another look at the list. "I'm surprised that she bothered even pretending to give me a choice. She's never hesitated to bend me to her will before."

"Hmm." Tesner's low humming noise didn't reassure Niall at all.

"What do you mean, hmm?"

"Maybe it's because she can't influence you as much anymore. You're old enough to get people to listen to you now, not like when you were a child." Tesner stared at Niall long enough he began to shift uncomfortably.

"What?"

"Did she say anything about your appearance?"

"No, why?" Niall rubbed his palms across his borrowed sweatpants. "Oh, you mean my clothing?"

Tesner shook his head. "I was more thinking of the fact that you're pouring power out like a faucet. It's hard to focus when you're next to me."

Niall scratched his chin as he replayed his conversation with Clarabelle. "No, she didn't mention it. She didn't comment on my clothes, either." Strange, now that he thought about it. His mother never missed an opportunity to criticize. "I guess she had better things to worry about."

Tesner patted Niall's knee. "Maybe it won't be as bad as you think."

"Maybe." In his mind's eye he knew he'd rather be the third in a shifter sandwich than marry anyone on that list or any other. A strong, desperate need to return to Luka and Jovan struck him in the heart and left him gasping.

"Thinking about your shifters?" Tesner asked.

"Yes." He didn't dare say more. He'd learned young that the walls had ears, and although he trusted Tesner, Clarabelle did have the guard's sister. No one could be one hundred percent trusted within the palace boundaries.

"That's good. I mean, I guess that's good. I'll stop talking now." Tesner stumbled over his words.

Niall had never seen Tesner flustered before. "I've shocked you! I didn't think that possible."

Tesner laughed. "Sorry. I've just never considered the coordination needed to have a ménage."

Niall laughed. "There were some challenges, but we worked them out just fine."

His body burned from the memory. Damn, they ways they'd moved together. The places he'd been touched...

Tesner held up his hand as if warning off the memory. "Please — I don't want to know."

"I wasn't planning on sharing. Some things are just too personal."

Tesner stood. "I'm going to get back to guard duty. Call me if you need anything. Can I take this list?"

"Why?"

"So I can dig up dirt on them. You might as well know what you're getting yourself into. At least this way you can weed out the worst of the lot."

"Help yourself." It didn't matter which man had what going on since none of them would be a pair of sexy shifters who helped a young fae get over his virginity.

Chapter Four

"We can't go after him," Luka snapped. They'd been having the same argument for the past week. Jovan kept insisting they retrieve Niall, but Luka thought they should wait for him to return. Surely he wouldn't claim them, then vanish? Luka's neck still ached from where Niall had placed his fae bonding mark. As days passed with no communication, Jovan had become surlier with each hour and Luka's inner lion had risen up with equal aggression. They each bore scratch marks of their discontent.

"Sure we can. No one will spot us. We can make it look like a kidnapping. We just won't ask for a ransom." The wild expression in Jovan's eyes had also increased over the past seven days. Their lions were uneasy, pacing back and forth and snarling inside, all because the fae they'd fucked had left afterward. Why couldn't he have stayed there? He belonged to them, after all, both lions agreed.

"He had to go back home, Jovan."

"Why!" Jovan shouted. "Why did he have to go back? He belongs with us, not them! They don't treat him right!" Jovan's voice took on a low growl, the lion rising to the surface.

Luka's inner beast snarled back. "We can't go charging in there if we don't know he's in danger. We'll make fools of ourselves and possibly create a shifter/fae incident that will get us hunted!"

"There's something wrong in a castle where a beautiful man is a virgin and they need guards to drag him back home." Jovan's handsome face didn't change expression. If Luka didn't do something, his mate would charge in there after Niall and get himself killed.

"There are other reasons guards could come for him. Do you think he's a criminal?"

They'd gone back and forth over different scenarios since Niall had left. Why had guards come to fetch him? Why did he not look surprised? How come he didn't fight them? "No. I think he was hiding from someone but not because he's done anything wrong. He was too honest. He even told us he's a virgin."

"He was but we took care of that." Jovan's wistful smile twisted Luka's gut. They needed Niall.

"Yes, we did. It was a fine night. From what he said, I bet his mother was involved." Luka's skin burned as he remembered their intense evening together. They'd been unable to make love in their bed since. Too many memories and one great loss surrounded them when they slid beneath the covers at night.

As Jovan continued to pick at his favorite topic, raving about Niall's abandonment, Luka remembered their night together. He recalled in exquisite detail the fae's smooth skin and natural scent of lush meadows and moonlight. He hadn't even known the moon had a scent until he'd smelled it on Niall's body.

Luka's cat half gave a sad yowl. That's all it did these days. It was as if his inner feline was on strike. *Bring back the pretty fae or take the consequences.* "Jo, is your cat acting weird?"

"It misses Niall."

"What are we going to do about it?" Surely Jovan had a plan. His mate always had a plan—generally not one that would be practical or necessarily legal, but a plan.

He sat beside Luka until they touched from thigh to hip. "Don't worry, pet—one way or another, we'll get him back."

Luka nodded then rested his head on his lover's chest. "I just miss him. It hurts."

"I know, babe, I know."

Someone knocked on the front door. They both inhaled, trying to decipher the scent. Jovan stood to answer it when they couldn't determine their caller. Luka followed but stayed back, ready to pounce in case of trouble.

Jovan yanked the door open. "What?"

A messenger stood on the doorstep dressed in ridiculously expensive livery and holding a gold metallic envelope. "I'm looking for Jovan and Luka, animal shifters?" He barely held back his sniff at the introduction.

"And you must be the rude fairy we weren't looking for," Jovan snapped.

The messenger wrinkled his nose at Jovan. "By order of the queen I'm inviting you to the mating ball of Lord Niallvius Primrose."

A million questions flew through Luka's head. "He's getting married?"

His panic didn't fade with the commiserating look granted to him by his mate. "Luka, you knew he was getting married. He said so when he left here."

"I was hoping he'd changed his mind." Maybe only in ridiculously sappy stories did everyone end up together and live happily ever after. He rubbed the aching spot on his chest, hoping to smooth the twisted bitter edges of heartache.

"He hasn't picked his mate yet. That's the purpose of the ball." The messenger's snide tone had Luka curling his fingers to prevent strangling the man.

"Tell the queen we'll be there." Jovan snatched the invitation from the messenger's hand then slammed the door in his face.

Luka approved that action—better to be rude than a murderer.

"She might be wishing she retracted the invitation when she sees us," Luka commented. He snatched the envelope from Jovan to rip open the seal. "Fuck, it's true. They're holding our Niall a mating ball. What do you know about these? Can he pick us?"

Jovan scowled. "I don't know. Maybe we can find out when we get there. I'm keeping the possibility of kidnapping open. If Niall needs help, I'm not going to worry about interspecies politics."

"I know." Luka rubbed Jovan's back. "What do you say we go and find some clothes for this shindig?"

"Sounds good. I'm guessing they won't let us wear tight leather pants." Jovan smiled as he remembered his conversation with Niall.

Luka laughed. "Probably not."

* * * *

Jovan could hear music wafting out into the night. The fae queen's palace glowed like a jewel in the darkness, glittering and shimmering with exquisite architecture and magic.

Sparkling people dressed in gorgeous clothes and dazzling with jewels were lined up to go inside the ballroom. Guards stood on either side of the entrance, collecting invitations as guests passed.

"I've never seen so many jewels in my life," Luka whispered.

Jovan laughed. "Yeah, tempting, isn't it?"

In their poorer times, when they'd scrambled to get enough food to survive, Luka had lifted a gem or two from wealthy socialites. They'd long put those days behind them, but Luka sometimes muttered about his temptation to revisit their past.

A familiar scent stopped them in their tracks. "He's here," Jovan whispered. He'd almost thought it an elaborate hoax to lure them to this place and finish them off.

"Yes, he is," Luka agreed.

Jovan resisted the urge to push his way to the front and trample the glittering throngs. Luka almost vibrated beside him with the same restless energy. How would Niall react when he saw them? Had he missed them as much?

It took another thirty minutes to reach the entrance. Jovan handed over their invitations.

The dark-haired guard examined them with suspicion. "We don't let shifters in here."

Jovan hissed. "We were sent invitations. I'd hate to have to rip off your arms and beat you with them."

The guard paled. "Go right in, sir."

"That's what I thought." Jovan flexed his fingers, flashing his claws as he passed.

"Show-off." Luka grinned and bumped his shoulder against Jovan's.

"I only like one fae and he's not the one," Jovan snarled.

It didn't take long to locate Niall. They simply followed the crowd.

Luka froze a few feet away. "Damn, he's beautiful."

Niall stood on a small platform dressed in a black suit decorated with diamonds. Whatever his problems, Niall didn't lack for money.

Jovan nodded his agreement. "Yes, he is." He hooked an arm through Luka's and dragged him forward. This was not the time to be cautious.

Niall stood next to a petite woman who resembled him enough that Jovan suspected she must be Niall's mother.

"You be nice to Lord Borson. He made a lot of money in the stock market," Jovan heard her say over the noise.

"He's not going to be nice to anyone." Jovan stepped forward, ignoring the indignant noises of the man he pushed aside.

"Jovan?" Niall's eyes widened. "And Luka? What are you two doing here?"

"Leaving." The cold-faced woman glared at them.

"We were invited." Jovan folded his arms across his chest.

"I didn't invite you," she said.

"I did." A beautiful lady swept through the crowd. Everyone scurried out of her path as if she could move people by her charisma alone.

Jovan had never met anyone more powerful. He bowed and from the corner of his eye saw Luka do the same.

"Gentlemen."

Niall bowed low and his mother curtseyed. Neither of them straightened until the queen beckoned them upright.

"Your Majesty," Jovan and Luka said in unison. There could be no question over the identity of the lady before them.

"Why did you invite them, Your Majesty? They weren't on my list." Niall's mother's mouth turned up slightly in a stiff smile.

"Clarabelle, I invited them because I wanted to see who Niall had claimed."

"I didn't claim anyone!" Niall's face paled as he took in the shifters, his expression less welcoming than they had hoped.

The fae queen ignored Niall's outburst. Instead she examined Jovan with a piercing gaze before turning her attention to Luka. He almost sighed in relief when she moved her gaze away from him. "You two will make Niall excellent mates."

"No! Niall will marry a fae! That's why we're having this party!" Clarabelle shrieked.

"Niall, do you wish to marry any of these people?" The queen waved a hand to encompass the people around them.

"No, Your Majesty."

"And the shifters?"

"I'd be interested in pursuing a relationship with them." Niall's nervous smile wiped away the stress Jovan had struggled under the past week.

Pride had Jovan puffing up his chest. Niall smelled of fear but he had stood up for what he wanted anyway. He would be a worthy mate. Jovan's inner lion growled its approval.

"You will do as I say!" Clarabelle raised her hands and slammed a wave of power into Niall.

Niall screamed but stayed on his feet. He glowed from the magic pouring through him.

Jovan and Luka rushed to his side, each grabbing an arm and holding him up. Electricity rolled across Jovan's skin. He gritted his teeth but dug in his heels and remained strong. They couldn't abandon their mate. "You can't have him."

"Don't shift. I've got this," Niall said.

Before Jovan could ask what Niall was talking about, thunder rumbled through the ballroom and the room fell into silence.

Niall crackled with energy but this time, Jovan could feel the source was Niall. "I've had enough, Mother. I've survived years of your abuse, starvation and torture. What I won't do is give you my future. These are my mates and I claim them as my own."

"Are you mine?" Niall asked Luka.

"Yes." Luka kissed Niall's cheek.

"And you, Jovan?"

"Absolutely." Jovan leaned over and nipped at Niall's bottom lip.

Clarabelle clenched her fists. "You are my child and I'll do what I want with you."

"Let me bite her," Luka growled.

"No, she might poison you." Niall's relaxed stance eased Jovan's tension. "She's nothing but rotten inside."

"I'll show you poison," Clarabelle said.

"You'll do no such thing." The queen stepped between them. "Guards, throw her in the dungeon."

"What? You can't do that!" Clarabelle's shock made Jovan smile.

The queen tilted her head back and looked down at the woman before her. "I have ignored the warning signs for too long. I trusted you to take care of your offspring, hoping your maternal instincts would kick in. I apologize, Niall, for not taking action before."

"No!" Clarabelle screamed.

The queen smiled. "You thought you'd use Niall to take over my crown. I allowed this party so I could see who might be foolish enough to plot with you."

Jovan spotted a few men slipping away in the crowd. If Clarabelle had expected public support, she'd vastly overrated her pull.

Guards moved to surround Clarabelle. She struggled to get away but they grabbed her arms. Screams followed her across the ballroom as she shrieked her ill temper.

"I am sorry, Niall. I know nothing I do will take away your horrible childhood, but I hope by reuniting you with your mates I'm helping you find your future."

"Thank you, your majesty."

The queen tilted her head as she examined the trio. "I think it's best if you go reside with your mates. Leaving the castle will be good for you."

And would get the only man capable of challenging her for the throne out of the palace. The queen might only want Niall with them to prevent a coup, but Jovan would take their mate however he could get him.

"I will. Thank you." Niall nodded his head.

Jovan bowed his head to the queen. "That's an excellent idea, Your Majesty."

"Good, then carry on." After one more regal nod, she wandered away to visit with her other subjects and no doubt impress on them the futility of challenging her rule.

"Thank you for coming for me." Niall's smile glowed brighter than the ballroom lights.

"Always." Luka kissed Niall, a deep claiming embrace. When they finally parted, Niall had a dazed expression on his face.

"Are you sure you're my mates?" Niall asked.

"Yes." Jovan rubbed his neck. "You marked us with your magic when you left us. We've smelled your scent on us for days. We belong together."

Niall grinned. "Excellent. Let's go home so you can claim me back."

Jovan had never heard a better idea in his life. He might have a psychotic mother-in-law but with the support of the fae queen, they'd be just fine.

THE UNICORN
SAID YES

T.A. Chase

Dedication

Another wonderful anthology with some
amazing ladies.
Thank you all for continuing this journey with me.

Chapter One

Passing under the neon sign that read 'Unconventional', Ivan sighed as he stepped into the bar. As much as he loved his herd, he enjoyed the nights he could go out and not worry about them. His brothers were keeping an eye on the ladies and their children so Ivan could go have a drink or two.

"Hey there, Ivan. Good to see you," Wilma, the owner of Unconventional, called out from where she stood behind the wooden bar. "You want the usual?"

"Yes please, Wilma." He got there just as a shot glass of vodka slid down the smooth surface to him. It was followed closely by a bottle of Corona. Ivan snatched both before they could fall off the edge. He saluted her with the vodka then drank it.

He enjoyed the slight burn as it went down and hit his stomach. After taking a sip of his beer, he glanced around to see who else had decided to come for a drink. Ivan saw Angelo and started to walk over to say hi when the most intriguing scent hit him.

Being a unicorn shifter, Ivan would be the first to admit he wasn't extra sensitive to smells. He was much more a 'line of sight' kind of creature, but there was something about this scent that made him hard and took his attention from everything else around him.

Inhaling again, he followed the fragrance through the crowd to one of the corner booths. Ivan spotted the young man sitting there, elbows braced on the table while he stared down at his drink. There was sadness in the tilt of his head and pain in the lift of his shoulders.

"What did that drink do to make you look like that?" he asked as he stopped next to the booth.

The man jerked, almost knocking his drink over. Ivan caught it before it fell off. He set it back in front of the guy.

"I'm Ivan Brusilov. May I sit?" He motioned to the spot next to the enthralling human.

"Umm...sure. I guess."

He could tell, even through the scent that drew him to the man, that he was human, which was strange to see at a paranormal bar. After dropping down onto the leather bench, he fought the urge to bury his face in the crook of the man's neck. *Fuck!* He'd never wanted to do that before.

"Your name is?"

"Oh sorry. I'm Carney Ferguson." Carney held out his hand for Ivan to shake. "You're Russian."

"My family came from Russia," he admitted. Just because Carney was at Unconventional didn't mean he knew about paranormals, so Ivan wasn't about to say he'd brought his herd over after the Bolsheviks had taken over the country. No need for him to know how old Ivan really was. "You sound like your family is Irish."

Carney smiled slightly. "My father's side is. My mom's French."

Ivan grinned back. "An interesting blending of cultures. I'm all Russian. My parents met back in the old country. Are you here to drown your sorrows—whatever those may be?"

"No. Well, yes. I was going to, but I've never drunk before, and after taking a sip of this whiskey, I've figured out I don't like it." Carney frowned. "I'm not a very good Irishman if I don't like liquor."

"I don't know. I would think you'd hate to be a stereotype," Ivan teased.

Laughing, Carney nodded. "You're right. I should probably head home then. My family will wonder where I've been."

Allowing his instinct to override his usual reticent tendencies, he reached out to rest his hand on Carney's arm. "Please stay. I'll get you a soda or water. I'd like to hear what kind of sorrows a good-looking man like you would have to drown."

The blush staining Carney's cheeks fascinated Ivan. Everything about the man spoke of innocence. Yet Ivan didn't know how any person—human or paranormal—could still be pure in this modern age.

Touching Carney's warm skin sent a shot of electricity through him to Ivan's cock.

Could it be? Is Carney truly a virgin in every sense of the word?

"I'm sure you have other things to do. Probably came looking to hook up with someone. Isn't that what people do at bars?" Carney's voice held a question and a hint of shyness as well.

"Some people do, and I'll admit I have as well from time to time, but it wasn't what I wanted when I came tonight. I just needed to get away from my family for a while." Ivan shook his head as he thought about the noise of the herd when they got together.

Frowning, Carney sounded disappointed when he said, "Oh you're married."

"No." The lead stallion of a unicorn herd rarely settled down with one mare. It was his duty to continue the bloodline by sleeping with as many of the mares as wanted him. Those who wanted could leave and go to other herds. He had five kids—three sons and two daughters.

"You're not?" Carney narrowed his eyes at Ivan. "Yet you don't strike me as a man who still lives with his parents."

Ivan laughed aloud. "No, I don't. I've been the head of my family for years now, but unfortunately, there are a lot of us, and they drop in at all hours of the day and night. Thank God, I work from home."

Carney wrinkled his nose. "That doesn't sound very fun. I bet you get tired of that."

"It can get annoying once in a while," Ivan confessed. "I wouldn't have it any other way though. They're my kin, and I have to protect them."

He motioned for Samantha, the bobcat shifter who worked as a waitress for Wilma. When she got there, he ordered a soda for Carney and another beer for himself. She winked at him before whirling around to go to the bar.

"I like it here," Carney informed him. "I don't feel like such an outsider."

After finishing his first beer and setting the bottle aside, he studied the human. "Why would you feel like an outsider?"

"Because I was homeschooled all my life. My parents and relatives have a strict set of rules my siblings and I must follow. I've never been allowed to date or even just hang out with friends. Heck, I don't have any friends to speak of." Carney traced a circle on the surface of the table. "It's hard not to feel awkward when you don't know anything about the world around you."

Ivan scooted closer, pressing his leg and arm against Carney's, and the human shivered. He had the crazy need to kiss Carney, to learn his taste and see what kind of sounds he made while in the throes of pleasure...

Shaking his head, he tried to clear it. He wasn't here to get laid. It was just a night out for a drink or two and some conversation. "Is it a religious thing?" he asked, knowing there was some religions that chose to keep their children separate from the world.

Carney lifted one shoulder. "It's more of a family tradition, I guess. My parents were brought up that way."

Samantha brought their drinks to them, and Ivan paid her before turning back to Carney.

"You've really never gone on a date before? How old are you?" Ivan held up his hand before Carney could answer him. "Don't answer that. It's none of my business. Your age or whether you've dated."

"I'm twenty-five and I'm still a virgin." Carney blushed again, ducking his head.

"Oh my," Ivan whispered, knowing exactly why he wanted Carney so badly. A virgin to a unicorn was like offering catnip to a feline shifter. Something was hardwired inside him to be entranced by all that innocence.

It was how they used to hunt his kind in the old days. They'd almost been hunted to extinction because of their greed, but a few herds had survived in the Black Forest of Germany and out on the Steppes of Russia. Unicorns had hidden their true selves away for centuries until the truth about them had faded into legends and myths. Some of his kind didn't believe the virgin thing was real, but Ivan accepted that every shifter species had a weakness and his were virgins.

"Stupid, huh? I should've had sex already, but my parents kept us on a tight leash." Carney turned the bottle around in his hands as he spoke.

"How did you get out of the house tonight? I would think that a bar isn't a place they would want you." Ivan leaned back in the booth, keeping just the tips of his fingers on Carney's thigh.

Carney twisted to face Ivan, his dark green eyes so earnest. "It's my birthday, and they told me I should go out and celebrate. It's the weirdest thing. My father handed me some money and said I was old enough to go out and have fun. My cousin was supposed to meet me here, but I should've known he wouldn't show."

Ivan didn't like the sound of that. It was as though Carney wasn't important to anyone. What family sent their kid out to celebrate his birthday on his own? That was horrible. Hell, Ivan's birthday was always a huge, three-day celebration with the herd going out to the Cleveland National Forest to run among the trees. They'd camp out and stay out of sight of the humans when they were shifted.

"Well, how about I take you to dinner for your birthday? I know we just met, but I really am a nice guy." He motioned to Wilma. "You can ask Wilma. She's known me most of my life."

"I don't want your pity. I'm good just sitting here and watching people."

Carney did seem happy to just stay where he was, but Ivan found himself wanting to take Carney out and show him a good time. Treat him like a king instead of someone whose family couldn't be bothered with.

"I don't pity you, Carney. I think you and I might have a chance to be friends, and I'd like to get to know you." Leaning close to him, Ivan brushed a quick kiss over Carney's cheek. "Maybe I want to be the guy who takes you on your first date."

"How do you know I'm even into guys? Maybe I like girls." He winked.

"You're right. I don't know if you like boys or girls. And you might not know either, considering you've never dated anyone. We could go out as friends and you can work on deciding."

Carney squeezed Ivan's leg. "I don't need to decide. I might not have any experience, but I'm pretty sure I'm a six on the Kinsey scale."

"Listen to you. Your family must be pretty intelligent to homeschool their kids on the Kinsey scale and shit like that." Ivan was impressed.

"Oh, Dad just taught us the basics." Carney shrugged. "I wanted to know everything, so I went to the library and checked out every book they'd let me. I know a little bit about a lot of different things."

Nodding, Ivan said, "I think that's a good way to be. Rather than so focused on one thing that you can't see anything else."

"What do you do?" Carney shifted closer to Ivan as though he could feel the pull between them as well.

"I work as a translator. English to Russian. Russian to English. I get a lot of jobs over the internet, and it pays the bills." Ivan sipped his beer. "I just finished a large project that I'd been working on for a couple weeks. Needed to get out of the house."

"That sounds like an awesome job. I can speak French fluently, but that's the only foreign language I know." Carney's stomach growled, causing them both to chuckle. "Sorry. I didn't want to stick around to eat, in case they changed their minds."

Ivan slid out from the booth then stood, holding out his hand to Carney. "Then I think I should take you out for your birthday before you starve to death."

Carney studied him for a minute before taking his hand. "I'd like to talk to Wilma really quick before I make a decision."

"Sounds good to me." He was glad Carney wasn't just going to walk out of the bar with him. Ivan wasn't a psycho, but Carney didn't know that.

He led the younger man up to the bar. "Hey Wilma, can you tell Carney that I'm a good guy?"

Wilma shot him an amused glance. "Now why would I want to lie to the kid like that?"

Carney smiled. "Ivan wants to take me to dinner. I want to make sure he's not going to kill me and toss my body in a dumpster."

She motioned for Carney to move closer. When he did, she patted him on the cheek. "Don't worry, honey. He won't hurt you. Ivan's one of the good guys. Nothing like some of those wolves that come in here late at night."

Ivan felt his eyes widen. Would Carney think she was joking, or did he really know about paranormals? Was that why he liked Unconventional so much?

Chapter Two

Carney couldn't believe his luck. Maybe his birthday wouldn't suck ass after all. He hadn't been surprised when Carson hadn't shown up. His cousin was a good guy most of the time, but he wasn't known for remembering dates or things he was supposed to do.

Sitting in the corner at the bar had sounded like a good idea. He'd snuck out of the family house once before and had wandered into Unconventional while looking for something different. He'd discovered there was a whole other world filled with weird and magical creatures. Some of them looked human and others only acted that way.

Carney had been shocked when Ivan had approached him. The man was tall and bulky with muscles. His high cheekbones slashed across his face, making him look like a Slavic fashion model. His black hair curled around the nape of his neck, except for one lock that was braided in front of his ear. Ivan's eyes were like blue diamonds, cool and sharp.

He had the feeling that Ivan was a paranormal—possibly even a shifter, though Carney couldn't tell what kind. Whatever he was, Carney knew he was an alpha. Ivan gave off those 'I'm in charge' vibes.

When Ivan had sat and talked to him, Carney found he wanted to throw himself into the man's arms and offer him everything. Which was stupid. Carney was a virgin, and men like Ivan didn't go for inexperience. They wanted someone who knew how to give them pleasure. Carney had no idea, having only read about it in the books he'd borrowed from the library. Those were the ones he hid under his bed so his parents wouldn't find them.

And Carney wasn't gorgeous or even cute. He was rather vanilla with his blond hair cut short and big blue eyes. His teeth were slightly crooked, as was his nose from one of his brothers breaking it when he was ten.

Excitement had coursed through him when Ivan had offered to take him out to dinner for his birthday. He would be crazy to agree, but nothing as exciting as this had ever happened to him before. He wanted to take the chance and maybe get laid by the end of the night. It would be an awesome present.

"All right, Ivan. I guess you're taking me out to dinner." He smiled at Ivan.

"Wonderful. Wilma, remember I was the one he left with—in case something happens and they come looking for him." Ivan winked at him as he joked.

Wilma shook her head. "How can I forget you, Ivan? Now get out of here. Help the kid have a good birthday."

Ivan offered Carney his arm like a gentleman, and they walked out of the bar together. Carney's mouth dropped open when Ivan escorted him to where a black Mustang Shelby GT500 was parked.

"This is your car?" He wanted to run his hands over the curve of its hood.

"Yeah. Need a car with a lot of horsepower," Ivan told him, opening the door for Carney.

He sank into the soft leather seats, biting back a moan as he slid his hands over the sensuous fabric. A groan escaped when Ivan turned the engine over and the car growled as though it were a living animal.

His cock, which was hard from the rumble of the car, stiffened even more when Ivan laid his hand on Carney's thigh. He swallowed then licked his lips before he looked into Ivan's blue eyes.

Ivan bent over, kissing him on the mouth quickly, then settling back behind the wheel. "Let's go. Do you have any food allergies I should know about?"

Carney shook his head. "No. She might be French, but my mom doesn't cook fancy stuff."

"Good. I know a great vegetarian restaurant I've been meaning to try. Haven't found the time to get over there. You okay with that?" Ivan put the vehicle in gear, easing out of the parking spot.

"Vegetarian? I would've thought you were a carnivore." Carney set his hand on Ivan's thigh, loving the flex of the hard muscle under his fingers each time Ivan had to shift gears.

Ivan glanced at him quickly and Carney saw the man's desire for him burning in his eyes. "I like meat once in a while, but I don't eat it on a regular basis."

Nodding, Carney relaxed a little more. "That's cool. I'm open to trying different things."

"Hearing you say that makes me happy, Carney, because I think I'm going to love helping you experience new things."

The innuendo in Ivan's voice caused Carney to wiggle in his seat as his ass clenched and his skin flushed. *He's sex on a stick. God was smiling on me tonight when He had Ivan walk into the bar.*

To take his mind off Ivan bending him over the hood of the Shelby, Carney asked, "What kind of paranormal are you?"

Ivan tensed slightly and Carney rushed to reassure him.

"Don't worry. I won't tell anyone. I've known about your world since I was twenty-one. The first time I went to Unconventional, I got into some trouble with a vampire and a demon. A little scary, but Wilma helped me out and told me about you all."

"Wilma's a good lady. Her husband was a paranormal, though I don't know what kind. She opened the bar to give us a place to have fun without having to worry about being discovered. We try to be good while we're there because humans do sometimes wander in." Ivan drummed his fingers on the steering wheel for a moment then said, "I'm a unicorn."

Carney turned to look at him. "Seriously? That is so awesome. I didn't know there were unicorn shifters."

"There aren't many of us around. My herd only has about thirty members. We're slowly growing, but it's hard when we have to travel back to Russia or Germany to bring new blood in." Ivan shrugged. "I brought my family here in nineteen-twenty, right after the Bolsheviks took power in Russia."

"You're over a hundred years old?" Carney couldn't believe it. "You don't look a day over forty."

Ivan shrugged. "Shifters age at a different rate than humans. Some quirk of our DNA, I guess."

Carney tried to wrap his mind around the fact that the man he was going on a date with was at least a century older than him.

"If our age difference makes you uncomfortable, I can take you home. It won't hurt my feelings." Ivan stopped at a red light and faced Carney. "Even though you know about us, finding different things out about paranormals can be a little upsetting at times."

"No, I'm fine. It might take a little getting used to, but at least you don't look like your age." Carney snorted. "That would be terrible."

"I'd feel even more like I was robbing the cradle than I do now," Ivan confessed as he continued down the street before turning into another parking lot. "Here it is."

The lot was almost completely full, but Ivan managed to find them a spot. He didn't get out once he turned the vehicle off. Carney waited to see what he would do. Ivan moved slowly, encircling the nape of Carney's neck then bringing him toward him. Their lips met in a soft caress of a kiss and Carney trembled. He twisted his hands into the front of Ivan's shirt, needing something solid to anchor him.

He gasped and Ivan swept his tongue in to tease Carney's. He tasted like beer and some strange flavor Carney had never encountered before. Maybe it was unique to a unicorn—or maybe just Ivan. He sank into the kiss, letting Ivan take control and angle his head any way he wanted to deepen it.

Carney whimpered and wiggled, wishing he was closer to Ivan. Close enough to be sitting on his lap, but there wasn't enough room for them to be fooling around like that.

Finally, Ivan broke the kiss then brought Carney's forehead to his chest while Carney panted. He struggled to get his cock under control. If the kiss had gone on any longer, he was pretty sure he would've come just from that.

When his breathing had calmed down, Carney pushed against Ivan's shoulder and Ivan let him go. He flopped back into his seat, staring at him.

"Wow! I'm kind of glad you stopped when you did or I'd be messing up my jeans."

Ivan chuckled as he opened his door. "Come on. Let's go get something to eat. Maybe we'll take a walk on the beach afterward."

"Sounds great to me." Carney practically bounced out of the vehicle and dashed around the rear to plaster himself against Ivan.

Embracing him, Ivan met his gaze with an amused one. "You're kind of short, aren't you?"

Carney pinched Ivan's ass and the man yelped. "I suggest you don't call me short. I'm average height. You're the one who's huge. I'd love to see you in your other shape. I bet you're magnificent."

Ivan rubbed his cheek over the top of Carney's head. "Maybe someday you can go with me out to Cleveland National Forest. I'll shift and we can spend time on the trails there."

"Is that where you take your herd?" he asked as he stepped away. His stomach chose that moment to growl again and he giggled. "Sorry. I guess I'm hungrier than I thought."

He found himself being escorted across the parking lot and into the restaurant. They were seated right away. After ordering drinks, he propped his chin on one hand and studied Ivan.

"I can't believe you're a unicorn." He kept his voice low, not wanting anyone to overhear their conversation. "And you're gay. How appropriate. Now if only you did something with rainbows."

Ivan rolled his eyes. "I'm not entirely gay. I'm a three on the Kinsey scale. Bisexual." He winked at him.

Disappointment raced through Carney for a second. "Oh?"

"I had to be. As lead stallion, it's my job to make sure my bloodline continues on in the next generation. I have three sons and two daughters. Their mothers are members of my herd. Only one can stay with our herd when they get older. The rest must leave to find other families, so there is no inbreeding amongst us." Ivan took Carney's hand in his. "Trust me on this though, Carney. If you and I decide to date and have a relationship, I'm in it. I'm not going to be dating you until a better female prospect comes along."

Carney felt a little better. He tightened his grip on Ivan's hand.

"I will admit that if I was younger and didn't have children, it would be a different story. Even if we wanted to date, I still would've had to mate with a few of the females in my herd. I like them, but I've never been in love with any of them. They knew what needed to be done. Just so you know, I also never forced any of them into my bed. I don't use my authority as lead stallion to hurt people." Ivan sounded adamant.

He couldn't argue with that. He wasn't sure how he felt, knowing Ivan had children, but in a way, it wasn't any of his business. Keeping the herd bloodline going was an imperative for all species, and he had no right to judge how Ivan went about doing that.

"Do you have any brothers or sisters?" He wanted to know more about Ivan.

Their waitress returned with their drinks, then Ivan ordered for them both. Once she was gone, Ivan took a sip of his wine before returning to the question.

"I have two brothers and one sister who chose to stay in my herd. Two brothers and two sisters left to join others. We get together twice a year, plus stay in contact through email and phone calls. My brothers watch over the herd when I'm gone."

Carney laughed. "You have a big family like me. I have six brothers and sisters. Have to give my parents credit for homeschooling us because it was utter chaos at times in our house."

He started telling Ivan about some of the adventures he'd had with his family while they waited for their food. Ivan was fascinated by the activities Carney's parents taught them besides basic schooling.

"Are your parents survivalists or something? They took you out to the forests and taught you how to track animals?" Ivan shook his head. "It seems strange to me."

"We learned how to shoot and hunt as well. I'm still not clear on why, though I've always suspected my parents believed the apocalypse was going to happen at any time. They wanted us to be prepared for it." Carney took a bite of the bread their waitress had dropped off for them. He hummed as the butter melted on his tongue. "This is good."

Ivan agreed. "Yes it is. The bread is homemade here, and I believe the butter is locally sourced as well."

Carney sighed. "I would like to buy a farm out in the country and raise animals. I think it would be fun to do it all yourself." He paused when a thought hit him. "Okay. I wouldn't want to do the killing part of it. That was the one thing I hated when we went out to the woods. I hated hunting."

"I think you have a soft heart, Carney, and you don't like the idea of hurting anyone—or anything."

Joy rolled through him at Ivan's words. It was strange that he should understand Carney after only spending an hour with him—better than his entire family did after twenty-five years.

* * * *

Dinner had been one of the best Ivan had had in a long time. He'd loved listening to Carney talk about his family and babble on about whatever struck his fancy. Ivan hadn't tried to direct the conversation. He'd discovered it was the best way to learn about people.

After paying, he took Carney's hand as they left the restaurant then turned toward the beach. He waited at the edge of the sidewalk while Carney took off his shoes and socks before rolling up his pant legs. After tying the laces together, Ivan put them over his shoulder, more than willing to carry them for Carney.

"I'm glad it's a nice night out," Carney said as they wandered along where the waves washed over the sand. He squealed when the cold water hit his toes. "Yikes! That's cold."

Ivan chuckled and wrapped his arm around Carney's waist, pulling him close. "If you get chilled, let me know and I'll give you your shoes back."

Carney snuggled into his side. "I'm all right for now."

They strolled a little further away from the lights and other people before he stopped them and turned Carney so they were facing each other. Ivan slid his finger under Carney's chin to lift his head until their mouths met.

He dipped his tongue between Carney's lips, stroking it along Carney's. Ivan grabbed two handfuls of Carney's tight ass then flexed them.

"Oh!" Carney moaned, pressing tighter to him.

The hard length of Carney's cock enticed Ivan to rock their groins together. He traced the tips of his fingers along the seam of Carney's jeans, rubbing harder when he got to Carney's hole.

"God," Carney whimpered as he pushed back into Ivan's hands. "I want your hands on my skin. Please."

There was no way Ivan could ignore Carney's plea, so he fumbled with his belt then his jeans to get them open. Once he'd done that, he slipped his hands down the back of his pants to grope Carney's butt. Ivan massaged the smooth skin under his fingers, and Carney wiggled as he did so.

Sudden laughter caused him to jerk his hands out of Carney's clothes and shuffle back into the shadows of the piers. He fastened Carney's jeans before crushing the younger man to his chest. Carney whined in protest and Ivan smiled.

"Carney, I'm not going to fuck you on the beach where other people could walk up on us. Your first time shouldn't be like this." Ivan gave him a peck on the cheek before setting him away.

"But I want you to be my first," Carney told him and Ivan's chest swelled with pride.

He shook his head. "Not here and not now. Do you want to have dinner with me on Friday then spend the night? Maybe we could go to the forest and I'll shift so you can see me."

Carney's eyes were huge when he nodded. "Oh yeah. My parents might complain, but I'm old enough to go out on my own."

Ivan had thought that when Carney had been telling him about how he took online college classes because his parents didn't want him leaving the house. Overprotective seemed to be a little under descriptive when it came to the man's family.

"Then let's go find somewhere to get dessert. I'll take you home after that, unless you left your car at the bar?" He shifted on his feet, still hard from their kisses, but not aching or at the point where he would come in his jeans. That was something he hadn't done since he was young and hadn't had control over his body.

Carney shook his head. "No. I took a cab from my house. Are you sure about this? I think there's something else I'd like to have besides cake for dessert." He fluttered his eyelashes at Ivan, who chuckled.

"Flirting might get you another kiss, but it won't get you fucked here," Ivan told him.

He urged Carney to start walking back toward the restaurant. After taking Carney's hand in his, Ivan kept him close. He found that he enjoyed having Carney chatter in his ear about anything and everything that struck the man as they strolled along. As much as Carney might have wanted Ivan to take him right then and there, Ivan truly did want it to be special.

They stopped at an ice cream parlor, and Ivan suffered through watching Carney lick his ice cream cone. *Christ! I'm not going to be able to handle it if he treats my cock like that cone.* The sounds of pleasure issuing from Carney's mouth were have been enough to make Ivan come if he hadn't had complete control over himself.

Ivan had the feeling that sex with Carney was going to something special.

* * * *

After dropping Carney off at his house and waving as Carney disappeared inside, Ivan decided to return to Unconventional and have another drink. He was going to need a strong one to get rid of his blue balls.

"What a gentlemanly thing to do," he muttered as he drove back to the bar.

When he walked in, Wilma eyed him then motioned him over to her.

"Where's Carney?" she inquired with a narrow-eyed stare.

"I took him home after buying him dinner and dessert. We had a lovely walk on the beach and I kissed him." Ivan propped his elbows on the bar. "Can you give me a shot of Patrón and a Corona?"

Chuckling, she flicked his arm before walking away. When she returned with his order, she set it down in front of him then said, "You were a perfectly nice guy who kissed him but wouldn't fuck him on the beach where anyone could see?"

"Yes," he groaned. He slammed back the tequila then took a sip of beer. "I had to watch him lick an ice cream cone. I will never question my control again. I think I have permanent blue balls from this."

"From what?"

Montague Ramey, a witch and one of his good friends, took the seat next to him. Ivan couldn't help but smile at the sight of the tall man dressed impeccably in an Armani suit sitting amongst the patrons of Unconventional, who for the most part were dressed in T-shirts and jeans.

"Reef taking the night off?" Ivan asked after Montague's familiar.

"Yes. He doesn't like it when I come here. Says I'm mingling with the riff-raff." Montague even gave a little sniff of disdain like Reef probably did when he told Montague that.

Ivan nodded. "He's right, you know."

"Maybe, but I'm not interested in that. What's giving you blue balls?" Montague smiled his thanks to Wilma for the glass of pinot noir she'd set in front of him.

"Ivan's being a nice guy for once and not having a one-night stand," Wilma informed the witch.

Montague's dark eyes grew wide. "Really? I didn't think it was possible for you to turn down sex."

"I'm not turning it down. I'm simply postponing it. He's a virgin, Monty. I couldn't very well let his first time be on the beach where strangers could stumble upon us." Ivan picked at the label of his bottle.

"A virgin?" Montague wrinkled his nose in thought. "I didn't think there was such a thing in this day and age any more. You need to be careful, Ivan. You know what happens to unicorns that run into a human that has reached the age of eighteen and remained a virgin."

Ivan took another drink then nodded. "Sure. I know all the stories, but it's been centuries since we were hunted. I'm not worried about that."

Montague shot him a warning glance. "You should be. From what I've heard, there has been some talk about a resurgence of some of the old traditions."

"Fine. I'll keep my eyes open for people stalking me. Somehow, I don't see unicorn hunting making a comeback." Ivan didn't want to talk about the old days, and he wanted to get his mind off Carney for a little bit. "Why don't we go play some pool?"

The smile Montague flashed him was worthy of a shark—all teeth and predator. "I've been wanting to pay you back for the last time we played."

Ivan held up his beer for Wilma to see. "I'll have another one of these and another pinot for Montague. Tonight you just might have a chance at that, my friend."

Chapter Three

Carney rubbed his sweaty palms on his jeans while he stood in the hallway, trying hard not to peek out of the front window for the fifth time in the last ten minutes. He'd never been this nervous before. It wasn't because of Ivan. As strange as it seemed, he knew Ivan wouldn't hurt him.

"What's got you all worked up?" Jordan, the brother closest to him in age, asked as he wandered in from the kitchen.

"What are you doing here?" He deflected Jordan's question. He'd told his parents he was staying with a friend, which shocked them, but he hadn't explained anything else. Hell, Carney was an adult. He didn't need his parents' permission to do whatever he wanted.

Jordan shrugged. "Just thought I'd drop in to see what's been going on around here."

His brother had moved out of the house when he was eighteen. Jordan had always struggled against the family rules and had left as soon as he could, rarely coming back to visit. Carney didn't blame him. If he'd felt more social and better equipped to go out in public, Carney would've left with Jordan.

"Hey, are you leaving?"

Jordan's inquiry brought Carney back to the moment, and he looked to see Jordan motioning to the duffel bag Carney had packed and set by the door. Blushing, he shook his head.

"No. I'm spending the weekend with a friend." At least he hoped it would turn into the entire weekend and not just one night.

"A friend? Where did you make one of those? I thought the parents had you on a pretty short leash." Jordan looked shocked.

He didn't know if he should be offended that Jordan didn't think he could make friends or if he should take it to mean Jordan was surprised their parents had made the decision to allow Carney out of the house on his own.

"I'm not an idiot, you know. I can make friends." Carney huffed as he frowned. "I met him at a bar."

Jordan grunted. "A bar? Are you experiencing your teenage rebellion a couple years late or what? And you met *him*? So you're gay?"

Christ! He didn't want to be having this conversation. Not now. Not ever. Shoving his hands through his hair, Carney gritted his teeth. "Yes, I'm gay. Remember, my birthday was last weekend. Thanks for a card or call, jerk. Anyway, Dad suggested I go out and celebrate. Carson was supposed to meet me, but he never showed. I met Ivan at Unconventional, and he took me to dinner."

"Wow. You two are moving fast." Jordan stepped closer then rested his hand on Carney's arm. "Just be careful. You don't have a lot of experience with people."

"I know that, Jordan, but how can I gain experience if I don't go out and spend time with others?" Carney covered his brother's hand with his and squeezed. "Don't worry. I trust Ivan not to hurt me."

A wrinkle appeared on Jordan's forehead and he scrunched his nose. "Ivan? Why does that sound familiar? What's his last name?"

Carney chuckled. "What's with all the questions? You'd think you were my father instead of Dad. His last name is Brusilov."

Jordan hummed but didn't say anything. There was a knock on the door, and Carney jumped. He went to answer it, but Jordan got there before him. When he opened it, Ivan was about to knock again.

"Hello. I'm Ivan Brusilov, and I'm here to pick up Carney." Ivan smiled at Jordan, though his gaze went over Jordan's head to where Carney stood.

"My, my. Bro, you have good taste in friends." Jordan wiggled his eyebrows at him and grinned.

Carney blushed as he snatched up his duffel then shoved past his brother. "I'll see you later, Jordan."

"Wait a minute." Jordan grabbed his wrist and pulled him to a stop. He leaned in to whisper against Carney's ear. "Be careful and if something feels off, call me. I'll come and get you."

Surprise rushed through him at the concern in his brother's voice. They'd never been a close family, especially once Jordan had left. Carney smiled at Jordan as he patted his shoulder.

"Don't worry. I'll be okay, but I'll call if I think something's not right," he promised.

Jordan glanced at Ivan. "You treat him right, or you'll have to deal with me."

Ivan didn't laugh, even though Jordan was several inches shorter than him. He seemed to be taking

Jordan's threat seriously. Ivan covered his heart with his hand before bowing slightly. "I promise I'll treat your brother like a prince."

Carney giggled when Jordan rolled his eyes, but he didn't stop Carney from leaving. Ivan took the duffel from him as he joined him on the porch.

"I'm glad you could go out with me," Ivan told him as they strolled down the front walk to where a large, black truck was parked at the curb. "Did your parents give you any problems?"

"No," Carney said then sat. He waited until Ivan joined him in the cab before he continued. "They actually seemed rather excited when I said that you'd invited me out and I didn't plan on coming back until Sunday night."

Ivan's chuckle caused him to blush.

"Confident that this night will be so amazing we'll want to stay together the entire weekend?" Ivan joked.

Carney let his gaze drop to his lap and shrugged. "I was hoping."

He jumped when Ivan took his hand in his. Glancing up, he saw Ivan smile at him.

"I like that. Tonight is a hopeful night. I'm positive that we'll enjoy ourselves. I might have booked a campsite for the whole weekend as well." Ivan leaned toward him to nuzzle his temple. Easing back into his seat, Ivan took a deep breath then exhaled. "Let's get going."

Shivering at the sound of the engine turning over, Carney nodded. "Oh yes. I can't wait."

"Neither can I." Ivan leered at him before pulling away from the sidewalk. "It won't take us long to get to the forest and our campsite. My herd usually uses the same one when we go out there."

Carney wanted to bounce in excitement, but he fought the urge. Just because he was a virgin didn't mean he had to act like a spaz. He had to be cool, though Ivan knew he wasn't very experienced. Carney wanted to slap his forehead.

Not very experienced? Hell, I have no experience. My first kiss was in Ivan's car at the restaurant.

He might never have done anything like that, yet he was looking forward to learning everything Ivan wanted to teach him. Carney had the feeling that Ivan knew a lot about sex and making love.

"Are you going to shift? I really would like to see what you look like. Do the pictures and paintings I've seen represent you well?" Carney turned in his seat, placing his back to the door so he could watch Ivan drive as they headed east away from San Diego.

"Yes. I'll shift for you once we get out to the forest. I've seen quite a few paintings and tapestries with unicorns on them. I'd say they are close. We're bigger in size and more muscular than regular horses." Ivan shook his head. "Most of those artists never actually saw a unicorn. Even the females aren't as ethereal as the humans have made us appear."

Carney nodded. "I wish I could take a picture of you."

Ivan shrugged. "You can take one with your phone. Trust me, if you were to show it to anyone, they wouldn't believe you. They'd say you Photoshopped it or something."

"You could be right about that," Carney agreed. "I'd like to have it just to look at when we aren't together." He winced at how needy that sounded.

Reaching over to take his hand, Ivan flashed him a quick smile. "What do you do when you're not hanging out at the bar?"

"I want to get a degree in web design and computer repair. I like working on them, plus I think I'm pretty creative in coming up with cool websites and things like that."

"Really? I should have you check out my site and see if you have any suggestions on what I could do to spruce it up. I get a lot of my translation jobs from recommendations, but sometimes I have people search me out online."

Carney laughed. "I'd be happy to. Have you thought about doing some web ads? We could check out spots that would be the best place to put them. I took a class on that last semester."

Ivan tilted his head as though he were considering it. "We could do that. I'm making good money, but I could do more jobs. It's pretty easy for me to translate. We still speak Russian at home about half the time. We don't want to lose touch with our past."

"My parents tell us that everything they've taught us—like hunting and tracking—is a family tradition passed on from parent to child. I think it's a little weird to do it when we live in the city and aren't very likely to have to hunt to keep ourselves fed." Carney rolled his eyes at how ridiculous he thought his parents were.

Ivan chuckled. "Every family has odd traditions that only another member would understand. So that was one of your brothers that greeted me at the door?"

"Yes. That was Jordan. He's the second oldest, but he's rarely home anymore. He moved away when he turned eighteen. Guess he didn't wasn't interested in what my parents were selling."

"Are you close?" Ivan let go of his hand to downshift as they took the exit off the highway toward the forest.

He shook his head. "No. I wouldn't say I'm close with any of my siblings. I mean, we're family and all, but it's not like we tell each other our secrets. I was surprised when Jordan told me to be careful and threatened you. He's never done that before."

Ivan signaled as he turned. "From what I understand, you've never had someone come pick you up at the house either, so there's a first time for everything."

"Very true." Carney watched as they drove up to the park ranger station.

After rolling down the window, Ivan greeted the ranger. "Hey, Nigel, how's it going?"

The ranger stepped out then leaned down to look inside the car. "Ivan, good to see you, man. I see you're staying out here this weekend. Is the rest of the family coming out?"

Even Carney could hear the hopeful tone in Nigel's voice. Ivan shook his head.

"Sorry, man. Just me and Carney. When are you going to work up the nerve to talk to Maria? I told you she was interested in you."

Nigel dropped his gaze to the ground. "Yeah. Not sure how well having me in your family would work out."

"Better than you think. Can I get our tag?"

"Right." Nigel went back into the small hut then returned with a piece of paper for Ivan. "You know the routine. Display this on your dashboard, so if a ranger comes by, he can see it."

Ivan handed the paper to Carney. "Will do. Take care of yourself and grow some balls, man. Call her."

"I'll think about it." Nigel slapped Ivan on the shoulder. "Have a good weekend."

After the ranger moved away from the truck, Ivan drove down the trail, which wasn't paved. Carney understood now why Ivan had chosen to use the big vehicle instead of the Mustang. The ruts in the road would've torn off the undercarriage of the car.

"Is he a shifter as well?" Carney held on to the door handle to make sure he didn't end up hitting his head on the ceiling.

Ivan was quiet for a few minutes before he said, "Yes, but remember you can't mention anything about it. He's a cougar."

Carney nodded. "Ah. That would explain why he thought you might not want him to be part of the herd."

"I don't care. For the most part, we're more than the animals we change into. My human side keeps control of my unicorn side. Though there are shifters who are more animal than human. Just depends on the traditions of the particular species." Ivan slowed the truck down even more. "I trust Nigel not to hurt Maria, plus he knows we'd kick his ass if he did. We might be prey animals, but get enough us together, and we fight back. We can be quite dangerous if angered."

"Not only are you huge, you have a sharp horn in the middle of your forehead." He grinned. "I could see you being able to take on a cougar—whether he's a shifter or not."

Flashing him a smile, Ivan said, "Thanks."

Once they were farther into the forest, Ivan pulled into a campsite and Carney blinked at the small log cabin before them. He glanced over at Ivan.

"I thought we were going to camp in tents."

Ivan snorted. "Oh hell no. When you meet my sisters, you'll understand why we have a cabin. They don't camp. Roughing it for them is a hotel without room service, but this is the only place where we can shift without being seen. So we were able to convince the right people to allow us to build a cabin on this parcel of land."

Carney climbed out of the vehicle and strolled around the front of the truck to join Ivan as they walked up to the front door. "You don't lock the door?"

"Why would we? We don't leave anything valuable here. Just food. If people need shelter or something to eat, they can take what they want from this place. As long as there isn't any damage done, we're willing to share." Ivan motioned toward the back of the cabin. "Our bedroom is there. There's a loft."

Carney saw the open floor plan that included the kitchen and living room area. There was a set of stairs leading up to the loft, and he decided he'd check that out later on. He wandered down the short hallway to the bedroom. Peeking into the room, he saw a king-size sleigh bed. It had a bright blue comforter and piles of pillows.

"The ladies decorated it," Ivan commented as he stopped behind Carney.

"Are you saying you don't like it?" He grinned over his shoulder at Ivan.

Shrugging, Ivan chuckled. "It's not what I would've done. Bright blue really isn't my favorite color."

Ivan snaked his arm around Carney's waist, and he leaned back against the big man. They fell silent for a few minutes while Carney absorbed the heat rolling off Ivan. He wanted to burrow closer, maybe while naked.

"Here's your bag. You can put your stuff away, and I'll go get the rest of the supplies from the truck." Ivan bent to kiss him then handed him his duffel.

Carney entered the room before putting his clothes away. He hadn't brought a lot of things, but it was nice to unpack. It felt more like he was there for the long haul, not just a weekend. When he was finished, he stored his duffel in the closet then went out to find Ivan.

Chapter Four

Ivan glanced up from where he stood in the makeshift kitchen area. There was a wood stove where he'd cook dinner for them when they got hungry, plus it would heat the cabin at night. There was still a little bit of a chill in the air. He smiled when Carney appeared in the living room area.

"Get settled in?" He handed Carney a soda then got a beer out of the cooler for himself. "Or would you like a beer?"

Carney wrinkled his nose. "Soda's good for me."

"Not everyone likes alcohol, especially if you haven't had much of it before." Ivan shrugged. "Are you hungry?"

He placed his hand at the small of Carney's back, guiding him to the couch set in front of the fireplace. Ivan planned to light it later that night when they got back from him shifting.

"Not at the moment." Carney set his drink on the coffee table then turned to look at him. "I'd rather see you shift."

After leaning down and brushing a kiss over Carney's cheek, Ivan said, "I can do that. Let's put these back, and I'll take you out to the clearing we use to shift in."

"Is there like a ritual or something you have to do to change? You're not ruled by the moon like wolves, are you?" Carney paused then answered his own question. "No. You must not be since you're shifting tonight and it's not a full moon." Carney dashed back to the bedroom to get his boots.

Waiting, Ivan tried not to be nervous about how Carney was going to react when he saw Ivan's unicorn. Because he was the lead stallion, he was bigger than the others, about the size of a Clydesdale. The others in his herd were smaller, generally the size of an average Quarter Horse or Arabian. The females tended to be elegant with long, clean lines. The males were a little more muscular, but Ivan was the biggest and strongest, which was why he led the herd.

"I'm ready," Carney called as he rejoined Ivan in the kitchen area.

"Great. Let's go." He grabbed a lantern while walking out of the back door of the cabin. He knew they wouldn't be back until after sunset, and while he could see just fine in the dark, Carney couldn't. Ivan didn't want him tripping over downed trees.

He took Carney's hand in his once they were outside and guided him down the trail, deeper into the woods. Carney glanced around but stayed silent as they wound their way toward the clearing Ivan and his family used when they shifted.

The hair at the nape of his neck stood up as they came around the curve in the path closest to the clearing. The unnatural silence in the wilderness around them alerted him something else moved through the forest that night, and it had to be a predator to keep the creatures quiet.

After signaling for Carney to pause, he bent to whisper in his ear, "Stay here. I'm going to go check the clearing out. Something isn't right."

Carney shot him a worried look but didn't argue, just stepped to the edge of the trail into the underbrush. "Be careful," he murmured back.

"I will be."

Ivan and his herd hadn't lived as long as they had without learning how to be cautious. He reached down to pick up a sturdy branch from the ground as he approached the edge of the clearing. Shifting wouldn't help until he knew exactly what he faced. He didn't think it was another shifter—Nigel would've mentioned them being around.

Standing at the very edge of the clearing, he tried to pinpoint where the feelings of unease were coming from, but there didn't seem to be one single spot for him to focus on. It was as though he was surrounded by danger, and his unicorn hated it.

Suddenly, Carney screamed behind him, and Ivan whirled. He'd promised Carney nothing would happen to him, and he would do whatever he had to do to in order to keep that vow. As he came around the curve where he'd left Carney, Ivan slid to a halt when he saw Carney wasn't there.

A man dressed in green and brown leather stood where Carney had been. He looked like a huntsman of old. He held a bow in his hand with a quiver of arrows slung across his chest. There was an evil grin on his face as he spied Ivan.

"It's been too long since we've hunted one of your kind," he spoke and Ivan frowned.

"One of my kind?" He wasn't going to reveal anything.

The hunter laughed. "Don't deny it, unicorn. We baited the trap and you walked right up to it. I was all for killing you the other night on the beach, but my wife suggested we wait until you took our virgin boy to the woods. It's much more fun to chase our prey down. It's what we've been training for all of our lives."

Fear and betrayal surged through Ivan. "Your virgin boy?"

"Oh yes. Carney is a very sheltered child, but from the moment he was born, his destiny was revealed to us. He was going to bring our family back the glory it once had. In Ireland and France, our families were renowned unicorn hunters, and when we realized there was a herd in San Diego, it all became clear to us." Carney's father pulled an arrow from his quiver and notched it on the bow. "I suggest you shift and run, unicorn. This is the last night you're going to get to do that."

Ivan dodged the arrow the man shot at him before taking off. He tore his shirt from his chest, letting it drop to the dirt as he ran. There was precious time lost as he kicked off his shoes and stripped from the rest of his clothes. As soon as the night air hit his skin, Ivan allowed the power of his shift to overtake him.

In an instant, he raced along the forest trail on four legs. It always was disorienting when his vision changed from forward facing to the side angle view of a prey animal. There was a large blank spot right in front of him, but his hearing and sense of smell heightened.

The baying of a hound caught his attention, and his flanks shivered at the thought of being chased to ground by dogs. Yet if they were using them, Nigel would hear. Sound traveled far, even in the woods. He just hoped he could run long enough for Nigel to get help.

Ivan had heard the stories passed down from the herd elders about the hunts, how the humans would run the unicorns until they were exhausted then circle them around to where the trap was set. Inside the trap would sit a virgin, pure as an unmarred snowdrift. By the time the unicorn got to that point, the human part of their soul had been overtaken by the animal instinct and they would walk to their death.

He wasn't going to allow that to happen. He didn't know where they'd taken Carney, but if it was his family that hunted Ivan, Carney wasn't in any danger. As much as he wanted to hate the younger man for deceiving him, he couldn't. If there was one thing Ivan understood, it was family and how young ones didn't go against their elders' wishes.

An arrow embedded in the tree he'd just passed, and Ivan realized he needed to keep his attention on the present situation. He'd work out what had happened with Carney later. He needed to stay alive. Ivan didn't plan on dying that night or any night in the near future.

How well does Carney's family know Cleveland National Forest? Is this the place his parents took him and his siblings to train? He wished he'd asked Carney some more questions about that. Snorting, he shook his head in annoyance. Of course he hadn't asked because he was more interested in getting Carney into his bed than he was in learning more about Carney's family. It was that terrible craving all unicorns felt around a human virgin of a certain age.

Ivan ducked around a large oak tree then sprinted up a hill. There was a cave just on the other side of the small stream at the bottom of the hill that he could duck into and rest for a few. He'd have to shift to fit in, but if he could get there, he might have time to do it.

Splashing through the cool water, Ivan shifted before he climbed out. He squeezed into the cave and crouched, trying to catch his breath. As much as he wanted to close his eyes and curl up into a ball, he knew he couldn't. If they truly were tracking him with dogs, the water wouldn't fool the animals for long. Plus, if they knew about unicorn shifters, it was quite possible they knew about dog shifters and had gotten some of them to help out.

Ivan frowned at the thought of shifters hunting shifters. No. They would be real dogs. Dog shifters wouldn't be part of a pursuit of another species. It went against the code of conduct in the paranormal world, though Ivan wasn't naïve enough to think there weren't groups out there who tracked and killed others. The paranormals were no more immune to evil than humans.

A fresh burst of cool air blew over his shoulder, and Ivan twisted where he knelt at the entrance of the cave. The air meant there might be another opening somewhere in the back. He'd never taken the time to explore it thoroughly. *Wish I'd paid attention when the young ones talked about it.*

The space was too small for him to shift if he got cornered. The hunters could injure him then drag him out into the open. Being hurt would kick start his 'fight or flight' instinct, and he'd shift. They would be able to kill him and take his horn.

"You have to do something," he whispered. "You can't stay here. They will find you either way."

After pushing to his feet, he stumbled over a few rocks before he caught his balance again as he followed the scent of clean air through the turns and twists of the cave. Ivan didn't know for sure how long it had taken him, but finally, he found another entrance.

He stood in the shadows, studying the forest around him for anything that shouldn't be there. All of his instincts—human and shifter—told him his enemies weren't near. He still had a little distance on them. Staring up at the night sky, Ivan figured out where he was in relation to his cabin, the clearing, and the ranger's station.

"I won't have time to get to the ranger's station," he muttered. "They'll be on me way before that, but if I can get to the cabin, I can barricade myself in. There are guns there."

The herd kept a few rifles at the cabin to protect against bears. Hopefully, it would be enough to discourage them. Carney's family seemed to like the old-fashioned way of killing with arrows and spears.

Guns will alert Nigel and the rangers quicker than dogs will. Hunting isn't permitted in the forest.

That was what he would do. Get to the cabin, fire one of the rifles into the air and hope Nigel brought the cavalry.

Taking a deep breath, Ivan stepped out of the cave and shifted. He took the narrow trail down to the main path, though he didn't actually use it. Not knowing how close his pursuers were, he didn't want to make it easy for them to find him. Moving as fast as he could but being cautious about where he put his feet, he ghosted through the trees like his kind had for thousands of years.

A crack of a twig was the only warning he got before an arrow slammed into his left hindquarter. He neighed in pain and anger as he staggered. It wasn't a killing wound. Hell, it wasn't even one that would keep him from running. As he shot forward, the human part of his brain warned him that it was what the hunters wanted.

Yet the animal side had taken over once he'd been hit, and it wanted to get away from the creatures that wanted to kill it. All his unicorn could think about was fleeing and trying to find safety.

As Ivan raced through the woods, slamming into trees and leaping downed logs, he could tell he was being driven somewhere, and in the deepest part of his soul, he knew what was waiting for him at the end of this particular hunt. He just hoped he survived the trap.

Chapter Five

Carney stared at his younger brother, Sebastian, who stood next to him in the clearing. "What the hell is going on, Seb?"

Seb sneered down at him. "You seriously have no idea? Didn't you pay any attention to the lessons Dad and Mom taught us?"

He shrugged. "Not the ones when we went out into the woods. Why would I need to know how to hunt and track?"

"So you can carry on the family legacy, dumbass." Seb nudged Carney's foot with his boot.

"What family legacy? Why am I sitting here? Where's Ivan?" Carney could hear his voice getting higher and higher as he asked.

"The Fergusons are hunters. Dad's clan and Mom's family were well-known for being the best at trapping and killing unicorns."

Seb's prideful boast tore into Carney's heart like a lead bullet.

"Oh my God. You're kidding me." Carney shot to his feet, ready to run. He needed to find Ivan and explain he had nothing to do with this.

He cried out in pain when Seb grabbed his arm then twisted it behind him.

"You'll sit right here. We're waiting for the others to drive the beast to us. Because he'll be in his shifted form, once he sees you, it'll be like shooting fish in a barrel." Seb smirked.

Carney dropped to his knees, the pain in his shoulder and wrist overwhelming him. "You're crazy. You're talking about murdering someone. Ivan isn't an animal. He's a person."

Seb gave Carney's arm a slight jerk, and the resulting stab of agony shot through him, stealing his breath away. "He's an animal. All those freaks that can change shape are abominations in the eyes of God."

"So is this," Carney murmured as he let his chin drop forward to rest on his chest. He bit back a whimper when Seb let go of his arm.

"You were always the weakest of us, Carney. Why do you think our parents chose not to tell you about our plans? They knew you wouldn't be part of it, but they needed someone to be the bait. So they kept you in the dark and kept you innocent. They let you go out on your birthday because it was the right time. Jessica had just killed her first deer. We were all ready for the ultimate hunt—just needed our prey." Seb patted Carney on the head. "You did your job remarkably well. I wasn't sure you'd be able to attract anyone, much less the lead stallion of the local unicorn herd."

The ache in his arm didn't even begin to touch the pain in his heart. He knew the legends of unicorns being trapped using virgins as bait, but he never thought his own family would use him like that.

"That's why they let me go out by myself. They were hoping I'd cross paths with Ivan," he said.

"Him or one of the other herd members. They weren't particular when they first started this. Then they saw Brusilov drop you off and knew you'd bagged the biggest trophy of them all. A lead unicorn stallion's horn is far more powerful than a normal one. They're also harder to bring down, so they lead us on a better hunt." Seb growled. "I can't believe I got stuck guarding you. I'd rather be out there, tracking that beast."

Carney closed his eyes, resting his forehead against the trunk of the large redwood in the middle of the clearing. "Why aren't you?"

"It was supposed to be Jordan's job, but when he bailed at eighteen, I got stuck with it. I'm hoping next time, Dad will have Jessica or one of the others doing it." Seb tapped the tip of his bow on the top of Carney's head. "I'm a great shot with this."

Christ! He didn't want to think about Ivan being shot by his family. Carney would never be able to forgive himself if that happened. How could he have lived with psychopaths and never known it?

"Did Jordan know about all this?" He wanted to believe that at least one of his family members wasn't a horrible person.

Seb grunted as he kicked the tree root next to Carney's knee. "Yeah. He ran away the day after Dad told him the truth. The bastard."

"Thank God," Carney whispered. At least that meant Jordan wasn't hunting Ivan with the others.

The sounds of something large crashing through the woods brought Carney to his feet. He wanted to do something to take Seb down, to give Ivan a chance, but while Seb might have been younger than Carney, he was taller and outweighed him by quite a few pounds.

An enormous black unicorn dashed into the clearing, and the moon chose to shine down on him for a second. His flanks heaved. The whites of his eyes were noticeable as he rolled them, trying to see where the danger was coming from. Yet for all the panic and pain visible on every inch of the beast's body, there was a majestic glow to him. He was a creature of beauty and power as he stood there, assessing the situation.

Carney could see the human intelligence in Ivan's dark eyes and hoped that side ruled the unicorn's mind. He didn't want the curse of being in the presence of a virgin to wipe out all sense of self-preservation from Ivan.

"Go greet your lover," Seb ordered then shoved Carney out from under the shadow of the tree.

When he staggered into view, Ivan's gaze zeroed in on him, and Carney's heart dropped. He wanted to rush to Ivan, throw himself onto his back and beg for him to carry both of them away from these horrify circumstances. Yet Ivan's eyes clouded over with lust and longing, clueing Carney in to the fact that there would be no reasoning with the man inside the beast.

Ivan paced toward him, and Carney swallowed as he fought to hold his ground. Ivan was bigger than any horse Carney had ever seen. His black coat shined like polished onyx, making Carney's fingers itch to touch him. The single horn set in the middle of Ivan's forehead gleamed as though a swirled cone of silver had been delicately placed there by a goddess' hand.

He sighed when Ivan lowered his head and placed his nose in the center of Carney's chest. Reaching up cautiously, he ran his hands along the crest of Ivan's neck, causing the sensitive skin there to quiver.

"Oh my, you are so beautiful," he said softly, hoping Ivan understood him even while in this strange stupor being near Carney had caused. "I'm so sorry, Ivan. I didn't know about any of this. If I did, I wouldn't have accepted your invitation. Hell, I probably would've either ran away like Jordan or never left the house."

Ivan raised his head, his ears swiveling to catch the sound of Carney's voice and the approach of others. Carney knew his family drew closer, plus Seb stood hidden by the redwood.

"You need to get out of here, Ivan. You need to run and get help. Go find Nigel. Fight your animal and the urge to stay with me. Please," Carney begged. He didn't care what his family did to him as long as Ivan didn't get hurt.

Ivan huffed loudly, shifting to take the weight off his left hind leg. It was then that Carney saw the arrow wound. It looked as though the shaft and fletching had been broken off in Ivan's mad dash through the forest.

"Ivan, you're hurt," Carney stated the obvious. He eased slowly around, trailing his hands over the heavily muscled body and murmuring to keep Ivan calm.

"That's right, brother. Keep talking and touching him. The more you do that, the deeper into the trance he'll go. It'll make it easier for us to get close and slit his throat."

Seb's eager, bloodthirsty words spilled over Carney as though he'd been doused by a bucket of ice water. He jerked upright, and Ivan tossed his head in surprise, sidestepping away from Carney's touch.

"No. You're not going to get close to him. You'll have to kill me first." Carney stalked toward his brother.

"If we must." His father stepped into view behind Seb. "You do realize we have you surrounded. There is no way for you — or the creature — to get away."

Swallowing, Carney whirled when he heard a branch snap from the other side of the clearing. His mother and the rest of his family walked out, spreading out until they really did have him and Ivan trapped.

"You would really kill one of your children just to get your hands on a unicorn's horn?" He shook his head. "I can't believe you would be that twisted, Dad."

"You might look like me, but I'm pretty sure you're a changeling. No child of mine would side with a beast like this instead of his own family." Dad held up his hand. "I've disowned Jordan, so don't even bring him up."

Ivan must have thought Carney's father's gesture was a threat because he reared and struck out with his forefeet, screaming a challenge into the night.

"It was a good chase through the woods. The dogs got a work out and kept him moving," Mom informed Dad while Carney listened in horror. "I think this pack will be good to go when we start hunting the rest of the herd."

"Yes. They'll be vulnerable since the next lead stallion is still young. He's not ready to take over the herd." Dad's grin was evil personified in Carney's opinion.

He met the gaze of each of his siblings but found no sympathy — or anything else for that matter. They stared back at him as though he were a stranger and not someone they'd grown up with.

"Maybe we'll just ride out of here. I could get on his back and he could run you over," Carney bluffed.

"He's a unicorn, Carney. They'll never suffer the indignity of being ridden like a common horse," Jessica told him, her upper lip curling as though she thought he was an idiot. "Don't you know anything about unicorns?"

A warmth filled Carney when he felt Ivan press his chest to Carney's back. Something told him that if he could get on Ivan's back, this particular unicorn wouldn't throw him off. It was just that he didn't see how he could do something like that without them being shot.

"*I* know about unicorns, and what I know will get you all arrested."

They all froze when Jordan's voice drifted into the clearing. Carney peered over Ivan's broad back to see his brother step out of the forest wearing a black uniform and carrying a rifle. His mouth dropped open. It was the one sight he never imagined he'd see that night.

As the rest of his family whirled around, Carney watched as more people dressed like Jordan surrounded Carney's family. He began to relax as they relieved his siblings and parents of their weapons and took the dogs' leashes from his mother.

"Jordan, what the hell are you doing?" his father demanded while being cuffed by one of the black-clad men.

Ivan snorted and shook his mane when two strangers approached them. Carney moved to stand in front of the unicorn, hands out.

"Who are you?" He wasn't going to let anyone touch Ivan until he knew what was going on.

Jordan joined them once the others were detained. "Don't worry, Carney. This is Digby Randolph and Stacey Cash. They're doctors who specialize in shifter medicine. They just want to check Ivan's injury. Once they're done, he can shift, and I'll tell you everything. I promise."

Carney glanced over his shoulder at Ivan, who stood tense and ready to explode into violence at any second. Something told him Ivan didn't trust these people any more than he'd trusted Carney's family.

"You can stay right beside him the whole time," Stacey spoke up.

"In fact, we'd prefer it," Digby said. "He's bonded with you, and once that happens, His Highness will never trust another more than he trusts you."

"But he shouldn't," Carney protested. "I'm the reason he was injured in the first place. They used me as bait."

Jordan gave Carney's shoulder a quick squeeze, keeping an eye on Ivan as he did so. "That's true, but you didn't know about any of it. We all know if you had, you would've told Ivan as soon as you saw him."

"True." Carney swung around to touch Ivan's soft nose. "I would've told you the instant I saw you if I had known what they were planning. I swear to the Goddess."

Carney didn't necessarily believe in the Goddess — or any god for that matter — but he did know that Ivan did. If it helped Ivan accept what Carney was saying, then Carney would swear to every god and goddess that had ever existed.

Ivan heaved a heavy breath, letting his head drop to rest on Carney's shoulder. He closed his eyes, and every inch of the unicorn relaxed, though he still shivered because of his wound.

"I think that means he believes you, Carney," Digby pointed out as he moved closer. "I need more light over here."

Three more people jogged over to them, bringing lanterns with them. They held them so it lit Ivan's flank where the injury was. Stacey and Digby studied it for a few moments without touching him.

"Your Highness," Stacey said.

One of Ivan's ears swiveled back, though he didn't lift his head from Carney's chest. It was obvious he was listening.

"I'm going to have to get the head of the arrow out." Stacey caressed a spot close to the wound, and Ivan jerked his head up.

"How bad is it going to be?" Carney didn't know if that was what Ivan would've asked, but he was worried, so he had to say something.

Stacey and Digby stared at each other for a few minutes as though they were having a silent conversation then she shrugged.

"I don't know for sure. We'll numb the area. Heck, if he wants, I'll knock him out."

"We could take him to the hospital and do it there," Digby suggested.

Carney stroked Ivan's broad forehead. "Would you rather they did that? I'll ride with you the entire way."

Ivan nodded and Carney smiled. Maybe Ivan trusted him a little bit, though Carney knew they would have to talk when Ivan was healed and the rest of the situation was taken care of.

"All right. I'll call one of our assistants and have them bring a trailer to the entrance of the park. Do you think you can make it there or should we have it brought closer?" Digby asked Ivan.

Carney remembered how rough the road was leading up to the cabin. To ride over that in a trailer wouldn't be much fun. "I think we'll walk out to the ranger station. If we take it slow, you should be okay," he told Ivan, who snorted and shook his entire body as though he was impatient to get moving.

"All right. Let's get going. Are the prisoners ready to be moved as well?" Jordan shouted.

Turning slowly, Carney glanced over to where his entire family stood, handcuffed and under guard. "Jordan, what's going to happen to them?"

His brother slung his arm around Carney's shoulder and gave him a hard hug. "I don't know, Carney. They broke the law, and they have to be punished. Even the kids need to learn that hunting unicorns isn't permitted anymore."

"Are you serious?" He hadn't realized there were laws about that sort of thing.

"Yes. When unicorn shifters started to become rare because of the poaching, a group of concerned paranormals warned the hunters that if another unicorn was killed, the humans themselves would become the hunted. The paranormal community does its best to protect its citizens. It doesn't always work, but when I discovered what our parents were up to, I went to find help. They're enforcers for the community." Jordan motioned to all of the people dressed in black.

"I'm not in trouble, am I?" Carney glanced back to see Ivan walking carefully behind him, limping slightly. "I didn't know about any of this."

Jordan smiled when Ivan reached out to push Carney with his nose.

"As long as His Highness doesn't press charges, you'll be fine. Something tells me Ivan understands, though you can talk to him after he shifts back," Jordan explained.

"Why do you call him Highness?"

"He's the lead stallion of a herd, which is the equivalent of being royalty," Stacey informed him from where she walked beside Ivan.

Carney inhaled sharply. He was falling for a king. Then he shook his head. He couldn't be falling in love with Ivan so soon, not even with the spell of being a virgin placed over the unicorn. He pushed that thought to the back of his mind. Carney would examine that later, after he knew Ivan was going to be okay.

Epilogue

"Oh my God, Ivan! Please!" Carney begged as he lifted his ass off the bed.

Ivan wrapped his lips around the flared head of Carney's cock, sucking as hard as he could then pressed the tip of his tongue into the slit. He gripped Carney's hips to pin him to the sheets so he wouldn't choke Ivan by shoving his entire length in without Ivan being ready.

While he bobbed up and down Carney's shaft, Ivan trailed his fingers down over Carney's slightly furred balls to caress his taint. Then he slid them further to rub his puckered opening.

Carney shuddered and tried to close his legs, but Ivan's wide shoulders made that impossible.

"No one's ever touched me there before," Carney confessed.

Ivan popped off Carney before grinning up at him. "I would hope not. That's why it's called being a virgin."

Carney rolled his eyes and punched Ivan in the shoulder. "Smart ass. You know what I mean."

"I do and I plan to do more than just touch you there before the night is over," Ivan warned.

He discovered he loved the way Carney became tongue-tied when he said things like that to him. This was the first chance they'd had to be alone since the night Carney's family had tried to kill Ivan and take his horn.

Ivan's herd had stayed close to him because they were scared by how close they'd come to losing him. Jordan had kept Carney close while the rest of the Ferguson family had been charged with attempted murder. Ivan hadn't known about the laws prohibiting unicorn hunting either, so he'd been as shocked as the others when Jordan told them about it.

While Ivan healed from his wound and the trial went on, Ivan and Carney had spent time with each other, getting to know each other's favorite colors and movies—everything people dating learned about the person they were falling in love with.

He figured out he really did love Carney. It wasn't the pull he felt because Carney was still a virgin. Ivan knew Carney felt the same way, not just from the way he lit up whenever Ivan walked into the room, but from his touch and how well he took care of Ivan while he was healing. They hadn't said the words yet, though Ivan knew it was just a matter of time before they did.

"Are you going to continue?"

Blinking, Ivan came back to himself and realized he'd checked out for a minute or so while in the middle of making love to Carney for the first time. *Not the sign of a magnificent lover, jackass.*

"Sorry. Just got thinking about what we've been through lately," he admitted as he tilted toward the bottle lying on the pillow next to Carney's head. "Hand me the slick."

Carney glared at him but did as Ivan ordered, handing him the lube. Ivan popped it open then squirted some on his fingers. After closing it, he let it drop to the mattress while he teased Carney's hole again.

He took Carney's erection into his mouth, applying suction while pressing the tip of his middle finger into Carney.

"Oh!" Carney gasped, and his ass clenched around Ivan as Carney looked unsure whether he wanted Ivan to continue.

Ivan let him slip from his lips before he said, "If one bothers you, it's going to take a while for me to stretch you enough to take my cock."

"It just feels weird," Carney whined and Ivan chuckled.

"Try to relax."

Leaning down, he took Carney in all the way to the base where his pubic hair tickled his nose. He swallowed around his length and Carney cried out, but he also relaxed enough for Ivan to push his entire finger inside.

He kept working both Carney's ass and cock, keeping him a little off-center so he couldn't tense up. Carney's words slowly turned into babbling and incoherent sounds as Ivan coaxed him closer and closer to his first climax, but he didn't allow him to go over the edge. Ivan was selfish and wanted to be inside Carney when he came.

Finally, Carney grabbed hold of Ivan's head and pulled him off his cock. Ivan licked his lips as he looked up to meet his desperate gaze.

"Make love to me, my king," Carney murmured. "I want to come with you inside me."

He'd echoed almost exactly what Ivan had thought, and there was no way he'd deny his lover whatever he wanted. After rocking back onto his heels, Ivan snatched the condom he'd dropped onto the sheets when they'd started earlier. He tore open the foil packet then covered his shaft.

Fumbling slightly, he finally got the bottle of lube open before pouring some into his palm. After closing it, he stared at Carney as he tossed it over his shoulder, not caring where it landed. He groaned while he coated his length.

With the leftover slick, he prepared Carney a little more. He positioned the head of his cock at Carney's opening and kept his eyes focused on Carney's as he slowly sank in. Carney bit his bottom lip, but he didn't tell Ivan to stop.

When he was in as far as he could go, Ivan settled Carney's ankles onto his shoulders then leaned forward, almost bending Carney in half as he kissed him. They both groaned as the movement let him sink a little further in.

"You feel incredible," Ivan praised Carney. "So tight and hot around me."

Carney rolled his head from side to side. "I never imagined it would be so full. I can't believe you're inside me."

"It's almost like you were made to fit me."

Okay, so that was a corny thing to say, but Ivan felt like that. It wasn't just something he was spouting to get Carney to put out for him. In so many ways—not just physically—Ivan felt like Carney was the other half of his soul, and he planned to keep the human around for as long as Carney wanted to stay.

The need to move rocketed through him, and he began to thrust in and out, keeping a slow, steady rhythm. His pleasure rose higher when Carney joined in, rocking up to meet each stroke. When he achieved the right angle and nailed Carney's gland, he grinned when Carney shouted his name and trembled.

Ivan made sure to hit it every time after that, driving Carney wild. He was also growing closer to his own climax as his balls drew tight to his body and pressure built in his groin. Ivan's smooth movements became jerky and faster until he plunged in and out of Carney with an almost wild abandon. Carney held on to him, encouraging him with moans and groans.

Suddenly, without warning, Carney came, spilling his cum over his stomach, and some even landed on his chest. When his inner muscles clamped around Ivan's cock, Ivan's orgasm exploded through him. He threw back his head and shouted as he filled the condom.

He had enough presence of mind to lower Carney's legs before he collapsed on top of the man. Ivan knew he had to be smothering him, but Carney didn't protest, and Ivan wasn't entirely sure he could move right then. Carney trailed his hands along Ivan's sweaty back, tracing the line of his spine.

Unsure whether it had been seconds or hours, Ivan finally decided he needed to move. He grasped the base of the condom before he eased out of Carney, who winced.

"I'm sorry. Are you really sore?" Ivan cupped Carney's face with his free hand.

"I'm sure I will be tomorrow, but I'm not complaining." Carney gave him a big grin. "I'm so happy right now."

Leaning down, Ivan brushed a kiss over Carney's lips then climbed out of bed. He wandered into his bathroom, took care of the rubber and washed up. He got a damp cloth before returning to the bed. After cleaning Carney off, he tossed it back toward the other room.

He got them situated under the blankets, snuggled together with Carney's head resting on his shoulder while Carney played with the hair on Ivan's chest. He could tell Carney wanted to ask him something, but seemed rather unsure how to go about it.

"Just ask me, Carney. I'll answer it if I can." He rolled Carney over onto his back so he could look into his eyes.

Carney licked his lips and took a deep breath. After exhaling, he blurted, "Do you love me?"

What else could he say? Ivan, the unicorn king, said, "Yes."

BLOOD ON THE MOON

Jambrea Jo Jones

Dedication

So I asked my Facebook group to help me with a few things for this story! Carol Cobun aka Beth, thank you for helping me pick a witch to use in my story. Ro DuBose, thank you for all the great links because they help out so much, Becky Faith Reeves, thank you for gifting Montague and Kishar with their names and Cinders, thank you for Reef, it's a great cat name.

I'd also like to thank Devon, T.A., Carol, Amber and Stephani. It is so great to work with you every year and to see you every year at GRL. It is so wonderful to be a part of the Totally Bound family.

Chapter One

Montague Ramey left the bar Unconventional after beating his friend Ivan Brusilov in a game of pool. He had no idea why he put up with the unicorn. Ivan persisted on calling him Monty no matter how many times Montague insisted that was not his name. Of course, he'd have no excitement if he didn't have Ivan in his life. Playing pool with his friend was about all the excitement he'd have that week. Maybe he should have had another glass of wine before he left for home. It wasn't like he was driving. And his house wasn't that far from the bar. No matter, he had a bottle at home he could dip into. He didn't have to work at the television station on Saturday. It was his weekend to...do nothing.

God, his life was boring.

It was midnight, the witching hour. He laughed at himself. His coven probably wouldn't find it funny, but it was made up of a bunch of older ladies who were set in their ways. It was the only coven around, so he made do. His adoptive parents, being fully human, had done what they could to embrace his magical powers. It had come as a surprise when puberty had hit and his body had gone crazy. His parents had searched for a coven close to home, and when they'd found the group of older women, the coven had been happy to take him on as a prodigy.

Once he'd been accepted, his parents had moved to be even closer so he could seek assistance when he had questions about his powers. Puberty was a bitch, and he'd needed the help.

Montague had been fresh blood for the coven, who all had daughters and granddaughters they wanted to marry off to a magical being. It was a small community and they were happy to have him. At first, it had done nothing for his social life—he was introduced to the eligible women—but once the coven had found out he was gay, they'd started looking for a good man for him.

Luckily, there weren't many gay men around for them to throw his way. He'd joined when he was fifteen, so that could have been very embarrassing and traumatized him for life. They meant well. He knew that.

After his parents died, Montague had taken over the cottage he'd grown up in. It settled his soul, being in the home his mom and dad had loved so much. Sometimes he could feel them surrounding him. One of the perks of being magical.

Montague looked up at the moon and stopped walking. Blood on the moon. That was bad. Very, very bad. Something was about to happen and it wasn't going to be good. The hair on the back of his neck stood on end. Montague needed to get home—he'd rather read about the results of the blood moon than be involved in it. He was up for adventure, but he wasn't crazy. He hurried his pace, making sure to keep an eye on his surroundings.

The best thing for a witch to do was batten down the hatches and wait the night out. Maybe put out some protective spells or something to keep the bad away from them. Being magical drew the attention of the universe, be it good or bad. He should contact the others in his coven, but right now he needed the safety of his home. His coven was probably all asleep by now anyway, so he'd check in tomorrow to make sure they were okay.

Montague all but ran to his little cottage, wasting no more time being outside than he had to. He fumbled with the keys. He would blame it on the drink even if he hadn't had much—it was more fear than anything else. He'd lost his adoptive parents on a night with a blood moon. His heart ached thinking about not being able to help them on the day they'd died.

They'd been so good to him. He couldn't have asked for better parents. Most humans would have freaked when their son started to levitate in bed. Not his. Goddess he missed them. He flipped the light on and put his keys on the table by the door. Trying to catch his breath, he laid his head against the door while turning the deadbolt.

Reef, his black cat, weaved between Montague's legs. He bent down and picked Reef up. He needed the comfort after thinking of his parents. It was like Reef knew he was upset.

"Hey, kitty." Montague rubbed his cheek against the cat's side. It soothed him in a way alcohol never would.

Reef meowed back. Sometimes he wished his cat could talk. At least he didn't feel as alone with the animal in his house.

About a month after his parents died, he'd found Reef meowing at his door. He hadn't been going to bring him in at first, but there had been something about the poor kitten that'd had him ushering him into his home and heart.

"We need to be careful tonight, Reef. Blood on the moon. We both know what that could mean. I need to go grab my Ague amulet. I'd grab the African Violet one, but I think the Ague might be more effective. What do you think?"

Some might think it was weird he talked to his cat, but if he didn't, Montague would be lonely. Most days he didn't mind, but sometimes the solitude during his downtime was too much and Reef helped combat that.

"I wish something exciting would happen."

A crack of thunder shook his house.

Montague should have known better than to tempt fate on a powerful night. What had he just brought down on himself? He should have left good enough alone, the blood moon should have been all the excitement he needed. He set Reef down, brushed the cat hair off of his suit jacket and hurried to his bedroom. He rummaged around the chest at the end of his bed until he found the amulet he was looking for. He slipped it over his head and felt better. More at peace. Maybe he should meditate. Clear his mind enough to go to sleep.

He went in to the living room to light a few candles. Something about candlelight always helped him get in the right frame of mind. Once he had them lit throughout the living room, he turned off the overhead bulb. He sat on the floor with his legs crossed and his hands on his knees, palms up. He took a few deep breaths. In and out. In and out. A nice, slow rhythm to help his meditation. He should have taken his suit off, but he was so frazzled he hadn't even thought about it.

A thump at his door startled him. Montague gulped and turned around to look at the door, like it would have the answers. The thump happened again. It wasn't a knock, it almost sounded as if someone was throwing their body against the door. He'd seen those horror movies, and now he was going to do what every stupid person did when something happened on a scary night—he was going to open his door.

* * * *

Kishar Nichelson shivered in his fur coat. He wrapped it tighter around himself, but it wasn't helping. He was so cold and his whole body hurt. For the life of him he couldn't remember what had happened to him or where he was. Kishar had woken up in a ditch beside a motorcycle. His head had hurt and the cold hit him hard as soon as he'd regained consciousness. Kishar couldn't get warm.

He was thankful for the fur coat, but what he really wanted was a nice fire and maybe a bed. He was tired on top of everything else. Now the motorcycle had stalled out and he didn't think the night could get any worse, but that is when it usually did.

There wasn't much traffic, so he pushed the bike along the road. The quiet was eerie, almost unnatural. Probably the effect from the blood moon. Kishar might not know how he'd ended up where he was, but he had the rest of his faculties intact. He knew he was an incubus who hadn't fed in a long time. Kishar felt a sense of urgency—not just because of his injury. More was going on—like someone might be chasing him, which seemed odd, but what did he know? He'd woken up in a strange place with a bump on his head. He could have wrecked the motorcycle, but it felt like more than that. He was going to trust his instincts on the matter. It could be his brother, or even one of his cousins. They had it out for him. The gay thing wasn't too much of an issue, but the fact that he didn't want to feed off of humans and kill them had them after his blood. His parents were no better — they'd tried to force his feeding for years.

It was easier to feed off other paranormals. They were a hardier lot and wouldn't die when he fed unless things got out of hand. Kishar was too in control of himself to let that happen. The fact of the matter was, most paranormals didn't like to be thought of as dinner. They were higher up on the evolutionary scale. He had a few he could go to when things got too bad, but right now he was contemplating sexing up a human if he had to. Just a taste would ease some of his cold.

Thoughts like that were dangerous. If he was thinking of feeding from a human, he was at rock-bottom. Whatever accident he'd been in had made him more vulnerable to his incubus side.

There were lights ahead, maybe a town or something. He was going to have to find someone to have sex with. His power was draining so fast, and he'd need to be in top form. Maybe the power surge would help him remember why he had the urge to drop the bike and run toward the light.

Kishar should be getting ready for — something. He hated being unsure. The urgency was getting stronger. Like he was supposed to — save someone? He fell to the ground, the pounding in his head overwhelming him. It was stronger than the cold or the need for sex.

Someone had done a number on him. He was sore, but not in the way he would be if he'd had a motorcycle accident. He took stock of his body — it was more as if someone had beaten him and left him for dead.

The gap in his memory might give his attacker the advantage, but his memory would come back to him, he was sure of it. Once he'd healed his body, his memory would return and he'd take down whoever had thought to bring him down.

Kishar might not like to kill, despite being born an incubus, but there was no way he'd let someone cold-cock him and let them get away with it. It wasn't in his nature. One of the reasons he still tolerated his family was that they knew they couldn't mess with him and not get some payback.

He clutched his head, not like it would help the pain go away, but it gave him something to do. Maybe he could just stay on the ground and hope someone would find him before he perished. If only he'd fed earlier.

But his life wasn't about 'if onlys'. He was stronger than his nature.

"Get your ass up. Now," he demanded of himself through gritted teeth.

Kishar didn't know where the strength came from, but he managed to get to his feet. He was done with the bike for now. He'd leave it where it was and save his strength to get to the houses that had to be beyond the lights.

He put one foot in front of the other, taking small, shuffling steps. A crack of thunder and a slash of lightning had him stopping in front of a house. It was a little cottage and it looked like it might be warm inside. His whole body shook. The craving was getting strong, the need for sex harder to fight.

The house called to him, the thunder and lightning showing him the way. He just hoped whoever was in there would be strong enough to withstand what he'd need. He started up the walk. When he got to the door he slipped and his body slapped against it. That didn't help the aches in his body. Trying to gather himself, he put his hands on the door and pushed away, only to thump back in to it. The control he was so proud of was slipping away second by second.

The door opened and he fell into the doorway. He looked up and standing above him was a god. The man had a suit on, and had short, dark hair. And he looked warm. Sexy. Hot. Kishar wanted to climb him like a pole, but he couldn't get off the ground.

"Help." It was all he could say—everything was getting dark.

He blinked once and again...nothing helped. He was fading. Fast.

Chapter Two

Montague didn't know what to expect when he opened his door, but it wasn't the man who fell through it. He could be a serial killer and Montague had lucked out because he'd passed out, but he doubted someone who was going to do him harm would say help before going under. At least it wasn't something out of a horror movie, because it could have easily ended up in bloodshed on a night like tonight. Even with his protective amulet. Morning couldn't come fast enough.

First thing to do was to get the man off his doorstep. He wasn't going to let the guy stay in his doorway and he couldn't leave him outside on a night with a blood moon shining in the sky. Of course, he wouldn't have left him out there on any night. It just wasn't in him not to help someone.

When he bent over to pick up the guy, he noticed that he had red rings around his eyes. He wasn't human. Montague wasn't sure what he was. He picked the guy up in a fireman's carry. The man was very cold to the touch even through the fur coat he was wearing. Something was very wrong and he had no idea what because he didn't know what species the individual was. Maybe he was supposed to be cold. What did Montague know? At this point? Nothing.

If ending up with a dead paranormal in his bed was his excitement, he wanted to take his wish back. Leave it to him to bring the odd to him by wishing on one of the most powerful nights. He should know better. Damn that moon.

Montague kicked the door closed so Reef wouldn't sneak out. He managed to get to his room and put the gentleman on his bed. He needed to warm him up, maybe. Montague was worried about how cold his visitor's skin was. It wasn't that cold outside. Good thing he had a fireplace in his room. One of his many indulgences he'd added on once the place was his.

First he struggled with getting his guest under the covers. For now he left the fur on, hoping it would help. Reef actually jumped on the bed and curled up against the stranger's chest. Usually his cat would run off when people were around, hiding until it was just the two of them again. He would take that as a good sign. Animals were usually a good judge of character, with his cat more on point than most. He had a special bond with Reef and would trust his judgment. Right now he just hoped he wasn't putting the guy in danger by warming him up. Time would tell.

He left the two on the bed and started the fire, all the time contemplating getting both of them naked and warming the guy up with body heat. Normally he wouldn't even think of getting naked with an unconscious stranger, but this could be life or death. He wouldn't have time to do his research to find out what species was now unconscious on his bed, at least not until he could warm the guy up or he woke up. Montague had never seen someone with a bright red ring around the eyes unless it was cosmetic, but it didn't appear that way in this instance.

The eye rings stood out against the pale skin, which appeared to be almost translucent against the black fur. Montague was actually surprised the guy wasn't tinted blue with the chill his body was throwing off.

Finally the fire was going nice and strong. Now he had to figure out if he should get under the covers with or without clothes. He knew skin on skin was the best, but he just didn't feel right about it. What if his visitor woke up? Montague didn't want him to think he was taking advantage of him.

What he would do was change out of his suit. He'd already had it on too long. He used it like armor. When he was outside of his home he always wanted to appear put together and proper. Few knew he was more than what he seemed. His friend Ivan being one of them. At home he put down the shield.

He took off his jacket and set it on a chair. He'd have to take it in to get dry-cleaned. Montague rummaged around in his drawers and found an old, comfortable pair of sweatpants and a T-shirt.

It wasn't the kind of first impression he wanted with the attractive stranger, but his heath was more important than Montague's pride.

He switched clothes and got behind the stranger, bringing their bodies close together. He started to shiver. The stranger hadn't warmed up at all. Reef was still curled up in front of the guy, and that should have brought his temperature up a smidge. There was no way he was going to be able to share enough body heat with both of them dressed.

Montague would start with shirts, it would be innocent enough. Being this close to someone was having an effect on his cock. It didn't help that all his senses were becoming attuned to the stranger in his bed. A musky scent rolled off the stranger's body with the cold. Montague wanted to bury his nose in the guy's neck, but that would be overstepping what he needed to do. Right now his mission was to warm the stranger up and figure out why he'd stopped at his door.

Montague took off his shirt before struggling with the fur coat and shirt of his bed partner.

"Here goes nothing."

He wrapped his arms around the human icicle and couldn't suppress his full body shudder. *So. Cold.* Reef licked his hand and shifted on the bed. Montague figured his cat was getting comfortable. It was actually nice having someone in his bed. Of course, it would be better if the guy was awake and aware of his surroundings.

Montague closed his eyes and focused his energy into being warm. The guy started twitching and moaning. It had an immediate effect on Montague's dick. It twitched along with the frozen guy. The sounds he was making drove Montague crazy. He was rocking his hips—like his control was gone.

He freaked out a bit when the guy turned and grabbed his face, kissing him for all he was worth. The sensation was odd. Like the man was sucking his essence from his body.

Kishar didn't know where the wonderful warmth was coming from and he didn't care. It had been ages since he'd reveled in the glorious heat that now surrounded him. Acting on instinct, he turned and kissed the man in bed with him, drawing in the power from the body lying beside him. The strength from just the kiss warmed him. What would happen if they had sex? The man flailed around a bit before settling into the kiss.

He shivered, but this time not from the cold, it was from the wonderful sensation of warmth and joy that pulsed through his body. He opened his eyes to get a look at the stranger who was saving him. The face of his savior was strong and handsome. He remembered looking up before passing out. The man was tall, with short dark hair and plump lips. A walking wet dream.

Why did he deny himself this high? He nibbled at those red, plump lips. He needed more, but first, he had to let the stranger know what was going on. What if he was human? The kiss alone could kill him. It was that thought that had him pushing the gorgeous man away from him.

"Sorry. I'm so sorry." The man looked flummoxed.

Kishar was confused. He should be the one to apologize.

"You have nothing to be sorry for." Kishar leaned back. Something hissed and jumped off the bed. He turned to see a black cat racing toward the door.

"But I do. I took advantage of you in a weakened state. It's not at all proper. I'm sorry."

He forgot about the cat and focused on the man in bed with him. It wasn't proper? Who thought that way? Two horny men in bed with no shirts on? That was a go for most men on the planet. Come to think about it— hadn't he had his coat and shirt on when he landed in the doorway? He had more important things to think about right now. Where his clothes were could wait for a later time.

"No. I'm the one who started it." And luckily he hadn't finished it.

He didn't want to have to take care of a body—one of the reasons he hated being an incubus. Of course, having to kill to survive was the biggest suckatude.

"You're flushed." The man reached for his face. "You aren't as cold as you were before. Are you okay? Shoot. Sorry again. It's very rude of me not to introduce myself. I'm Montague Ramey." He held out his hand.

It was an odd juxtaposition of proper and naughty. Here this guy was introducing himself all nice and polite when they'd just been sucking face not even five minutes ago.

"Pleasure meeting you, Montague. I'm Kishar Nichelson." Kishar clasped both of his hands around Montague's, holding them tight and not really shaking them.

The chemistry was there between them. It was almost like another entity in the room.

"Your eyes—"

He dropped Montague's hand and brought his fingers to his eyes. Shit, he'd forgotten the rings. Had they disappeared? The kiss should have at least lightened them a little. There wasn't much light in the room however, when he'd passed out at the door, they had to have been bright red.

"I—" Kishar had no idea what to say. Some humans didn't know about the paranormal world.

"It's okay. I know you're not human. Don't freak out on me. I'm a witch." Montague shrugged like it was no big deal.

"Incubus," Kishar whispered, not sure how Montague would react. Most other paranormals stayed away from his kind. The bringer of death. He was a parasite.

"I don't know much about incubi—just that they need...sex. Oh, I see." Montague cleared his throat. "The kiss helped you."

"It did. My kind usually kill when they feed," Kishar blurted out.

"That's why you pushed me away."

"Yes." Kishar wasn't sure how he should react.

Montague seemed more curious than anything else. At least he didn't throw him out of the bed or kick him out of the house.

"I feel fine."

"I took some of your life force when we kissed. It's a curse. Paranormals can usually handle it because of the longer lifespans and magic." Kishar looked at Montague's mouth.

Now that he knew the other man wasn't human, he felt better about the situation. He could feed, if Montague was willing, and he looked very willing.

"You're still chilled. How long has it been since you've—um—fed?"

"About a month."

"Why so long?"

"I don't want to kill anyone, and it's hard to get other paranormal men to agree to sex that could leave them weak. It's hard to trust a parasite."

"Don't call yourself a parasite!"

Montague sounded horrified. *That* got to the man? Not the fact that having sex with Kishar could kill him?

"It's the truth. We take life to live."

The conversation was getting a little awkward. He felt like he should be dressed for it. Kishar crossed his arms over his chest.

"Hey. None of that now." Montague traced a finger across Kishar's lips.

He stuck his tongue out and licked the tip of Montague's finger before sucking it into his mouth. Now that Kishar knew Montague wouldn't die from a kiss and that he should be able to withstand the sex, Kishar's instincts took over.

"We're going to fuck now. You okay with that?"

In answer Montague rolled him over and pressed him into the bed.

"Tell me what you need."

"I need to be inside you. Skin on skin."

"Condom?"

"We can use one, but it won't have the full effect."

"Okay. Okay. Wait here." Montague scrambled off the bed and left the room.

Kishar hoped he hadn't scared him off. He could mesmerize Montague—it was in his repertoire of tricks as an incubus. Most of his kind would have used it right away, human or not, but that wasn't in his nature, much to his parents' horror. He got out from under the covers and wondered if he should take his pants off or not, but before he could make a decision Montague rushed back into the room holding something in his hand.

"Magical lube."

"What?"

"No need to worry about the condom with this stuff." Montague wiggled the bottle and smiled, pushing his sweats off before jumping onto the bed.

Montague was going commando and Kishar hadn't had a chance for a good look because of how fast the witch had jumped onto the bed.

It seemed unnatural for the man to be so... unencumbered, but Kishar liked it.

Chapter Three

Montague was almost giddy, which was totally out of character for him, if his coven could see him now they wouldn't recognize him. He didn't know if it was because of the kiss, but he didn't care. This was the kind of excitement he'd wanted—a strange man in his bed that he could help through sex. And he didn't have to be his proper self. It was almost a relief for him. Kishar had no idea who he was or who people expected him to be. All he had to do was feed Kishar's soul and make him stronger.

It was odd to jump on the bed feeling carefree, but something about Kishar was calling to his inner free spirit that he'd thought he'd locked away after his parents died.

Usually he'd want to know a bit more about someone he brought to his bed, but the excitement of the unknown was calling to him. He'd been so bored for a long time. His friend Ivan would be egging him on, like a devil on his shoulder. And Montague *had* been the one to wish for excitement. He wasn't one to look a gift horse in the mouth. He would take Kishar falling on his door as the gift it was.

For the first time he felt as if a spell was being cast on him, and he was going to go with it and live in the moment. Would he regret it? No. The only regret would be if he didn't go through with it. Now that Kishar had color back in his face and the red rings were fading away, Montague got a good look at Kishar. He had dark hair and almost black eyes. On closer inspection, he noticed the eyeliner surrounding the eyes—it had been lost in the red. It looked good on Kishar. His body was still pale, but it fit him, and it allowed his pretty pink nipples to stand out against his skin.

Montague tossed the lube onto the bed within easy reach because first he wanted to taste Kishar. It had been too long since his last sexual encounter, and that had been a rush job in a dark alley with some random man whose name he never did get.

Now was different. He was in his home with a man who needed sex to survive and Montague was going to make sure he did what he had to for Kishar.

"I'm going to taste you, Kishar. I want to lick you from head to toe before you fuck me into the mattress. I'm hoping I won't come so I can fuck you. If I can't hold out, there is always next time. Because there will be a next time." Montague hovered over Kishar's body, propping himself up on his elbows.

"But—" Kishar was shaking his head.

"No but. There is a pull there. Can you feel it?" Montague looked down at Kishar.

"Yes." Kishar looked right back, not blinking.

Montague felt something click, like this was meant to be, and was happy he wasn't the only one feeling this connection. Like they belonged. He didn't think fated mates were real and he'd have to look into it, but not right now. They had other things they needed to do. Like warming Kishar up.

"We'll explore that later, but for now..." Montague licked at Kishar's mouth.

Kishar opened for him and sighed into Montague's mouth. Montague lingered on the kiss, letting it slowly build up until Kishar began moving his groin, looking for friction. The material from Kishar's pants against his naked skin was driving him crazy. It was so hot, being completely nude while Kishar still had his pants on, but it was time for them both to be naked.

Montague ended the kiss, nibbling his way down Kishar's body. He nuzzled the incubus' neck, inhaling the musky smell, taking it into his body and reveling in the way it made him feel tingly inside. He scraped his teeth along Kishar's chest, heading for the pretty pink nipples that teased him with their very existence.

"Montague!"

Still using his teeth, he moved over the nipple before sucking it into his mouth, soothing it with his tongue. Kishar tasted—fresh. There was no other word for it. Like a cool spring day that Montague wanted to relish.

He pinched the other nipple, not wanting it to feel left out. The need was stronger than it had ever been before. He ran his hands down Kishar's sides. He squirmed.

"Tickles." His tone was breathy.

"Mmm. Noted." Montague did it one more time because he could.

It was time to get Kishar completely undressed if Montague wanted to taste him. And he needed to hurry, because he was too excited. He might blow before Kishar could even get inside him. And he really wanted to be fucked.

He scrambled with the pants, unbuttoning them and shoving them down the incubus' body. Kishar kicked his feet and pushed his pants off the end of the bed.

"You feel so good, but still chilled." Montague kissed Kishar's belly.

"I'm always cold." Kishar bit his lip and moved his hips to rub his cock against Montague's.

"Let's see what we can do about that. Grab the lube. I'm going to turn around so I can suck your cock and you can get me ready." Montague turned and shoved his ass in Kishar's face.

Kishar was quick on the uptake. He squeezed Montague's ass, rubbing his hole. It was almost too much. He had to focus on Kishar's dick to help him not think about what Kishar was doing to his ass.

He grasped Kishar's cock and licked the head, swirling his tongue around it, sucking at the pre-cum. He hummed before taking it to the root.

"Fuck."

Montague didn't stop what he was doing, he wanted Kishar so out of control that his instincts would take over and he'd stop being so careful.

Kishar was going insane. Everything Montague was doing had him burning up inside. And now he had to focus on opening the witch up for his cock. He slapped the bed, trying to find the lube. If he didn't hurry up he was going to come before he was inside Montague. It would help, but not give him the full charge penetrative sex would.

"Stop. Stop. I'm gonna... Montague!" He was grasping Montague's ass as tight as he could, but it wasn't helping him. He should be pinching himself. The pain would bring him down from his high. Get him off the edge. He shouldn't have gone a whole month without feeding his supernatural side. If only he could he'd get rid of the hunger and be more human, but that wasn't going to happen.

Montague turned around. Kishar hadn't even had time to lube him up. Montague took the lube from him and swiped at himself. He was whispering something Kishar couldn't hear. He didn't care—he just wanted Montague to hurry.

He was wiggling on the bed, there was no way he could control himself. He was so close to the edge that he was looking down the side ready to fall off.

"Shh. Deep breath. That's it. In and out. You've got it."

Montague's voice soothed him deep inside, somewhere no one had ever touched before. He hadn't noticed because he was too busy panicking that he was going to come too soon, but Montague had placed his palm on Kishar's chest. The hand was warm. Was this magic? If it was, he liked it.

He was still hard and ready to come, but the edge he'd been riding backed off. He was in tune with Montague. He put his hands on Montague's hips. He had straddled him and looked like he was ready to rock Kishar's world.

Kishar couldn't believe it when Montague took his cock in hand and began to sink onto it. There was no way he'd had time to prepare himself. Kishar wasn't huge, but he was of good size with considerable girth. He didn't want to hurt the man who was helping him.

"Slow. Fuck. Montague!" He'd meant to tell Montague to not hurt himself, but he was having trouble thinking.

"Magic." Montague grinned down at him.

"Magic." Kishar nodded.

He'd forgotten he was with a witch. It could make things interesting, but thinking was overrated at that moment. Montague began moving up and down, with both hands on Kishar's chest to balance himself.

They stared into each other's eyes. Kishar could feel the power surging through him and see the blue sparks flowing into him. He wondered if Montague could see it as well. His whole body was now on fire. He grasped Montague's hips tighter and thrust up again and again. Montague's body began bouncing on his.

"Kishar. Feels. Good. So. Good. Please."

Kishar took charge. He flipped them so Montague was under him, took his legs and threw them over his shoulders, bending his lover in half while he pounded away. Montague's hands never left Kishar's body. His eyes never wavered from Kishar's.

They were connected on more than a sexual level. It was more intense than anything he'd ever felt before. Montague was doing something with his ass, making it squeeze Kishar's cock in such a delicious way. He was going to come too soon. He wanted it to last forever, but he could see Montague tiring. He needed to finish this before he took too much.

"Come for me, Montague." Kishar took Montague in hand and stroked his dick.

"No. More." Montague shook his head and bit his lip.

"I'm—too much. Please. Come." He wasn't beyond pleading.

Montague closed his eyes and gritted his teeth, but he came, squeezing Kishar's cock even more. He threw his head back and screamed Montague's name. It was like an explosion in his body. He was on fire and couldn't stop moving, milking Montague as much as he could. He brought his hand up and licked it clean, the taste firing his senses even more.

It was like a bright light all around him. He'd never felt this invigorated before after sex. He'd feel healthy, but this was more than his incubus being full and happy.

Montague was patting his chest. "Good. All. Good." Montague was breathing heavily under him.

He made to move off, but Montague wouldn't let him.

"You okay?" He put his hand over Montague's.

"You're warm." Montague smiled at him.

"I am. But what about you?"

"Good. Oh, so good."

Kishar looked him over and he seemed okay. No gray tinge like someone who'd been drained too much. He actually had a rosy glow about him. It was very odd.

Montague's penis finally softened enough to ease out of Kishar's body. They both groaned, missing that connection. If he had to use one word to describe what had happened, he would have to say — magical.

He moved beside his new lover, but didn't go far. Montague still radiated warmth, and Kishar may be warm again, but the cold always crept back in. They both were quiet for a few minutes. Montague was the one who broke the silence.

"Why my door?"

"Hmmm?" Kishar didn't really understand the question.

Montague moved so he was on his arm looking down at Kishar.

"Why did you come to my door?"

"I was weak. I had wrecked my bike. Some of my memory is gone. Your door was the first one I saw. I kind of stumbled on it."

"You wrecked your bike? Like...motorcycle?" Montague's brow crinkled. He looked worried.

"Yes." Kishar had never had anyone worried about him before.

He didn't know how to handle the emotions that flooded his body. It confused him even more than waking up not knowing where he was and what he was supposed to stop.

"But you're okay, right?" Montague sat up and ran his hands over Kishar's body.

"It takes a lot to kill an incubus." Kishar winked at Montague.

Chapter Four

Montague woke up a bit out of sorts. It took him a second to realize there was someone in his bed with him. It was Saturday. He didn't have to work, and he had an incubus in his bed. A beautiful man who he couldn't believe he'd had sex with the night before. Usually on a blood moon night things went wrong, but for him everything had gone right.

He was trying to figure out what had woken him. It was his phone. It was chirping beside his bed. He fumbled for it and almost dropped the damn thing, but finally opened it.

"Hello?" His voice was gravely. It had to be all the screaming from last night's romp.

"Montague. Honey, is that you?"

"Yes, Mira, it's me." He had to smile picturing the small white-haired lady on the other end.

"Dear, we need you at the coven house as soon as possible."

Montague sat up in bed. Mira might sound calm, but something was wrong.

"What happened?"

"Tilda is gone." Mira's tone was even and calm.

How could she be calm if one of the members was gone? Unless she'd left on her own, but why would Mira be calling if Tilda had gone on vacation?

"Gone?"

Tilda was one of the younger witches. Meaning she was in her fifties instead of her sixties or seventies like the others. She was sweet, and had a daughter she'd tried to match him with when he'd hit puberty.

"Yes. Someone kidnapped her."

He could imagine her sitting in a rocker with one hand in her lap and the other holding the phone, with a half made quilt resting on her legs, because again, Mira made it sound like nothing was overly wrong. How could she be so calm? Maybe he'd heard wrong.

"How do you know?" Montague was hoping for some sort of clarification.

"We were on the phone talking about the blood moon and worrying about everyone when I heard a crash and a scream. Tilda yelled at me to help, but by the time I got there she was gone."

"Mira! Why didn't you call me sooner?" Montague jumped out of bed and looked around for some clothes.

"Calm down. There was nothing you could do, sweetie. I figured I'd call everyone over and we could scry for her this morning."

"Let me clean up and I'll be there as soon as possible." Montague rummaged around in his drawer, looking for some boxers and socks.

"We'll be waiting for you, dear." Mira hung up the phone.

"Who was that?"

Montague turned around to see Kishar sitting up in bed, rubbing his eyes. He wanted to crawl back in there with him, but with Tilda missing he had more important things to worry about. The world was going to go on—he couldn't live in a bubble with his new lover, despite how much he wanted to.

"A member of my coven. One of the women was kidnapped last night during the blood moon."

If it was possible, Kishar paled. He looked like he had last night before they'd had sex. Almost translucent.

"Kidnapped...witch... Oh fuck." Kishar scrambled off the bed.

"What is it?" This was the reaction he'd expected from Mira, not Kishar.

"I remember." Kishar put his fist to his mouth.

"Remember what?"

Kishar removed his hand so he could speak. "Why I was trying to get here. And that on my way here someone ran me off the road." Kishar paced back and forth.

Montague stood in front of Kishar and grabbed his shoulders.

"Calm down and talk to me." Montague pulled Kishar into his arms and stroked his back. Kishar laid his head against Montague's chest.

"My family. They heard about a coven here, and something about a paranormal bar. They figured it'd be easy pickings. They'd grab a witch and maybe another paranormal if they could so they'd have food for a while. Remember, I told you that paranormals are harder to drain. Humans usually die after the drain from the sex. Some can't even handle a kiss from an incubus or succubus."

Montague squeezed Kishar tight.

"Why were you headed here?" Montague wanted to believe that Kishar wasn't the bad guy.

What did he know, though? They might have some connection, but they still had just met.

"I needed to warn someone."

The tightness of his body left at those words. He was going to put his faith in Kishar and hope he wasn't making a bad decision. After all, Reef liked Kishar, and Montague's cat was picky. That had to be a good sign.

"Well, now you have. Get dressed. We're going to go to the coven house. You might be able to help us." Montague moved away, but still stood in front of Kishar.

"You don't blame me?" Kishar looked nervous.

"Did you send your family here?"

"No." Kishar shook his head.

"Do you want to kill and drain people?"

"No." Kishar hesitated a bit with his answer.

Montague hoped he was getting through to his new lover.

"Then stop worrying. We can use a bit of your blood to scry for your family. That might be easier than trying to find Tilda." Montague moved away so he could get the stuff he needed for a shower. No way was he going to the coven house smelling of sex.

"Scry?"

"Yes, it's how we search for people. A supernatural GPS. You'll see when we get to the coven house."

"Are you sure you want me there?"

"I do. You and I aren't finished. We have a lot more to explore." Montague squeezed Kishar's shoulder, pulling him closer and kissing his forehead.

"You feel okay this morning?" Kishar hugged Montague to him.

"Never better. Fully energized."

Montague walked to his closet. They needed to get to the coven house as soon as possible.

"You shouldn't be."

"What was that? I shouldn't be? Why is that?" Montague had walked into his closet to pull out a suit.

"Because I drained some of your power."

"Maybe the others in the coven will know." He shrugged. "Come on, let's shower, but no funny business, we need to get going." Montague headed for the bathroom.

Kishar was at a loss. Montague should be sluggish after last night, or at least dragging a little. If anything, the witch looked well rested and full of life. And now that Kishar's memory had returned and he recalled what his family had planned, the guilt was strong. It was like another part of him that hung on and never let go. But it wasn't like he could have stopped them by all by himself. His guilt didn't care that they were powerful when together. They hated him with a passion. If they were angry, he was the first for it to be taken out on. He did his best to stay out of their way, but it was hard when he worked in the family auto shop business. They were all he'd ever known. Once they'd started talking about actively taking people to feed when they didn't need to, Kishar had known he'd have to leave. He'd waited too long, it seemed.

Now someone had been kidnapped, and from what Montague had told him it was someone who had a family, not that it mattered one way or the other, it just seemed worse. He knew his brothers and Mom wouldn't have gone for the older ladies in the coven. He'd bet the last dollar in his pocket they'd been pissed when they figured out the coven was made up of woman in their sixties and seventies. If they'd known about Montague they would have been on his doorstep in a heartbeat. He could be thankful they didn't do their homework.

They'd be back. No way would they be happy with just one witch, if she was the only one they'd taken last night. Who know how long the witch would last with the five of them feeding off her.

There was the bar that catered to the paranormal—Unconventional. They could take their pick, like an all you can eat buffet of sexual energy. It would be a big draw to take more people. Kishar couldn't let that happen. Maybe they could go to the bar and warn... someone—because if they got tired of snatching witches from their homes, they'd go with plan B and hit up that bar.

"You coming in?" Montague yelled from the bathroom.

It jolted him out of his pity party for one. They had to take action. Sitting there thinking about things wasn't going to cut it. The sooner they cleaned up and headed out, the better. Maybe the coven could help, if they didn't kick him out first. Most people didn't like incubi or any of the bottom feeders, as they were known. He hated being looked at as if he wasn't worth anything. Killing wasn't something he ever wanted to do—it went against his very nature. He was an anomaly.

He walked to the bathroom to find Montague already naked and in the shower. He took a moment to look at the witch, watching the water and soap cascading down his body.

"Get in here. I'm almost done." Montague opened the see-through curtain and held a hand out, pulling Kishar into the stall.

It was actually pretty big. It fit both of them. Montague leaned over and pressed a quick kiss to Kishar's lips. There was a zing of power behind it that Kishar wasn't expecting. It had never happened before in his experience. Sure, he would pull some power from it because it was his nature to drain life force, but it wouldn't make him burn. He was turned around so he was facing the water with his back against Montague's chest.

Montague lathered Kishar's hair. It was getting too shaggy—he needed to cut it because it was beginning to bother him. All thoughts of his hair slipped from his mind as Montague massaged his head. He leaned his head back and enjoyed the moment. Who knew when he'd be cared for again?

"Turn around."

Kishar obeyed, not even thinking, just doing what felt right. He stared up into Montague's dark brown eyes.

"Close your eyes."

Again, he did as he was told. Montague rinsed his hair. The water was warm and he never wanted to leave this moment.

"Okay, let me just—" Montague moved his hands over Kishar's body, soaping him up. "Just rinse off. God, I want nothing more than to make you dirty again, but we have to get going." With another kiss, Montague was out of the shower.

It was time to stop thinking he'd hit the jackpot, to remember his place in the world. He was sure the coven would talk sense into Montague. It was, after all, his family that had kidnapped one of the members.

He hurried up and finished showering. Montague had left a towel for him. Kishar dried off. He wasn't looking forward to getting back into his dirty clothes, but he didn't have many options. He'd left home without anything but the motorcycle and the clothes on his back.

"I'm sorry, but I don't have much that I think will fit you. I only have a handful of casual clothes, I mostly have suits. Anything I get you will be too big. I have a

T-shirt you can wear, but pants will be a problem, unless you mind sweatpants? They have elastic on the bottom so you can pull them up some." Montague held out a shirt and some sweats. He had on a pair of dress pants and nothing else.

"Is this—formal? I'm afraid I'm a jeans and T-shirt kind of guy." Kishar took the clothes.

"No. I—might have a thing for suits."

"Nothing wrong with that." Kishar smiled.

He bet Montague looked hot in a suit. He couldn't wait to see if he was right. He put the pants on. They weren't too bad. They had about the same waist size—it was just the length that was off. Montague had to be over six feet, maybe closer to six foot five. He was tall enough that at five eleven Kishar had to look up at him.

"That is so fucking hot."

Kishar stopped what he was doing and looked at Montague. The witch was adjusting his pants. He now had a blue dress shirt on, but not buttoned.

"What?" Kishar looked around.

"The fact that you're free balling in my sweats." Montague licked his lips.

Kishar laughed. "Well—maybe, if you still want me after we finish up this kidnapping business, you can take them off me and we can have more fun. Once we figure out why you're so energized after I fed from you."

Montague dropped the tie in his hand and rushed over to Kishar.

"Not maybe. You will come back here with me so we can explore this." Montague kissed him.

Kishar forgot everything but being in the witch's arms.

Chapter Five

Montague kept looking at Kishar. He was having a hard time believing the man was there, and was afraid he'd disappear if he didn't keep watch. Stranger things had happened the night after a blood moon.

They were walking to the coven house. It wasn't too far from his place. He loved his house—it was in the center of everything. Except the television station. He had to drive there, which was a disappointment because he enjoyed walking. It helped him clear his head and think about things.

He took Kishar's hand in his. No one would care, and not many were up this early on a Saturday anyway. Not that he'd care. He had a feeling if he didn't hold on, Kishar might run. He'd turned a bit skittish since he'd remembered why he had shown up in town.

Montague didn't know much about incubi, but Kishar had a very low opinion of himself. It did sound like he'd grown up with some rough characters, but paranormals were more than their species.

"It'll be okay, you know." Montague squeezed Kishar's hand.

"How do you know that? They could kick me out or call some—law or something. My family took one of yours." Kishar looked over, frowning.

"That's right. Your family. Not you. *You* came to warn someone." Montague didn't know how to convince Kishar that things could be good and he wasn't responsible for the actions of his family. Maybe the coven could help.

"Fat lot of good that did." Kishar jerked his hand away and crossed his arms over his chest.

"Did you crash your bike on purpose?" Montague would try for logic.

"What? No. Of course not." Kishar shook his head.

"Then none of this is your fault and we will fix it. Just give us time."

The coven house was in view now. He wanted to get Kishar in the right frame of mind before he introduced him to his magical family.

"We might not have a lot of time. I have three brothers and a sister, with my mom as the ringleader. I wish I could get Damkina away from them. She is young enough—but if she starts feeding on your witch, I don't know what that could do to her." Kishar chewed on his bottom lip.

It was giving Montague dirty thoughts, but now was not the time.

"What about your father?" He was curious about family, having been adopted at such a young age he couldn't remember his biological family.

"My father? That is what you got out of all that? He hasn't been around for a long time. I'm pretty sure my mom killed him." Kishar shrugged.

"Bloodthirsty lot, huh?" How had Kishar turned out so normal if he came from such a violent family?

Montague needed to do some research. The more he knew, the better he could help Kishar.

"You have no idea."

Montague was happy Kishar was talking to him, even if it was a bit disturbing to see where he'd come from.

"I think your sister might be okay, I mean—look at you." Montague took Kishar's hand back and tugged him toward the house.

"But I'm an anomaly."

"That is a good thing." Montague winked at him.

The stopped on the walk up to the house. He tried to see it through Kishar's eyes. It was a big two-story house. A couple of the coven members lived there. He'd stayed for a bit when his folks died. It was a neutral color. A beige-ish brown. It didn't stand out at all.

"We're here." Montague pointed to the house.

Mira came bustling out of the door. All five foot of her with her short curly white hair. She looked like someone's grandma. No one would guess she was the head of a coven and one of the most powerful witches in California.

"Oh good. You're here. And you brought a friend. I'm afraid the scrying isn't going too well." She was wringing her hands together.

Montague let go of Kishar so he could hug Mira. She thought of all of them as her children even though most of the coven was her age.

"Is everyone here?" Montague figured they would have all spilled out of the house as soon as they saw he'd brought a friend.

"No, dear. Not yet. I didn't want to scare anyone." Mira patted his shoulder and stepped back.

"What about Tilda's daughter? And on the phone you said, 'we'll be waiting for you'." Montague wondered why Mira hadn't called in the troops. They might be scared, but they could help with the scrying.

"If we can't find her mom soon, I'll let her know. And Agnes was here, but she was tired so I sent her home. We need full energy for this and, Montague, you're almost as strong as I am. I think between the two of us we can fix this. Now—who is this?" Mira pointed at Kishar.

"This is Kishar. He's here to help."

Mira grabbed Kishar and hugged him. Kishar looked at Montague, his eyes wild, like he'd never been hugged before. And maybe he hadn't.

"Thank you for helping. Let's get inside. Maybe you can have better luck locating Tilda. We can do a location spell, but sometimes those can be wonky. Scrying is better."

"Montague said something about using my blood?"

"Why would we do that, dear?" Mira looked puzzled.

Kishar cleared his throat. "It was—ahh...my family that—well..." Kishar rubbed the back of his neck, his face going red. He was looking down at his boots.

"Kishar is an incubus and his mom and siblings are the ones who took Tilda. When Kishar found out what was going on, he came here to try and warn someone, but he was in an accident and too late. He passed out on my doorstep."

"Oh, you poor thing. Here, sit down." Mira helped Kishar to a chair. "I've never met an incubus before. We must talk after we find Tilda." Mira patted Kishar's hand.

"They could be feeding on her right now. We need to hurry." Kishar sat on the edge of the chair, his back ramrod straight.

Montague just wanted to hug him close and never let him go. If anyone needed comfort it was his incubus.

He'd convince him to stay and explore this thing between them. Just thinking about losing Kishar hurt his chest, and it had only been one night.

Kishar was confused. The little old lady should have kicked him out and—cursed him or something. Instead she'd hugged him and more or less welcomed him into her home, making him sit in some high-backed flowery chair that might have been comfortable, but he couldn't relax. He watched her bustle around. Montague sat on the arm of the chair like he belonged there. He had his hand on Kishar's back, rubbing it. It was soothing. He finally let himself sink into the chair. His worse fears weren't answered, and it made him a bit discombobulated—not a feeling he'd usually associate with himself, but being in the atmosphere of the coven house made him feel like he was on an episode of *Leave it to Beaver*.

"This won't hurt a bit." Mira grabbed his hand and pricked his thumb with a straight pin then squeezed a drop of blood to the surface.

She had some sort of crystal in her hand and smeared it in the blood before releasing him.

"Thank you for your offering, Kishar. It is appreciated." Mira bowed her head before turning around and walking to a table off in the middle of some sort of great room.

He began to wonder if he was under a spell. The past few hours had been nothing if not surreal.

"You want to watch or sit here?" Montague kissed his temple.

"Um—watch?"

Montague laughed. "You don't have to, I just wanted to ask. You're more than welcome to sit here."

"No. No, I want to watch."

Montague held out a hand. Kishar looked at it moment before taking it, allowing the witch to help him out of the chair.

"It's interesting. I was maybe thirteen the first time I saw it, and I was amazed."

"Why so late?" Kishar figured a witch would be learning stuff as soon as they could.

"I was adopted. We didn't figure out I was a witch until I woke up in mid-air. It scared both me and my parents. I crashed down onto my mattress. After that, my mom started to do some research and found this coven. We talked to them, and once we were comfortable, we picked up and moved here." Montague was leading him to the table as he talked.

"You're lucky."

"I know."

"Where are your parents now?"

"They died the last time we had a blood moon."

Kishar didn't know what to say to that. It was horrible to think he'd lost his parents, but at least he'd had the coven to fall back on.

"I—"

Montague held out a hand. "You don't have to say anything." He had a sad smile. "At least this blood moon was better. Well, parts of it." Montague brought Kishar close and hugged him.

"You are one of the best people I've ever met." Kishar couldn't believe his luck. Maybe fate was finally working in his favor. He could have woken up to someone who threw him out and left him for dead. Not many people would help an incubus. Most of the population thought it would be better if they were all dead.

"You need to get out more," Montague teased.

Kishar smiled. What was it about the witch that made him happy? Whatever it was, he wanted more. As much of it as he could get. Not just for the sex, which was beyond wonderful, but because his soul was lighter just being next to Montague.

"Hey, Mira, once we're done here, Kishar and I have some questions that you might be able to answer." They'd arrived at the table.

Mira had the crystal on a string and she had it hovering over a map, slowly moving it in circles. She nodded at them, but that was the only acknowledgement she gave that she'd heard.

He wasn't sure what to expect, but it wasn't for the crystal to slam onto the map sticking straight up. He jumped.

"Got 'em!" Mira leaned over to peer at the map.

Montague followed suit. "Is that—it is. Someone of Kishar's blood is at Unconventional. That can't be good."

"What's Unconventional?"

Montague looked over at him. "The local bar."

"Oh. Shit." His family was going to Plan B.

He just hoped this didn't mean the witch, Tilda, was dead. There would be a hole in these people's lives if she was taken from them in this manner. No one should have to go through what Kishar's family was putting these people through, though it would mean there was at least one less person feeding. He had to look at the positive or he'd cry.

"Yeah. We need to get over there and warn Wilma." Montague stood up and took a step back from the table.

"Can she stop them?" Kishar hoped she was some kick ass paranormal who would give his family what they deserved.

"No, she's human, but she owns the bar. She's tough, but there will be others that can help. Alexi, the bartender, or even Wilma's son, but first we need to get there." Once again, Montague held out his hand.

Just that small bit of kindness was enough to bring Kishar to his knees. Until that moment he hadn't realized how the simple contact of a hand in his would make him so happy. He was putting his trust and faith in someone who was, for all intents and purposes, a stranger.

"I'll be here when you get back, dear, and we can talk. You take care of that boy, and both of you come back safe." Mira toddled over and made them both bend down so she could kiss their cheeks.

And with that kiss, the tiny woman undid him. That was how his mother should be with him, but she hated him, and this woman who had just met him treated him with more kindness than he'd ever known. He vowed at that moment to do everything he could to bring his family down. This town would be safe if he had to take his last breath to make it so.

Chapter Six

Montague raced toward the bar. Kishar was beside him, not missing a step. They had no idea what they would be walking into, but they had to make sure no more people were kidnapped and used as a food supply for Kishar's family. He understood the need to survive, but there were better ways, so people wouldn't die. Like…asking for consent. There had to be a better way for incubi to feed. He knew he'd gladly be a source for his lover.

But, who knew how long Kishar's family had been at the bar. They could be walking into a massacre. They also didn't know who all was there. Montague got the feeling that Kishar's sister, Damkina, was too young to be in a bar. That left his mother and three brothers. His mind was racing with different spells they could use to contain without hurting. He wanted to go the non-violent route if at all possible, but he would do what needed to be done.

Kishar might not like what his mother and brothers were doing, but they were still his family. Montague had seen how upset the situation was making his new lover, and he hoped he would be able to comfort him if things went wrong. It was a real possibility that someone would die. It just wouldn't be them. Not today. Not when he'd found something to live for. They still had too much to explore.

And there it was. The bar. Had he just been there yesterday, playing pool with Ivan? It seemed so long ago. His life had changed so much in the span of a day. Not even a day. Montague took a deep breath and reached for Kishar's hand. They had to do this together. A united front against who knew what.

"You ready for this?" Montague squeezed Kishar's hand.

"No, but let's get this done." Kishar's whole body stiffened.

They were as ready for battle as they could be. The pair headed to the door. Montague didn't hear anything amiss as he pressed his ear to the door. It *was* kind of early—the place wasn't even open yet. Had they kept people hostage since last night?

Montague pushed the door. He was expecting it to be locked, but it swung open easily. He didn't know what he expected to see, but it wasn't a little girl sitting on a bar stool while three couples danced on the dance floor. Off to the side at a table was an older woman. He wondered where Wilma was. It didn't look like any employees were there. How had the Nichelson clan gotten into the place? And who were they dancing with... Was that Tilda? She seemed to be dragging a bit. That didn't bode well.

"If it isn't the prodigal son, come home. I knew you'd find your way back to us soon. Well, if you were still alive." The woman at the table spoke.

She had a husky voice that might have enticed him if he swung that way. She had the look of Kishar about her, but seemed — harder.

"You know better. What the hell is Damkina doing here?" Kishar pointed to the bar where the young girl waved at him.

"She has to learn sometime. Puberty isn't that far off and she'll need to start feeding." She shrugged as if it was no big deal.

"She's ten!" Kishar threw his hands in the air.

"So?" Now she seemed bored. "You were that age as well when you broke your mama's heart with the whole 'I like men and don't want to kill people' whine you had going on."

"What kind of mother are you?" Montague couldn't believe what he was seeing. Even after hearing Kishar talk about his family, he'd thought there would be a little bit of love, but he should have known better. How could a mother encourage her ten year old to watch them murder innocent people?

His comment piqued her interest. It was as if she'd seen him for the first time — her focus had been on her son. When talking to him she'd had a sneer on her face. Now she was all smiles.

"A good one. It's survival of the fittest, and my family will be the best out there. We'll rule the paranormals soon. Never worry about being hungry again...or cold. So. Cold. Do you know what that is like? Being so cold you don't know when you'll be warm again? Never again. It's better this way — easier. Why don't you come over here, my pretty? I don't know who you are, but your energy is off the charts. Come on." She gestured him to her table, patting the seat beside her.

"Montague, meet my mother, Tammuz. On the dance floor are my brothers Lahmu, Tiamat and Shamash. I'm not sure who their partners are."

"I won't say it's a pleasure to meet you, Tammuz. And whatever it is that you're trying to do to get me to go over to you won't work." He wondered why that was.

Montague felt the pull, but he was able to ignore it.

"I see, so you're with the abomination. I should have killed him at birth."

He was still holding Kishar's hand. He pulled him close and kissed the side of his head, whispering to him, "You don't worry about what she says. I've got you and I'm not letting you go."

Kishar gave a slight nod, but he was still pale. It had to hurt to hear those words from his own mother.

"You need to leave, Mother, before something bad happens."

A moan from the dance floor caught his attention. Tilda had dropped to the floor. Enough was enough.

"Stop!" he yelled at the top of his lungs. The whole place vibrated with the strength of his words.

The force of his emotions along with what Kishar was going through lent power to a spell he didn't know he was casting. Everything and everyone froze.

Kishar had no idea what Montague had just done, but he couldn't move. There had been a moment where it felt as if the building would fall around him, then—he was frozen. He could move his eyes and that was it. He noticed he wasn't the only one paralyzed. The dancing had stopped and his mother was in the middle of standing.

Montague touched him and he was able to move again.

"What did you do?" Kishar rubbed his arms. His body was numb.

"I think I let my emotions get the better of me. Let's get the three innocents out of here, then we'll deal with your family."

"What about Damkina?"

"You're going to think this is crazy, and maybe it is since we just met last night—but this feels like it was meant to be. Call it the magic of the blood moon if you will, but we belong together. We can take Damkina with us. Teach her a better way." Montague looked unsure of himself for the first time since they'd met.

"Is there a better way?" Kishar didn't know if he could help Damkina.

"There has to be. The coven will help us search for it. I promise."

Kishar was overwhelmed—not just by the offer to help his sister, but by the fact that Montague was correct. There was a bond there. And maybe it could explain why he hadn't drained his lover, but filled him with life. There was a myth out there that a mated incubus could feed off his lover and not kill them or steal their life energy. No one he knew believed it, but maybe, just maybe, he could have faith.

"We can talk—after. We do need to get those three away from my brothers. Can we do it without unfreezing them?"

"I think I can. Tilda should be easy because they aren't touching. I'll get her first."

They walked over to the dance floor. Montague touched Tilda's shoulder.

"Oh thank the goddess. I was hoping you'd come." Tilda scooted away before standing up. "What was that spell? I don't think I've seen it used before." Tilda stumbled.

"I've got you. Careful." Montague wrapped his arms around the witch. "I don't know. I was so angry at Kishar's family and hated what they were doing—I just shouted. I'd been working spells in my head most of the way here and something connected."

"Emotional magic is usually the strongest, my dear." Tilda patted Montague on the shoulder.

Kishar watched the byplay of the two. That was how family was supposed to be. He wanted to give his sister that, not the evil his mother spouted about. Montague had to be right, there was a better way. After all, how had the incubi before him survived? They would have been exterminated with all the dead bodies popping up. The paranormal world wouldn't have wanted the exposure.

"Tilda, I'm going to release the other two. Can you take them to the coven house? See if they need any help. Kishar and I will take care of his family."

Tilda nodded. When Montague went to touch the second person, he ended up unfreezing Tiamat as well.

"What the hell, Kishar!" Tiamat moved toward him.

"What did you expect, Tiamat? You can't come here and kill these people or kidnap them for a meal. It shouldn't work that way."

"It's all we've ever known."

"There has to be a better way, and these people will help us find it. Tiamat—I had sex with the witch. Not only did I not drain him, but he was energized after."

Tiamat looked over at Montague. "No way."

"It's true. I wouldn't lie." Tiamat was the only one of his brothers who was hesitant about their mother's ways.

If he could convince him, they could start a new family, here, with Montague.

"What about Lahmu, Shamash and Damkina?"

"We both know that Lahmu and Shamash will never go against Mother. Damkina we can keep here with us."

"Mother won't allow it." Tiamat shook his head.

"Your mother won't have a choice." Montague had all of the hostages freed. Tilda led them out of the bar. "How did you get inside the bar?"

"We waited until it was close to closing time Mother slipped inside and waited for everyone to leave before letting us in."

"You're lucky Wilma and her son weren't here. We're going to deal with this now. Are you with them or us?"

"I don't want to fight my mother, but I'm done with how she treats Kishar, and if there is a better way, I want it. I won't lie, it doesn't bother me as much as it does Kishar if I accidently kill someone because it is about survival, but this new direction my mother is going is no good." Tiamat looked firm.

He hoped Tiamat wasn't playing them. Kishar would have to have faith in this as well as Montague.

"Good. I'm going to let your brothers and mother go." Montague closed his eyes and waved his hands.

Tammuz stumbled and was furious. "What the hell did you do?" she screamed.

"You're done here. If you give me trouble, the coven will help me bind you. Be warned, we will keep an eye on you. Don't make me do something I don't want to." Montague had his arms crossed over his chest with a stern look on his face.

He was so hot, Kishar wanted to climb him right there in the bar and have his way with him. The suit on top of that stern take-no-shit look was a total turn-on.

His mother continued to charge them. She wasn't going to go down without a fight, and he wasn't going to let Montague bloody his hands. He could do this.

Kishar moved spotted a knife on the bar. He grabbed it and stood in front of Montague.

"Don't make me do this, Mother."

"You don't have the balls."

She lunged at him and he plunged the knife into her stomach, pulling the blade up to create a deep slash. Tammuz would need to feed to heal, and she wasn't going to be allowed to do that.

"Fuck, Kishar, what did you do?" Lahmu and Shamash yelled in union.

"What had to be done. I suggest you leave now and figure out a better way to feed. Don't make us come after you. I'll have my ear to the ground and will know if you start killing."

Lahmu and Shamash left the bar like the cowards they were. Damkina was bawling at the bar. He wished with everything in him that his sister hadn't witnessed this, but he'd done what he had to do.

"Tiamat, please get Damkina. We need to get to the coven house."

"I'll carry your mother," Montague knelt down.

"No!" Kishar cried out.

"Why not?" Montague was confused.

"She can feed from you, healing her wounds. I'll take her to the house. She can't feed from me."

"Will she die?"

"Maybe. If she doesn't feed? Right now she is weak, so we should take advantage of it."

The standoff over, it was time to start his life, once his mother was taken care of. Then he and Montague could figure some things out. It was time for him to be happy.

Epilogue

Montague was bored no more—he didn't have the time to be, and he loved every minute of it. It had been a month since the battle with the incubi after the blood moon. Kishar's mother had survived the knife wound. He had mixed feelings about it. He was happy that Kishar hadn't killed his mother, but the woman still had a hold on her sons. She was in some sort of paranormal detox, sorting out a better way to feed. Maybe after she was done she'd be able to be a good force in their lives. He was being optimistic, but he wanted Kishar to have a mother who loved him. Mira did her best, but she wasn't his mother. Tammuz had gone a little crazy when her husband and lover had killed each other. It explained some of the things that happened, but not all of them. At least Kishar had some closure on his father and knew his mother wouldn't kill him.

Incubi and everyone else could coexist—it had been done for centuries. Montague was slowly teaching Kishar that an incubus wasn't the underbelly of the supernatural. He'd get there eventually.

Lahmu and Shamash had been found by Tilda and they were staying at the coven house learning to feed without killing—their mother's influence was strong with those two. While some knew of the existence of the paranormal, it was better that stray bodies pointing to the unnatural didn't show up. Nobody wanted a mob of people with torches and pitchforks. People as individuals were great—it's when you grouped them together they got scary.

Tiamat and Damkina had purchased a house not far from him. He'd finally convinced Kishar to move in with him—his lover was stubborn. Of course, he didn't begrudge him helping out with his sister. She'd forgiven him for stabbing their mother. She knew Tammuz had needed to be stopped. It was traumatic, but the coven helped as much as they could. Damkina had visits with her mother once a week. It was hoped it would be good for both of them. Time would tell.

Tiamat and Kishar had opened an auto shop in town that kept them both happy, and if he wasn't mistaken, Tiamat's mate was in town. He'd been hanging around Samantha, a waitress at Unconventional. He couldn't wait to tell Kishar.

Mira had told them that the myth Kishar had heard was true. When an incubus found their soul mate they could feed from them and not kill them. It was like a feedback of energy. Montague didn't fully understand it, but he didn't need to as long as it worked. Kishar was never cold for long anymore, and that made him happy. Montague never wanted to see the red-ringed eyes again.

There had been talk at coven of getting some younger witches to join. Damkina was actually the first. She didn't share the brothers' father. At some point Tammuz had been with a witch. No one knew if that was her lover or someone else. Tammuz took needing sex to feed as her own sexual playground, which was why'd she had five kids.

Everyone was surprised that Damkina was also a witch. The coven had taken her under their wing. Damkina had taken to her new life and she was doted on by her brothers—all four of them. She had Montague wrapped around her finger as well. He wondered what it would be like to raise a child, but that might have to wait because Mira was stepping down as the head of the coven and he was training to take over. Montague would want to have time to spend with a child, and he'd have to talk to Kishar to see what his lover would say. Montague knew they'd make great fathers. He wanted a big family, and he was getting some of that with the coven.

, Life would never be the same again, and he had the blood moon to thank for it. He never thought he'd welcome a blood moon, not after his parents had died, but this one had more than made up for it. Not that he didn't miss his parents every day, but it didn't consume him like it did in the past.

"Montague, where are you?" Kishar shouted.

"Back here." Montague was working on paying some bills. Some of the boring stuff that had to be done so he could get to the fun stuff.

Montague stood from his desk and stretched.

"Hey. We're meeting Ivan and Carney soon. You about ready?" Kishar walked up to him and kissed him.

"Mm...we could..." Montague gave up talking so he could nibble at Kishar's neck.

"No." Kishar pushed him away from his neck. "We skipped out last time because you got all horny. We're going to go have a night out." Kishar patted his chest.

"You're turning down sex?" Montague pouted. That usually worked in his favor and Kishar would give in.

"No, saving it for later." Kishar winked before kissing him again. "Now hurry up." Kishar went to the closet and tossed some clothes on the bed. "Put those on." Kishar smacked his ass and left the room.

"Jeans! Kishar, I can't wear this!" Montague held the pants away from him. Where was his suit that was his armor? He didn't leave without one on. He knew he had some clean ones in there—they'd just gotten them back from the dry-cleaners.

All he heard was laughter floating back to him. The things he did for love. He'd miss his suits. Maybe. He still wore them for work, but he could get used to jeans and a T-shirt. Montague smiled and got dressed. He couldn't wait for the night to be over. He had plans for his incubus, but first he would enjoy a night out with friends and hope another blood moon wouldn't happen anytime soon. He wasn't sure how much he could take now that his life was no longer a series of boring events, and he didn't want to push his luck that the next one would be as lucky as this one had been for him. Sure, some tragedy had happened, but they'd all lived through it and life was better than ever with his incubus at his side and in his bed. Life would be eventful from here on out.

Montague whistled and made his way to the front of the house and a night of good times.

A SLIVER OF SUNSET

Devon Rhodes

Dedication

A mixed bag of shout-outs for this one...

For Kris and Mike. Many reasons for thinking of you with this book, between your name, your profession, your beautiful city of residence and the cancer scare.
Love you both and can't wait to see you in October!

To Sue, for Peter.

And, as always, to my compadres in Unconventional crime—you're the best!

Chapter One

Angelo took one last long look at the incoming waves then reached for inner strength as he rose from the sand and turned his back. It would be a long time until he felt the embrace of the sea again…if ever. It would about kill him to see the ocean every day and not dive into its cool, welcoming embrace.

Yeah, and it'll definitely *kill me if I do.*

Although the last thing he wanted to do was laugh, he snorted. Life was really bizarre sometimes.

"You okay?" His sister Nezetta was hovering as usual. He'd told her he'd be okay going to the doctor by himself this morning, but she'd shown up while it was still dark to go for one last swim together. They'd made sure to come out of the water well before dawn then sat on the beach until it was time to go.

"No. But I will be once I get this inhibitor crap over with." And the chemo to follow.

They began walking down the Pacific Beach boardwalk, dodging the occasional early morning runner or cyclist, passing a few sleeping homeless people who hadn't been chased off.

"You want some coffee?" Angelo checked his phone. "Kono's should be open by now."

"What I want is for you to stop pretending that this is just some ordinary day." Nezetta's voice rose, but rather than angry, she sounded scared.

It was very rare that ocean shifters ever became sick, which is why he'd gotten to such an advanced stage of leukemia before it had been diagnosed. He'd lost weight, fought fatigue and made excuse after excuse for how rundown he felt. It had been so gradual that he'd forgotten that, as a paranormal, he shouldn't be feeling any of those things.

Angelo stopped and took his sister into his arms. "I'm not pretending. You know I'm not the woe-is-me type. I'm just trying to enjoy the last couple of hours before everything goes…into unknown territory. 'Kay?"

She blew out a huge sigh. "I just wish I'd known how bad things were getting with you earlier. I mean…" Shaking her head, she didn't bother to continue what they'd both gone over hundreds of times, it seemed.

They started walking again. "Yeah, well. Who knew, right? I'm the only one of us I know who's even been sick, much less with something that could kill me. But hey, you know I've always been different."

"You're not *that* special. Get over yourself, Angel." It was forced, but Angelo appreciated her effort at banter.

The truth was, she alone had noticed his low energy and change in behavior, but had told him later that she'd chalked it up to Angelo being lazy.

Then he'd come down with pneumonia.

Pneumonia! Like some old, fragile human.

He'd gone to a doctor who treated wereshifters, and she'd treated his illness but, concerned with his overall health, she'd sent a blood sample to a para-friendly lab for a CBC—complete blood count.

Everyone had been incredulous about the pneumonia, but the bigger shock was still to come. The blood test results had proven that his illness wasn't a random fluke, that his people *weren't* immune to human diseases after all. After taking into account the typical differences between normal blood and para blood, it was still impossible to argue with the diagnosis—one of the worst types of leukemia, affecting white and red blood cells as well as platelets.

He'd struggled and finally kicked the lingering pneumonia, but in a few short weeks, his numbers had worsened. The aggressive cancer called for an equally aggressive chemotherapy treatment. But given his shifter side, it would only work if he accepted a course of inhibitors to keep him human for the duration.

Which meant his swim this morning would be his last one for a long time.

"Let's skip the coffee and find somewhere for brunch and stuff ourselves," he suggested. "It'll probably be the last time I can get down a full meal."

She gave him an irritated look. "Okay, fine—you win. I liked it better when you weren't doing woe-is-me. Why do you always have to be right?" Changing direction, she headed toward a side street. "Let's grab my car and go to Werewolf. I'm craving chicken fried steak. Plus it's hilarious to watch all the visiting paras who walk in and don't realize it's a normal-owned restaurant."

He laughed. "I always wonder how they came up with that name. They get plenty of para business, though, so who knows? Maybe they did it on purpose."

"No *way*," she argued, as he'd known she would, and they settled into a façade of their usual sniping as they strode toward the car. And if they both knew there was a lot that was going unsaid, they were in agreement to mutually ignore the elephant in the room, at least for now.

* * * *

The sun was at that blinding spot above the horizon, not quite sunset but low enough to really fuck with drivers heading west, when he finally managed to shake Nezetta after a long day on her leash. She'd dropped him back at his apartment after the lengthy round trip to Los Angeles for his appointment. The first inhibitor shot had been somewhat anticlimactic at first. Other than burning a bit when the nurse had slowly depressed the plunger, feeding the highly regulated substance into his bloodstream, nothing had seemed different.

"Just wait," the nurse had promised when he'd asked if something was supposed to happen. "You'll notice it kicking in later today."

Nezetta had offered to stay with him or have him come to her place, but he'd firmly turned her down and sent her packing. He knew she'd be back tomorrow and likely he'd have a dozen texts from her before the night was over, but that was her way of coping with the unknown.

His way of coping was going to be a few drinks at his favorite beachside bar, Unconventional. There were always plenty of distractions to be had there. Maybe Jovan and Luka, the lion shifters, would be there and he could find out how things had gone with the cute little fae he'd introduced them to. He hadn't seen them for a while.

Angelo doubted Roman would be there—not while his newly turned vamp boyfriend Bodi was still only able to be out at night. Roman and their third, Alexi, were possessive to the point of being humorous to watch when Bodi was around other people.

Nothing was laughable about the connection between the unicorn prince Ivan and his mate Carney. Instead, their love for one another was palpable and made Angel's chest ache with longing for his own lifemate. It was both hard to see, yet impossible to look away from.

Someday...if time doesn't run out for me.

He had to park several blocks away but that wasn't unusual. In fact, the neighborhood he parked in almost always had something available even during prime times, so he usually headed there first instead of even trying to find something closer.

Humming, he crossed the last street and came around the corner toward Unconventional.

But it wasn't there.

Angelo stopped short, prompting a huff from a couple that had to separate to walk around him, and squinted at where the entrance to the bar should be. Now there was a rather uninviting, narrow alleyway splitting the block in two between the seafood restaurant on the left and the tacky tourist souvenir shop on the right.

What the fuck?

At a loss, Angelo took a few steps forward then continued around the side of the restaurant to double-check. Yes, it was definitely the right place, but Unconventional was just...gone.

He returned to the front of the building and stared at the alley. It was giving off some serious *fuck off* vibes. Although Angelo had never heard of such a thing, he came to the conclusion that there must be some sort of magical protection on the bar so that only paras could find it—and now that his shifter side was being chemically suppressed, he was blind to it too. It was the only thing that made sense, and it was logical in a way, if it was true.

Either that or the inhibitor was causing him to hallucinate.

I need better drugs if this lame hallucination is all I'm going to get out of it.

He laughed then shook his head. "Well, damn." So much for getting his drink on tonight.

"Hi. Are you meeting someone?"

Angelo turned in surprise at the voice close by his side. An attractive dark-haired man smiled at him, but when Angelo didn't respond right away, the inviting expression began to fade a bit.

The human took a step back. "Or are you waiting for a table?"

Wait, was he a para? Fucking inhibitor. It was like he was wrapped in cotton. He didn't get a paranormal vibe from the guy and he didn't look like any type in particular. Then again, so many paras could cast glamours, so with his repressed senses, who the hell knew?

"I haven't been able to get in," he admitted.

The guy frowned and studied him then surveyed the full outdoor seating of the restaurant. "Well, happy hour should be wrapping up soon…"

Oh. He hadn't meant Unconventional. So…a human. Glad he hadn't said anything more revealing and not sure what else to do since the man showed every intention of continuing the conversation, he fell back on social niceties. "I'm Angelo."

"Dominic." He extended his hand for a brief, firm shake. "Want to join me for a drink or a bite to eat maybe? I can check to see how long the wait is. Unless you have other plans."

Interest shone in Dominic's warm brown eyes, calling to Angelo. It wasn't exactly the best time to start anything, but the distraction, even just chatting over drinks, would probably do him good. He wasn't usually the one-nighter kind of guy, but if more came of it, why not have a fling? Two more days of inhibitor shots then he'd start heavy-duty chemo and sex would be a distant memory.

That decided him. "I'm all yours."

Dominic smiled. "I'm very glad I took a chance and said 'hi' then."

"Me too. Let's go see about that table." And with one last glance at where the missing bar should be, Angelo followed Dominic into the restaurant next door.

Dominic couldn't believe his luck. Hoping it would hold, he checked with the hostess. The wait wasn't too long, so he put his name in for an outside table then turned to Angelo. "Want to wait in the bar, or outside? Maybe walk on the beach?" He knew he might be coming across a bit strong, but Angelo was scrambling his brain. He was gorgeous, yes, but something else about seeing him standing there on the boardwalk had tugged at Dominic.

A shadow crossed Dominic's face and his smile dropped for a moment. "The bar is better for me, if that's okay with you."

"Great," he hurried to agree. Scanning the bar area, he spotted a tall table with one stool. "There's a table, but looks like one of us'll be standing."

"That's not a problem." Angelo grasped his wrist and shouldered his way through the after-work crowd. He seemed to have regained the confidence Dominic had first seen when he'd come striding around the corner toward the restaurant.

He'd been texting the friend he'd meant to meet who had just bailed on him when he'd looked up and seen...well...an angel. He'd watched as Angelo had stopped short as if he'd just remembered somewhere else he had to be. Then he'd walked right past Dominic, close enough that Dominic had caught the scent of his shampoo, perhaps. Angelo's attention had unfortunately been on the building, so he hadn't caught his gaze.

Dominic had sighed and thought about ships passing in the night. Then Angelo had turned around and come back his way, so when he'd paused that time, Dominic had acted on impulse and took the opportunity to approach him.

Now, here they were.

Angelo released the gentle grip on his wrist and leaned in. "Go ahead and take the stool. I don't mind standing."

The thing to do would be to decline and offer it back but he'd done two twelve-hour shifts in the past two days, and the hit to his pride would hurt less than his feet did right now.

"Thanks." He hopped up onto the stool then turned it so that he was facing toward Angelo, who was standing so close in the limited space that he was almost between Dominic's legs. Swallowing as awareness flooded him, he met Angelo's gaze and they both smiled. "This is nice."

"Yeah." Angelo turned his head and Dominic fought to keep from leaning forward a few inches to taste that corded neck. "Not sure we're going to get a drink anytime soon, though."

"You're probably right." Then, before he really thought about what he was saying, he continued, "Actually, do you want to get out of here? I have some drink and food options at home and a partial view of the sunset."

"Partial, huh?" Angelo was one of those people who could lift one eyebrow and make it look effortless.

"Well, a sliver between a few houses of people who have way more in the bank than I do."

"Works for me." Angelo took a step back, and for a moment Dominic was disappointed, then he realized that he was giving him room to stand up so they could leave together. They worked their way back to the entrance and took their names off the waiting list. When they were back outside, Angelo asked, "Are you walking distance, or...?"

"Pacific Beach, actually. I drove down here to meet a friend, but they had something come up at the last minute."

They figured out they were parked within a block of each other. It didn't really make sense for either of them to leave their cars down here. So Dominic gave Angelo his home address for the navigation on his phone, then climbed into his car and headed out, hoping that Angelo wouldn't change his mind, while simultaneously wondering if he'd lost his, picking a guy up in the late afternoon and taking him home.

Chapter Two

He needn't have worried. Angelo was visible right behind him, or nearly so, the whole way home. Parking wasn't always easy on his block, so he wiggled his way in partially on his front walk and lawn to give Angelo enough room to squeeze in between his car and the hedge separating him from his neighbor.

They both awkwardly contorted their way out of their cars, laughing, which broke the tension and slight worry that had built in Dominic on the way there.

"Come on in." He unlocked the front door and led the way inside then closed it behind them.

"Thanks." Angelo stopped in the cool foyer and, wasting no time, surprised Dominic by reaching out and cupping his face with one hand. He turned into Angelo's touch, brushing his lips over the palm.

It was as though that was the signal Angelo needed. He stepped in closer and kissed Dominic hard, curving an arm around his waist to yank Dominic up against his lower body, where he was already sporting a promising erection. The light manhandling was hot as hell and Dominic moaned into Angelo's mouth, bringing his hands up to rest on his chest.

Angelo softened the kiss enough for Dominic to catch his breath, then he slid a gentle hand into Dominic's hair, using the other one to alternate between cupping his ass and locking around his waist. One small step, and Dominic was pressed to the wall with Angelo's weight pinning him there as they kissed.

Dominic pulled away to say, "We move to the bedroom now, and we might still be able to catch the sunset after."

Angelo grinned. "Well, I did come here to see the sliver of sunset, so it would be a shame to miss it." He braced his hands against the wall on either side of Dominic's head then gave him one more quick kiss. "You want to do this, right? It's a bit fast. I know my own mind, but I don't want to pressure you into anything."

"Hell yes." Dominic grabbed Angelo by the belt loops and pulled him back flush to him. "I'm the one who invited you here." He led Angelo through the living room down the hall to his bedroom. He crossed the room to open the French doors out to the deck.

Angelo came up behind Dominic and slid his arms around him. "Nice place."

"It's small, but I wouldn't be able to live anywhere near the water if it wasn't. And of course there's the sliver. But only from the living r—" He sucked in a gasp as Angelo found a nipple under his shirt and tweaked it. Dominic rotated his ass and it was Angelo's turn to catch his breath. He glided his hands across Dominic's abdomen then upward, taking his shirt up with the motion. Dominic half turned and kissed Angelo again, then pulled his T-shirt over his head.

Angelo hummed and finished turning Dominic to face him, then zeroed in on his bared nipples, tongue flickering against Dominic's skin. He licked and tasted, kneading Dominic's ass in counterpoint to his mouth.

"God," Dominic whispered, gripping Angelo's shoulders. "Yeah." He arched toward Angelo's mouth. No one had ever focused quite this much time on his chest before. Angelo nibbled and lightly bit at one of Dominic's nipples, creating a tidal wave of sensation. Dominic needed a touch on his cock…now. He blindly grabbed one of Angelo's hands as he moved to give attention to his other nipple, and placed it pointedly on his erection, holding it there.

Angelo chuckled against his chest. The vibration made Dominic moan, and he ran the fingers of both hands into Angelo's hair to keep him there.

"Huh-uh. You've made it clear you want something else," Angelo murmured. He hoisted Dominic into the air then a few steps later dropped him onto his bed.

For expediency, they each took off their own footwear and managed to undo their pants before they came back together as though gravitational attraction had kicked in, Angelo pressing him into the mattress. Angelo still had his shirt on, though, so Dominic returned his kiss while scrabbling to slide the fitted button-down shirt out of the way.

"Hold on." Angelo sat up, keeping their lower bodies in contact, and quickly unbuttoned his shirt. With it open all the way, exposing a taut and muscular torso, and his pants undone and hanging loosely from the points of his hips, he looked like sex on a stick.

"Pants off. Shirt—all that." Dominic was shucking his own pants and underwear as he bossed Angelo around. He obviously wasn't getting the sense of urgency. "You're still dressed," he accused.

"Okay, okay." Angelo finally got with the program, his gaze raking Dominic's nude form from head to toes as he revealed his full glory.

"Damn." Dominic couldn't stop gawking. Angelo was aptly named. Probably one of the most beautiful men he'd ever seen anywhere, much less in person and naked.

Angelo was obviously very comfortable in his skin, but there was the slightest tinge to his cheeks as he crawled up over Dominic then rolled them so that Dominic was on top.

He blinked to get his bearings then leaned down to kiss the angel beneath him.

Angelo pushed his tongue into Dominic's mouth as he trailed his hands up the backs of Dominic's thighs. He explored Dominic's ass and hips and back with his big hands, then he traced his fingers down farther, nudging Dominic's ass cheeks apart.

Fighting for air, Dominic sucked at Angelo's tongue like he'd love to do to his cock. Angelo shifted beneath him, kissing him harder. Meanwhile, he stroked over Dominic's pucker down to rub beyond, to his perineum. "Lube?"

Dominic broke from the kiss and fumbled in the nightstand basket. Angelo took the tube from him, and while he was messing with it, Dominic mouthed his way down to Angelo's neck. He ran his teeth along then nipped.

Angelo's breath caught again. "Fuck." His voice had gone deeper. "That's good." Dominic did it again, harder, and Angelo groaned and arched into it. He was back to his teasing of Dominic's ass, now with slick fingers. "Love that. You gonna leave a mark on me?"

Dominic pulled back to look at him. "You want me to? That's a pretty visible spot." He didn't know if he'd be brave enough to walk around and go to work with a hickey on his neck at his age. "How about down here?" He leaned in to lick at Angelo's nipple again then sucked just above, almost atop his heart. As he did, Angelo worked his fingers into his hole. Pulling hard with suction in sync with Angelo's fingering of his ass, he applied himself to raising a nice purple welt on Angelo's smooth pectoral. His cock was hard as iron and he couldn't keep from rubbing against Angelo's abs and equally hard erection.

He would be happy to just frot, but God, it had been forever since he'd been fucked. He wanted to make the most of this incredible, spontaneous situation. "Fuck me."

Angelo smiled, a slow, warm spreading of his kiss-swollen lips. "You have anything?" He rolled them again so that he was kneeling up between Dominic's legs.

"Same place where I got the lube. Just ignore the rest of the junk, please."

After rummaging around for long enough to make Dominic cringe and swear to get organized, Angelo finally came up with a rubber. Instead of putting it on, though, he spread Dominic open and resumed his torturous stretching and teasing of Dominic's ass.

"You're killing me," he groaned. He was already edging an orgasm just from all the damn foreplay. "I don't need *that* much prep. I mean, it's been a while but..."

"I want it to be good for you."

"Trust me — it will be. How could it not *be*?" This last came out as an undignified squeak as Angelo withdrew his fingers to pick up the packet. "Thank God."

As soon as Angelo was covered, he yanked Dominic halfway up his thighs so that his entrance was resting against the tip of Angelo's cock. Breathing raggedly, Dominic begged with his eyes. *Come on.*

Grasping Dominic's hips, Angelo began to press into him with little thrusts that claimed a bit more depth each time. He rocked his way in until he was fully seated, then leaned down, elbows resting on the comforter on either side of Dominic's head. He didn't kiss him, but the intense eye contact from that close was nearly as intimate as one.

From there, the motion began once again, and the first good thrust had Dominic tossing his head back with a gasp. It was as though Angelo knew his every desire, met them and exceeded them. He could only hold on for the ride as he careened to the edge much faster than he wanted.

His hands came to rest on the firm, muscular globes of Angelo's ass. The flexing not only speared Dominic on Angelo's thick cock, but rubbed his own erection between their abdomens. It was perfect, it was...was...

"Ah! Oh God!" he yelled as he came hard, spurting warm cum between their sweat-slick bodies. It was almost too much sensation as Angelo didn't cease his movements but did prop himself up in more of a push-up position, taking the friction away from Dominic's sensitized cock.

The position displayed Angelo's beautiful body, and Dominic couldn't resist sliding his hands over his chest, his abs. He slid a thumb across the mark he'd made over his heart and Angelo groaned. "Dom..."

Another stroke of his thumb appeared to trigger Angelo's orgasm. He froze in place, hard against Dominic, his shaft stretching him like no other, then with a harsh exhalation he thrust again, and again, slowly coming down from where he'd gone, his eyes opening to meet Dominic's.

Angelo pulled out gently then lowered himself, still supporting most of his weight, and Dominic cradled him with arms and legs. *Wow.* That had probably been the best sex of his life — and he barely knew the guy. He could feel the cooling cum between them and for once wasn't in a rush to go wash up.

The only thing that would make it better would probably be...

Angelo leaned down to press a tender kiss to Dominic's mouth then smiled. "That was fun." He seemed to be in no hurry to move, which was fine with Dominic. They kissed and petted for a few more minutes, then Angelo sat back.

"Let me go take care of this and I'll be right back."

A bit of feeling around on the side of the bed while Angelo was out of the room netted Dominic his own underwear, which he used to wipe off with, then he turned on his side, looking out of the open doors.

Oops. Hopefully his neighbors hadn't gotten an earful.

He was already drifting off when Angelo came back and, to his pleasure, climbed back onto the bed instead of getting dressed. He spooned Dominic from behind, toying with Dominic's hair. "You feel good," he murmured.

"So do you." This time when he drifted he went all the way under and when he came back up, Angelo was gone.

It didn't come as a shock, but Dominic couldn't help but be disappointed they hadn't had time to have a drink and talk or maybe go for round two. He turned over and sat up to look for his phone and found it sitting on top of a note on the bedside table.

Thanks for a great evening. This isn't a brush-off, but I have a lot going on right now. It'll be a while before I can do anything like this, but I know where to find you. You'll definitely hear from me again sometime, and maybe we can see that sliver of sunset together.

Angelo

Dominic sighed and smoothed the paper, then folded it neatly and put it into his top drawer. It was a nice sentiment, but he wasn't going to hold his breath.

Chapter Three

One week later

"This isn't working." Doctor Carter pushed the computer keyboard away and leaned forward, resting her elbows on her knees. "Your numbers are continuing to worsen, and what we're doing isn't even slowing it down."

Angelo swallowed, glad that he'd insisted upon having Nezetta drop him off rather than come in with him. "Does that mean…?"

"We're not giving up, Angelo. Not by a long shot. What we need to do is change direction." She sighed. "I wish I knew how a bone marrow transplant from a different species would work. I can't chance making you weaker than you are, though." And Nezetta, the only other one of his kind living in this area, was not a match—she'd been tested and eliminated. They had feelers out to other parts of the world, asking for any possible donors to be tested, but it didn't look promising. "So what I'd like to do is admit you and do general radiation followed by infusion chemotherapy."

She held up a hand when he was about to protest the hospitalization, obviously expecting his reaction. "The infusion isn't like your current injections, where you're in and out. These take several hours a day and you're going to be weak as a baby. And your immune system, which is already low, is going to be non-existent by the time we're done. This is our best chance to get on top of this, though." She stopped speaking and he could read the seriousness in her eyes.

He gave a bare nod, jiggling his knee, though his energy level was at the lowest it had ever been. He looked down at his arms, a patchwork of slow to heal, violent bruises from his chemo injection sites. At this point, he was willing to try anything. This was no life.

"Okay. I've already put orders in place pending our discussion here today, so we can either admit you tonight or first thing in the morning."

Angelo froze. "So soon?" Before she could respond, he continued, "Sorry. That's kind of a dumb question. Sooner the better, right?" He was talking more to himself than to her.

She nodded. "I know it seems like it's really rushing, but there's no reason to wait and every reason to start."

And all he could you was nod in return. "All right."

* * * *

A light tap at the door at dawn preceded Nezetta poking her head in, mask in place over her nose and mouth. "Ang?" She stepped in, revealed her gowned and gloved form...one gloved hand thankfully holding one of those cheap nylon backpacks that were so handy.

"Hi, sis. Thanks. You're a lifesaver." All of his electronics except his phone were dead. He'd packed his e-reader and laptop in his rolling case in the rush to get checked in to the hospital, but had forgotten their chargers, along with a few other odds and ends that would make his stay a bit more tolerable. Not that he had much energy to do more than lay around and doze. But at least now that he could charge his electronics, he could email and read online articles, plus check in with the others he worked with at San Diego's big aquatic theme park to see how things were going.

There was a small but passionate group of shifters who worked for animal rights around the globe, and the ocean shifters tended to gravitate toward places like his employer. It made sense because of their affinity with other sea-dwelling creatures. Plus when they occasionally slipped into their other form in the tanks — always after hours and only when trusted comrades were around and could cover for them — they could communicate on a simple but effective basis with the animals and find out more information.

The long-term goal, ideally, would be for Angelo to be unemployed. The larger mammals especially were kept in such a cramped and unnatural space compared to their usual unfettered, huge ocean territories, put together with no thought to their pods or groups of origin. It was stressful and unnecessary and Angelo hoped that someday all of their work, both shifters' and humans', would bring a stop their captivity. In the meantime, he and others quietly worked from the inside to do what they could to make them all as comfortable as possible until...

Angelo swallowed a sigh. Probably not the best to be thinking about his charges' demise when his own life was hanging in the balance.

She shifted, his warrior sister, looking strange to his eyes with all of the protective garb, though he knew it was to protect him, not her. "I can't stay — I really have to get to work."

"No prob. Tell everyone hi for me."

She was barely back out of the door before the next person came in. "Here's your breakfast tray, Michelangelo. I made sure they didn't put on any coffee or applesauce this time."

He tried to manage a smile for Beth, the kind, older oncology nurse who'd been on throughout the night, though even the sight of the covered dishes made his stomach turn over. He wasn't planning on looking under them. Thankfully his sense of smell was messed up. "I appreciate it."

She gazed at him with sympathy. "Try to eat a little bit if you can." She checked the complicated drip set-up on his IV. He had three different bags going — one was his chemo infusion, one was low pain management and of course, saline. "Did you manage to get any sleep last night? There's a doctor's order for a sleep aid if you need it," she offered again, as she had around three when she'd come to check on him and found him playing a game on his e-reader.

Only a few days into his incarceration and he already knew the routine. "Nah. I'll try to nap later on. By the time it would kick in, the doctors will be starting their rounds. Besides, maybe I'll get tired enough that it'll help me sleep better tonight."

She smiled. "There is that. Okay, I'm off to shift change. Your day nurse will be in in a little while. If you need anything in the meantime — "

"I'll call," he finished for her. "Got it."

Once she'd gone, he shoved the rolling tray table with the meal on it off to the side and swung his legs over the edge. He was sick of lying on the bed. Maybe he'd try the chair for a while. Thankfully they hadn't enforced the hospital gown thing—not entirely anyway. He had one on over his sweats.

Rolling the IV stand along with him, he carefully crossed the room and eased down into the chair. Nezetta should be back later today but it would be a while.

God – soooo bored.

He eyed the drawer with his phone in it. *Rules, shmules.* He needed conversation. Wishing he'd thought of it before he'd gotten settled in the chair, he decided to wait a little while before getting it out. After all, most of his friends were night owls and probably wouldn't be too happy about a phone call around sunrise.

Angelo settled for opening up the bag his sister had delivered to pull out the cords then plugged in his stuff to charge. He considered booting up the laptop that was on the table next to him to check his email.

A knock at the door. *God. Grand Central Station has nothing on this place.* How the hell did anyone ever get well in a hospital? They were constantly coming in at all hours to poke and prod you, or demand your attention for one thing or another. *Poor humans.*

Poor me.

"Come in," he called, but it was already swinging open to reveal a male nurse he hadn't met yet, holding an IV bag. The nurse stopped short and shocked brown eyes met his over the top of the ubiquitous mask.

He was having a hard to figuring out why the nurse looked so surprised at his appearance—yeah, he looked like crap, but...

"Angelo?"

The voice brought things back into focus with a jolt. *Wow, small world.* Immediately, he regretted not taking the time to try to look a bit more normal, but that was a joke. He wouldn't look better until this was all over with…hopefully.

"Hi, Dominic. It's good to see you." And he meant that.

Dominic crossed the room, the stunned look morphing into concern. "Angelo. Um, I take it you prefer that to Michelangelo?"

He gave a weak laugh, hoping his breath wasn't horrible. "Yes, definitely."

"Don't blame you. I'll change it on the status board then." The absent response had nothing to do with the sharp way Dominic was assessing him head to toe with his eyes. "So…" He trailed off.

"Yeah. So." Angelo shrugged.

"How are you feeling? Miriam said you didn't sleep much last night." Dominic slipped into nurse mode, checking his tubing then disconnecting an almost empty bag that fed into the port in his chest. Angelo didn't notice which one and didn't bother asking. The staff knew what they were doing.

"Not exactly the best environment. Plus I'm too tired to sleep, if that makes any sense."

Dominic hooked up the new bag and adjusted the flow. "It does, but I wish you'd let us give you something to help you. There's nothing wrong with accepting help even if you normally don't. Your body needs rest now more than ever. Can I check your port site?"

"Sure." Angelo reached up to untie the top fastener at his neck then shrugged the hospital gown from his shoulders to pool at his waist to give Dominic full access. He'd lost weight, plus was somewhat paunchy and soft from all of the fluid moving through his system. Not exactly sexy. He wished Dominic could have seen him at his best.

Dominic was quiet for the time it took to complete his task. His gaze flickered up to meet his once he'd finished his examination. "I guess this is what you meant about having a lot going on." He rested a hand against Angelo's chest over his heart in a warm, more than nursing touch. "I'm sorry."

"You don't have anything to be sorry for."

He sighed. "I'm sorry you have to go through this. I'm sorry I thought that your note was a polite brush-off." Dominic patted his pec then dropped his hand. "I guess it wasn't exactly great timing."

Angelo worked his gown back on up over his cooling shoulders. He was chilled almost all the time now—an unpleasant feeling for someone not used to it. "You can say that again. Right when we met, I was getting my inhib…um, the round of chemo before this one." Despite their short acquaintance, he was comfortable with Dominic, a bit *too* comfortable if he'd almost said something shifter related. He'd have to watch that. He was almost certain that Dominic was human at this point—very few paras were in the medical field, and with all of his recent health problems, by this point, he knew the few in the area who treated their own kind.

Dominic gave him a long look and pressed his lips together. "Right." Like a switch had been flicked, he morphed back into nurse mode, and Angelo instantly regretted the loss of their connection. "Okay, I need to get back to the station. I'll be in later, but call if you need me before then." He grabbed the empty bag and left without another word, leaving Angelo wondering at the sudden change in demeanor.

Had it just been Dominic remembering professionalism and having it crash back into place, regretting his personal touch while on duty? Or had he been quick enough to pick up on Angelo's slip and realized he was dealing with a shifter somehow? But that didn't really make sense. Even someone in the medical field might not know what an inhibitor was. It was seldom used — mostly just on criminals, traumatically injured shifters needing surgery, or the occasional female having a problem pregnancy. As far as he knew, he was the test case — a guinea pig for everything to do with a cancer-riddled para — and would be every step of the way.

Goodbye anonymity. If this all worked, he'd probably be in every medical journal there was.

Yeah, and if it doesn't *you likely still will be.*

But in that case he wouldn't be around for it to matter.

Chapter Four

The traffic in front of him was heavy, people riding their brakes, so he slowed down with a sigh. Dominic couldn't deny that he looked forward to going into work every shift now. It was particularly hard to stay away on his days off, too—not that he succeeded in that very often. He'd had special patients before that he'd gone out of his way to check on during his downtime, but nothing like the way he was drawn back to Angelo's side.

It had been one of the biggest surprises of his life when he'd walked in to meet his new paranormal patient, rather optimistically named Michelangelo, and had been met with the sight of *his* Angelo.

It had taken most of that shift to get over the shock of having the man he hadn't thought he'd see again pop right back in his life, albeit under completely different circumstances.

The past couple of weeks had been tough to watch as the drugs had broken Angelo down. It was especially hard since as a shifter of some sort, Angelo had probably never been incapacitated for long his entire life, if at all. Of course, Dominic had eventually worked out that Angelo had no idea the staff was aware of his status. He chuckled. For a very smart guy, Angelo must have some serious blinders on about who knew of his abilities. He'd known from first sight—well, maybe not first. He'd suspected that Angelo had been headed into Unconventional that afternoon, but then he'd plausibly redirected about going to the restaurant next door, so Dominic had had his doubts.

All those had been erased when they'd gotten up close and personal in the bar. He had those eyes, that intensity, that Dominic had only ever seen from the shifter sort of paranormals. Angelo had seemed reticent about mentioning it, though, so Dominic had respected his lead. Now, it had gone on so long that it was becoming ridiculous, especially now that Angelo was improving.

Out of the blue last week, a bone marrow donor who was a similar paranormal to Angelo had been found somewhere in Europe. With the lack of improvement from the chemo, it hadn't been hard for the oncologist to convince Angelo and Nezetta that a transplant was worth trying. They would know right away whether his body would reject the transplant, and they wouldn't be any worse off than before, really, because at that point it had been grave.

So far, they couldn't have asked for better results. The transplant had slowly been taking and working inside Angelo the past few days, and it was too soon to visually see a difference—Dominic knew that—but he was improving. The numbers in his bloodwork were promising.

He pulled into the parking garage at the hospital on autopilot, still thinking about Angelo and whether it was futile to expect anything beyond the friendship they'd been building while romance was out of the question. The biggest question he had was one he didn't know the answer to—it seemed like all the paras had the whole mate thing happening. And from what he knew of how they reacted to their mates, he wasn't it for Angelo. Of course, that didn't mean they couldn't have a relationship, at least he didn't think so. But if it wasn't the real deal, shifter-wise, was it worth risking his heart?

Because like it or not—mates or not—Dominic knew he was falling for his angel in a big way, and he had no idea what to do about it.

* * * *

Angelo's head was a little less fuzzy today, so he checked his email finally. It was really pilling up but not much of it was worth anything. Still, he worked his way through it probably even more conscientiously than usual just because he had nothing but time to do so.

An email from an address he didn't recognize almost ended up deleted unread, except that the subject line that read 'Hi Angel'. Since most spam usually shortened his legal name to Mike or Michael, he went ahead and clicked it open.

Not sure if you remember me but we worked together about a year ago. I wasn't there too long because family business called me back to Australia.

Oh, right. The Aussie shifter, Jenna. Dolphin trainer. She'd been a nice enough gal, super strong and hard-working, though a bit quiet—especially for a werewolf and an Aussie. But she had taken turns helping the ocean shifters in the tanks after hours, which was unusual for a werewolf. They typically didn't like getting wet.

I heard through the grapevine that you're sick and that you have cancer, and it was a complete shock and revelation. You see, I haven't been well for ages and our pack medic had no idea why. Of course, it had never occurred to me to see an actual doctor.

Angelo's heart sped up. Somehow he knew what was coming.

I decided to go against the pack and seek a shifter doc on my own. Turns out I have leukaemia as well. My guy in Melbourne would like to confer with your doc if possible, so I've given you all the contact information below. It would mean a lot if you could have yours get in touch with what's worked and not — that sort of thing. I wish I could travel to the States for treatment, but I can't even do my own laundry — what a joke.

The note went on as she unloaded her frustrations, all of which he completely understood. She ended with a heartbreaking plea.

I really need your help, so I hope you get this. I can't work, I can barely shift. I just can't go on like this — death would be better than living at ten percent.

Concerned, he quickly looked at the date — three days ago. Thank God he hadn't just deleted it or ignored his crammed inbox and missed it.

He typed off a quick email telling her that he'd gotten her message and to hang in there, he was getting the information to his doctor today. Cursing the fact that

Doctor Carter had already done her rounds early this morning, he rang the nurses' station.

"Can I help you?" an unknown voice answered.

"Yes, could I have my nurse come in, please?"

"Sure thing."

After sending a quick message to Nezetta to stop by when she could, he set his laptop aside just before the nurse on duty came in—Beth, not Dominic. He knew Dominic wasn't scheduled to be there today, but somehow he'd still expected him to come through the door. More wishful thinking than expectation, he supposed. Though the attraction between them was still simmering away, it was banked by the reality of his situation. But in the meantime they were getting to know one another, and Angelo liked everything he'd seen so far. Dominic's visits, both on duty and off, always comforted Angelo and left him missing the man when he was not there.

"Hi, hon, what can I do for you?"

"Could you please get a message to Doc Carter for me that I'd like to see her or talk to her today? It's kind of important."

Beth frowned slightly as she crossed the room. "Can I help you with something?"

He shook his head. "I'm fine. I just really need to talk to her about something that came up suddenly. It's…hard to explain. And sort of time sensitive."

"Of course. I'll leave a message with her service if I can't reach her directly." Beth hesitated then laid a cool hand on his arm. "You know that we're aware of your…unique situation and trained to handle it, so if it's something to do with that…"

Angelo had been half-distracted, thinking about the time difference between there and Australia, considering whether to call Jenna, so it took him a moment to process what the nurse had just implied. "What? I mean, I heard you, I just..." He had no idea that the staff of the hospital oncology unit knew he was a shifter.

Beth sighed. "I had a feeling. Of course we know. The treatment protocols and medications—it's all geared toward your makeup, and different than what we'd use with humans."

It made sense. So much sense that Angelo was a bit irritated that he hadn't considered that before getting hit over the head with it. But all he could think was that Dominic knew he wasn't human and he'd never let on. Why? Angelo wasn't sure he had the mental clarity to process that along with what Jenna was going through, so he focused on the more urgent of the two.

"I feel pretty stupid that I didn't think of that. Don't worry—it isn't to do with me or my treatment. I just found out that another"—he couldn't believe he was discussing this openly with a human—"shifter I used to work with has leukemia as well, and she's hoping Carter will share information with her doctor in Australia. Her email just now seemed so hopeless..." Exhaustion was starting to kick in now that the burst of adrenaline had subsided.

"Oh! I see." Beth's caring nurse's nature and empathy for the person she'd never met was written all over her face. "That is definitely an emergency and I'll let her know as soon as possible, all right? Don't you worry."

He picked up his computer again and saw that there was already a response from Jenna in his inbox.

Thank you so much. You have no idea how relieved I am to hear from you. Are you doing any better? I actually have to start getting ready for a doctor's appointment this morning. Let me know how you're doing and I'll tell him information will be coming soon. Sort of a cosmic laugh that the two strongest shifters who ever worked in that hellhole could be brought so low. If I didn't know better, I'd think there was something in the water. LOL.

Glad that he had been able to do a little something for her, he smiled slightly as he closed down the screen. His smile faded as her last words finally sank in.

Something in the water…

Chapter Five

Dominic tried to sneak past the nurses' station but Beth spotted him.

"The cat's out of the bag. Well, not a cat, I don't think. Not a wolf, either. Hmm..."

"What on earth are you...?" Dominic twigged to her meaning when she nodded toward the end of the hall where Angelo's room was. "How did that come up?"

"He's just had me send a message to Doctor Carter. Evidently another shifter he knows has been diagnosed and wants to discuss treatment options."

Dominic frowned and leaned on the chest-high counter to look at the screen where she was noting the call in Angelo's chart. "Oh, that sucks. And weird, too. Maybe it's one of those things where more of the paras have blood cancer than they know—it's just now getting diagnosed?" he speculated.

"I don't know about that. Anyway, he's awake and looking pretty perky compared to earlier this week, thank God." It was always satisfying for all the staff when one of their patients was on an upswing. "I'm sure he'd like a visitor if you have some time."

Way to pretend that he hadn't made a special trip here for just that purpose. "Thanks, Beth."

Dominic washed up and automatically donned the universal precautions gear that was still required for Angelo's room. If he wasn't mistaken, pretty soon that would be lifted. It would be nice to talk to him without a mask for a change.

He knocked then cracked the door. "Angelo?"

"Come in."

The flat tone was at odds with Beth's report of a few minutes ago. "Are you feeling okay?" He strode across the room.

"How do you think cancer happens?"

The non sequitur had Dominic mentally scrambling. "Well, there are several different contributing factors." The impatience on Angelo's face had him summarizing, "But for the most part, it involves exposure to a carcinogen that mutates cells within the body. When they replicate to the point where their numbers increase, that's when you see cancerous growths or altered blood or bone marrow, like you. I'm sure the doctor can explain it better than I can. Why? What's up?"

"Exposure..." Angelo muttered, absently rubbing the tips of his fingers with his thumb. He opened his mouth, shut it then took a deep breath. "You must think I'm pretty dumb for not realizing the staff knows that I'm..."

"A shifter?" he finished for him when it became clear he wasn't going to continue. "Of course I don't. I have to admit, though, I knew before I even spoke to you. Well, maybe not for sure, but I was pretty certain. You guys have a...look—a way of holding yourselves. And with you, I could almost feel it. It was probably you not being well that threw me a little bit. That and the fact that you weren't going into Unconventional."

"I, um...couldn't find it."

What? For some reason that made him laugh. "You were standing right in front of it. In fact, at first I'd thought you were going in."

"I swear to God, there was a dark alley there instead of the entrance. I'd been there a hundred times or more, but that day...nothing. So"—he cocked his head—"humans can see it?"

"Well, yeah. Why wouldn't we be able to? It's a bar."

"Huh. That's just weird. I had thought maybe my senses being repressed—you know, because of the inhibitor—made it so I couldn't see it, like humans, I'd assumed, but I guess I'm off base with that theory."

Dominic perched on the edge of the mattress near Angelo's blanket-covered legs. "I don't know what to tell you. Maybe I'll ask Wilma sometime. She knows pretty much everything about the place."

Angelo leaned forward. "You even know Wilma," he marveled. "How is it I've never seen you there before?"

Dominic should have seen that question coming. He sighed, wondering if what he was about to say would make a difference in how Angelo saw him. *Might as well just get it over with.* "I used to date a vamp. After we went our separate ways, I stopped going. I haven't been in there for a long time."

Angelo stared at him and squinted. "So you weren't headed there that day. Huh. What are the chances that we ran into each other right in front of Unconventional then? I mean, if I hadn't had whatever strange lapse that kept me from going inside..." He trailed off and his eyebrows rose.

"You wouldn't have been standing there when I walked past," Dominic finished. "I'm getting the feeling that some higher power planned for us to bump into each other."

"Higher power? What...you mean, like...the bar itself?" Angelo chuckled. "I've heard of and seen a lot of crazy things, but a sentient...business isn't one of them."

"Hey, you never know. I've long ago quit making the assumption that all that exists is limited to what I can see."

They smiled at each other and Angelo just touched Dominic's pant leg. Little touches like that had been their only contact over his stay in the hospital oncology unit—Angelo not having the energy to do more than that, and Dominic trying to respect the patient-carer relationship that was necessary while they were here. After Angelo was well and discharged home, though...

He startled at the unconsciously positive thought, then was chagrined by his surprise. Of course he'd believed all along that Angelo would recover, because the opposite was unthinkable. Or at least he'd tried to, but his usual pleasant objectivity was ruined by his increasing attachment to Angelo.

There was a brisk knock at the door, and Dominic jumped up, not wanting to be caught sitting on a patient's bed. "Hi, Angelo, you wanted to see me? Hello, Dominic." Doctor Carter strode across the room.

Dominic walked over to sit in the visitor's chair while Angelo explained his friend's situation. By the end, the doctor's face was grave.

"I have to say, I'm very concerned that, after not hearing of a shifter with cancer before now, there's another case. Either it's more common than we thought and it isn't being diagnosed, or..." She paused.

"Or there's something in the water." Angelo's voice was uncharacteristically bitter, and Dominic was focused on that so it took a moment for the penny to drop.

"In the water." She pursed her lips. "You say she did the same job as you—but she's a wolf shifter?"

"Not exactly the same, but similar. And even though she was a wolf, she was still a good swimmer and was a trainer with the dolphins. She couldn't communicate with them or the cetaceans, but she swam in human form and helped us with things that required strength or manual dexterity. She's one of the strongest weres I know."

Dominic tried to imagine what sort of shifter Angelo was that he could 'communicate' with ocean mammals. It boggled the mind.

Later, after they were alone in the room, he opened his mouth to ask, then closed it again.

"Hmm?" The conversation with the doctor seemed to have taken a lot out of him. Angelo was lying back on the bed with his eyes closed and Dominic hadn't made a sound, so he had no idea how Angelo had known he was going to say something.

"Nothing. I should probably go and let you rest." He stood from the bedside chair but made no move toward the door, reluctant to leave his angel's side.

Angelo reached out and Dominic gently took his bruised hand. "Are you sure you can't stay?" His eyes dropped closed and he grimaced. "Sorry. I sound like a needy kid."

There was no way Dominic could walk away now—and he wasn't just talking about leaving the room. "I have nowhere I have to be."

He was sitting back in the chair when Nezetta walked in a short time later. He quickly released Angelo's hand, but wasn't fooling her from the smug expression in her eyes above the mask.

"Dominic, nice to see you." She kept her voice down in deference to her brother's nap. "Is he...?" She made a vague gesture.

"He's doing good today, just tired after the doctor's visit this afternoon."

"This afternoon?" Nezetta knew the schedule as well as he did at this point. Her gaze flicked to her brother then back to Dominic. "Come on—I hate whispering. He looks like he's out for the count. We can talk outside."

After studying Dominic one last time, he could only agree. The shifter looked to be in a deep sleep, which was a relief. He followed Nezetta out and they discarded their protective gear. "It's good to see him resting."

"Definitely. So, why was the doctor here this afternoon?" She didn't waste any time getting to the point as she walked down the hall with him toward the oncology entrance.

He waved at Beth as she walked down one of the other short hallways branching like spokes off a wheel's hub, then led Nezetta out into a visitor's waiting area. "Nothing about him, actually. I'm sure he'll discuss it with you as soon as he wakes up." He paused then, before he lost his nerve, continued, "Can I ask you something?"

"Sure." She settled onto a cushioned couch and he joined her.

There was no good way to ask. "I know this is going to sound lame and maybe prejudiced, but...what are you two? I mean, what sort of paranormals?"

She cocked her head, a slight smile teasing at her mouth. "It doesn't say in his file?"

"Just that you're 'ocean shifters' and you can communicate with orcas and so forth, but I'm not sure if there are multiple kinds, or..." He raised his eyebrows at her amusement. "It's not that funny."

"Sorry. You're just tiptoeing around so much, it's sweet. Really." She rolled her eyes. "I suppose the best way to describe us is mer-people."

He froze. "Like..."

"Yeah, I'm a 'mermaid'. Though, for the record, I hate that term, and we never use it."

"Noted. Um..." He wondered if he dared to ask for more information or should just do some research on his own.

"Yes, we can shift to our other form in the water, but it's at will—we don't automatically grow a tail if we get splashed. No, it doesn't hurt our feet to walk on land. No, we don't lure sailors to their deaths—that's sirens." She winked. "And there aren't as many of us here on the West Coast as you might think. The water's a bit cold for our people. We're originally from the Med."

"That's the accent. Well—you have it. Angelo doesn't seem to."

"I'm a *lot* older than him."

"I won't ask." Females of any species didn't appreciate references to their age. "So the birthdate on his paperwork is a cover?"

"No—he's really just a baby of thirty-three. But he's a strong male, so he had to leave our family's territory, and I chose to go with him. It was getting crazy crowded there, and after I lost my lifemate..." She stopped and rubbed a mark on her inner wrist with her opposite thumb. "Well, I just needed a fresh start."

"I'm sorry." He patted her arm, trying to ignore the disappointment that he felt at learning they were a race with lifemates. "But I'm very glad to have met you both, even if it's been under stressful circumstances."

"Well, we would have met eventually anyway — and I'm pretty sure you two met before the hospital. It's the only thing that makes sense." She gazed at him thoughtfully.

"What do you mean?" he asked, a bit uncomfortable with her scrutiny.

"The connection you two have. It had to have begun a while ago to be this strong now."

He was at a total loss.

She waved her hand. "But I keep forgetting you're human, and he's been sick. He hasn't had a chance to claim you, and knowing Angelo like I do, he probably hasn't done anything to let you know he's yours. Little perfectionist. Probably waiting for the 'perfect moment' after he gets well and out of the hospital."

"He's mine..." Dominic processed that and couldn't keep a smile from spreading his lips. "I'm his lifemate?"

"The connection is there and strong enough I can almost taste it. I have no doubts. And it doesn't seem like you do either by how happy you look to hear that. I was hoping our talk wouldn't put you off — not every human is happy to be matched up with a para. Many don't even know we really exist."

"Yes, well, he's not the first one I've dated. But," he hastened to add when her eyes narrowed, "he'll definitely be the last."

"Good. It's the job of the elder females to broker matches, so I can give my blessing to your mating, even though I'll bet Angelo would keep you even if I disapproved. But I wouldn't ever feel that way. You care for him — beyond your job, you make him happy and give him a reason to fight." She took his hands in her strong grip. "Thank you."

"No, thank *you*," he returned. Her confidence in the situation was infectious, and he was almost giddy with relief at hearing Angelo might be his, always. It explained his need to be near him, the uncontrollable urge he'd had to meet him that first day, the amazing sex—and his sensitivity to Angelo's condition and mood.

Now he had every reason to give up that last bit of control and finish falling for the man who'd claimed his heart.

Chapter Six

One month later

"Home sweet home." Dominic rested his hand on the small of Angelo's back and Angelo could feel the warmth of the touch through his shirt as Dominic guided Angelo into his home.

He'd been anticipating this day for such a long time. It had been torture waiting for the doctor's orders to go through, for all the paperwork to be put in place. He'd nearly walked out a dozen times over the course of the day, impatient to be alone with Dominic with no interruptions for the first time in forever, it seemed. Thankfully they'd gotten out of there before one more unappetizing dinner tray could be delivered.

Home—with Dominic. Exactly where he wanted to be. It had taken the cessation of the inhibitor, which had only been stopped once his transplant numbers had become the majority of his blood cells, for him to get a sense of who Dominic really was to him.

His lifemate. And it was a good thing, too, because he already knew—had known for a long time—that he never wanted to let Dominic go. Whether it was luck, chance or otherworldly intervention that first day they'd met, now it was a pure melding of halves to fill the lack he'd been carrying around his whole life until now.

He wasn't waiting another minute.

Giving a strong tug to the hand in his, he brought Dominic up against him and lowered his mouth to take his in a kiss. Dominic gasped into his mouth then returned the kiss full measure, sliding his hands around Angelo's back.

He walked Dominic backward, not breaking from the kiss until he was breathless and needed to see where they were going. "Here."

With a little push, Dominic landed back on the couch. He smiled up at Angelo then his eyebrows shot up when Angelo went to his knees before him. A frown began to form. "Angelo…"

He began to remove Dominic's shoes. "Just getting you comfortable."

"I wish you'd sit up here. I can take off my own… Angel, what—?"

His belt buckle was no match for Angelo's determination, and the button and fly were open a moment later. His protests were belied by the obvious erection pressing out against the cotton of his blue briefs.

"When I say comfortable, I mean naked," he clarified. "Now, lift up. Up." He was feeling better and could easily have moved Dominic but made himself wait for Dom's cooperation, which he gave after a long study of Angelo's face. "There you go," he praised, finally able to slide Dominic's pants and briefs down his legs then off. "You can do your top."

"Oh, I can?" The concern was still there, but growing warmth as well. "I suppose you wouldn't be initiating this if you weren't up for it." Dominic obliged by pulling his shirt over his head.

Angelo really wasn't as 'up for it' as he would like, but that wasn't surprising. He tried not to let that bother him, and he certainly didn't want to bring it up to Dominic, who would almost without doubt call a halt if he knew that Angelo was nowhere near an erection. His spirit was willing, even if the flesh was weak, and he didn't want to wait for the undetermined amount of time it might take for him to be fully functional again—not when Dominic was there and aroused and *his*…

He took Dominic's cock deep into his mouth.

"God, Angel…" The long dry period with only his hand for company while Angelo had been sick had him ready to shoot as soon as he pushed into that warmth. He didn't want to be selfish, but as long as Angelo wanted to get intimate, nothing on this earth could have prompted him to pull away.

His need to come spiked as soon as Angelo pulled off and started touching him along his inner thighs. "Angel."

"Yes?" Angelo cupped Dominic's balls in his palm while teasing behind them with his fingers. With his other hand, he stroked Dominic's chest in long, too-light brushes between his nipples.

Dominic shivered, bracing his hands on Angelo's chest. "Please," he groaned, rocking his hips into Angelo's touch.

Angelo leaned up to lick over one nipple as he zeroed in on the other, tweaking it between finger and thumb. He never ceased with his other hand, rubbing along his perineum and back to stroke Dominic's hole. Dominic wrapped his arms around Angelo's shoulders and held on tight, his writhing back against Angelo's fingers making no secret of what he wanted.

"Angel..." Dominic pressed his mouth in soft kisses along Angelo's neck to try to stifle his moans, nipping and licking the warm skin.

Angelo left off his torture of his nipples and grasped his chin to meet his mouth in a breathtaking kiss. "You...are so...hot," Angelo murmured between kisses before pulling slightly away from Dominic and rolling them so Dominic was beneath him. He met Dominic's eyes. "I never knew I could want someone this much." He kissed Dominic one more time, his fingers finding both of Dominic's nipples again.

Dominic moaned, arching up into the kiss and the touches. Angelo petted down Dominic's body, over his sensitive hip bones then between his spread thighs. He leaned in and slowly sucked Dominic's cock down to the base again in one smooth, hot move. He'd never been taken in so deep.

"Oh, fuck." Dominic's hands went to Angelo's head. The feel of the hair just starting to grow back brought him to reality, and he made an attempt to push Angelo back by his shoulders. "Should we be doing this? You're barely—"

Angelo pulled off to scowl at him. "I'm fine. Better than fine. Shut up and take your blow job like a man."

Dominic huffed out a laugh that turned into a gasp. Angelo's mouth was so hot and wet, it was a miracle he was lasting this long. Angelo pulled back, teasing the slit while he made eye contact then sucked Dominic back down again. Sliding his hands down Dominic's thighs, he encouraged him to spread his legs open wider, then took advantage of his vulnerability in breathtaking fashion—using a thumb to tease

Dominic's hole while using the other to rub the area behind Dominic's balls that was so sensitive.

He tried his hardest to keep from moving, but ended up rocking between Angelo's touch and his mouth.

"Babe—oh God. Teasing so hard."

That garnered him an extra hard suck up and off before Angelo smirked and stuck his fingers into his mouth, coating them with saliva. He ached for what was coming and pressed down against Angelo as he worked one finger inside. He'd barely been breached when Angelo simultaneously swallowed him back down and found his prostate.

Dominic shouted as he came, arching up off the couch. As he floated back down to reality, Angelo laved Dominic's shaft to his balls, then up over the sensitive head of his cock to get the last drops of cum.

He collapsed back against the cushion, reaching down to Angelo. "That was intense."

Angelo kissed his fingers, then joined him on the couch so they were cuddled together with Angelo's arm around him.

"That was how it will be for the rest of our lives. Well, maybe with a bit more activity on my part."

"I'm pretty sure the doctor wouldn't have approved of that...but I'm not sorry." They both laughed, and Dominic could sense that Angelo truly was satisfied by what they'd done. They would have plenty of time in the future for more of the sensational sex they'd had the night they'd met, and he had no doubt it would be even better with their bond.

"I'm the one to blame." Angelo stroked Dominic's thigh. "I've been thinking about getting you to myself for ages."

"Yeah?" Dominic loved hearing that. "Good, because I have too."

T.A. Chase

There is beauty in every kind of love, so why not live a life without boundaries? Experiencing everything the world offers fascinates T.A. and writing about the things that make each of us unique is how she shares those insights. When not writing, T.A.'s watching movies, reading and living life to the fullest.

Jambrea Jo Jones

Jambrea wanted to be the youngest romance author published, but life impeded the dreams. She put her writing aside and went to college briefly, then enlisted in the Air Force. After serving in the military, she returned home to Indiana to start her family. A few years later, she discovered yahoo groups and book reviews. There was no turning back. She was bit by the writing bug.

She enjoys spending time with her son when not writing and loves to receive reader feedback. She's addicted to the internet so feel free to email her anytime.

Devon Rhodes

Devon started reading and writing at an early age and never looked back. At 39 and holding, Devon finally figured out the best way to channel her midlife crisis was to morph from mild-mannered stay-at-home mom to erotic romance writer. She lives in Oregon with her family, who are (mostly) understanding of all the time she spends on her laptop, aka the black hole.

All of the above authors love to hear from readers. You can find their contact information, website details and author profile pages at http://www.pride-publishing.com.

Made in the USA
Lexington, KY
15 December 2018